Anita Sivakumaran was born in Madras and has lived in the UK since 2004. Her historical novel, *The Queen*, based on real events, has been made into a major television series. *Black Rain* is her second novel in the DI Patel detective series.

Also by Anita Sivakumaran

The Birth of Kali
The Queen
Sips that Make a Poison Woman

DETECTIVE PATEL SERIES

Cold Sun

BLACK RAIN

Anita Sivakumaran

dialogue
books

DIALOGUE BOOKS

First published in Great Britain in 2022 by Dialogue Books

10 9 8 7 6 5 4 3 2 1

A CIP catalogue record for this book
is available from the British Library.

ISBN 978-0-3497-0158-5

Typeset in Berling by M Rules
Printed and bound in Great Britain by
Clays Ltd, Elcograf S.p.A.

Papers used by Dialogue are from well-managed forests
and other responsible sources.

Dialogue Books
An imprint of
Little, Brown Book Group
Carmelite House
50 Victoria Embankment
London EC4Y 0DZ

An Hachette UK Company
www.hachette.co.uk

www.littlebrown.co.uk

For Nila, my lovely daughter

The little girl played in the sandpit while she waited for Daddy. She dunked her plastic watering can into a bucket of water her mother had given her. 'Be careful not to spill any,' she told herself sternly. Her mother had warned her that she wouldn't come every five minutes to fill it for her. She was very tired from working, and had gone to lie down for a tick.

The little girl didn't mind being left alone. Daddy would never have left her even for a minute. But Mama worked long hours at night so she could be with her in the day. Except then she was too tired to play with her. Like now.

The little girl poured the water into the sandpit and made mud pies. One for her, one for Mama and one for Daddy. If Daddy was here, he'd be in the sandpit with her, playing. She was bored.

'Hey, lil' munchkin.'

She looked up at the sound of the man's voice. Her face brightened. The nice man Daddy brought home the other day. The one who made Mama laugh. He'd even come to preschool yesterday with Daddy, made Mrs Bingham smile.

She waved from the sandpit. A queenly wave.

'Come here, darling. Give me a high five.'

She went over to the fence, held her hand up. The man reached down from the top of the five-foot fence. Barely had their hands touched, when she scooted away laughing, the man's hand grabbing thin air.

Her mother had told her not to talk to strangers, but the man wasn't a stranger. Her mother had also told her: don't go near the fence. Now the man said, 'Come closer, doll. Give us a high ten.'

The little girl went closer, both hands raised up.

The man held out his hands, said, 'Now you say high ten.'

The girl widened her stance, ready to scoot away like before and began saying, 'High ...'

She didn't finish. Simian arms swept down and scooped her up. She laughed at the sensation of being whooshed through the air, but the man didn't put her down.

He carried her away from her garden, her mother, her house. As he buckled her into a car seat, she thought: *Mama will be cross.*

'Hasina' pulled her scarf tighter around her head so no wisp of hair escaped, then approached the desk. Silently she handed the passport over. The check-in assistant, whose name tag read 'Clara', pored over the pages, looking for the visa stamp.

'First time?' she asked Hasina, who nodded. 'Business or pleasure?'

For a moment, Hasina was stumped. She didn't know. Duty, she wanted to say, and settled for 'Family'. It was the correct answer, in a way.

'Tom', the man assigned to watch Hasina, pressed a finger into his free ear to hear himself better. 'Target heading to Security gates. Do I move now?'

A female voice crackled in his ear. 'Sally on standby awaiting instructions.'

'Sally' had started off as a joke name. Aunt Sally, shepherder of girls. Then it stuck, became code for the female agent on tailing and interception duty. For some reason his code name was 'Tom Thumb'. Either to do with his tomato complexion or short stature.

Ben from the surveillance van stifled a yawn. 'Sorry, it's been a day and a half. Wait and see if she makes contact with anyone. Usually they send an escort.'

Hasina approached Security, joined a winding queue. Before

Tom could get close, a dense knot of men gathered behind her. Hasina disappeared into a branching queue. Tom was stuck behind a group of football fans with red Liverpool tops on. More and more of their mates kept joining the bunch in front of him, pushing him back. Hasina was nearly out of his sight. When he tried to push past the fans, one of them put a beefy hand on his chest, said, 'Oi, mate, wait your turn.'

The agent didn't want to draw attention to himself. Didn't want to scare off Hasina's contact. He spoke into his earpiece. 'Sally, got eyes?'

'Oh crap,' said Sally. 'She's going through. I'm stuck behind a pushchair.'

Tom pushed past the football fans, who began yelling after him, but he couldn't afford to let Hasina get away. He flashed his credentials at the security officers and made it to the Duty Free zone. No sign of Hasina.

Sally arrived, breathless, a minute later. They shook their heads at each other, then began a panicked search for the girl they'd been told strictly to never let out of their sight.

Hasina emerged from the restrooms beside Costa Coffee exactly as she'd been instructed. New clothes, new hair, new shoes. She'd left her small backpack – along with her passport and boarding card – inside a nappy bin, and now wheeled a sporty yellow case. As she walked past the two agents scratching around like gormless chickens, she flicked her hair over her shoulder. Then, arm in arm with the new brother who'd come to escort her, she started on the path to her new life.

The running man began wheezing but he couldn't stop. *You can do this, just get away.* He reached the deserted stretch between two roads and turned back for a quick look, easing the heavy shoulder bag to the ground.

Through the darkness spot-lit by street lamps, the rain was a shimmering, dazzling curtain that hid his pursuers. Terraced houses loomed either side of the empty road, all curtained and gone to sleep. The people chasing him were still out there.

He started running again, his lungs close to exploding. Only last week his daughter had urged him to take up running. 'Next week,' he'd told her. 'I'll start getting fit next week.' Now he may not have next week, or a next day. He'd focus on staying alive for the next hour.

Suddenly he caught sight of huge metal gates set back from the road, half-hidden by hedges. Pitch-black inside. He wouldn't be able to see anything if he went in there. More importantly, *they* wouldn't be able to see him.

He unslung the bag and threw it over the gates, then began climbing. He hadn't been good at it, even as a child. He slipped, the metal slick with rainwater under his fingers. He cursed, looked at the hedges towering over the gates, wondered if they'd hold his weight.

He tried again, and his weight pulled the gates apart, the latch sliding open as he fell. Ignoring the jarring pain in his ankle, he limped inside. He peered into the dark, blinking the rain from his eyes, not trusting this eerie place. Was it a park or woods? Were there animals in there?

He closed the gates as softly as possible. His hand slipped. The huge gate swung too fast, the latch clanged against the metal, the sound piercing weather and air. He heard a man shout, not far away.

Where was the bag? He groped around frantically, came upon a hard leathery edge. He scooped up the bag and ran along the wire fence blindly, hoping to come to the path's end and find some light, but only getting deeper into murk, the lights of any houses now too far away to discern.

Where was he? Some kind of woods? He'd never before in his life been surrounded by so much darkness. A primal fear awakened within him and his breath came even shorter than before.

The rain had thickened into black ropes. The bag's strap cut into his shoulder. He crouched down by the wire fence. The pitch-black soup surrounded him like a python, crushing. Making a quick decision, he heaved the bag over the fence, and heard it land somewhere far enough away.

He heard a step behind him and launched himself sideways, stumbled against a bush and fell.

Even through the hammering of his heart, he heard the silky whisper, 'Too bad, my friend. Things could've been different.'

He felt a sting on his arm.

As the darkness closed over him, the dying man spat out his last words, a final attempt at defiance. 'You'll never find it, you bastards.'

Chapter One

Barely had his lunch settled before Clive found himself trotting to the allotment. Sylvia made him. She didn't harangue him with words as such, but her eyes followed him about the room as he rinsed and filled the kettle, fetched the milk, stirred the sugar, placed a cup beside her on the little table. A wealth of meaning in those eyes; asking, asking.

So, the toast barely finished, the tea too hot to drink and abandoned on the dresser, Clive pulled on his wellies and mac. He didn't miss Sylvia's sharp tongue, truth be told, but this silent pleading . . . Pleading from a proud woman, the dread of his saying no. All this spurred him outside in biblical weather conditions.

Flapping open the broken umbrella, its steel tip a blur of dried mud from when he leaned on it while peering at the tomatoes to check their ripeness, he called, 'Back soon, me duck,' before opening the front door to the grey blizzard.

Bastard slugs. This May Bank Holiday, like so many in recent years, proving to be a washout. Now, Monday afternoon, a veritable storm raged, perfect conditions for slugs to rise and devour cottage vegetable gardens. In all the years that Sylvia had her ol' lottie, she'd kept on top of the slimy critters, her plot free of weeds, the soil pristine, nowhere for the grubbins to lurk. Now it wasn't so easy. The allotment paths were wheelchair unfriendly, to say the least. Clive did his best, but with his hips, he couldn't kneel or stay bent at the waist for more than a few minutes.

He felt a twinge in his right hip as he shuffled up to the gates. All Sunday he'd stayed in with Sylvia, resisting the temptation to turn the central heating on, nearly lighting some old newspaper and kindling that lurked in the hearth of the woodburner but denying himself that comfort. Instead, he'd busied himself googling solutions for the slug problem. This morning after breakfast he'd set to work on old Tupperware containers Sylvia had kept from when the children were little – she hated throwing anything away. He drilled holes into the lids and poured in the Foster's Lager, which would both attract and drown the slugs.

Clive pulled open the metal gates to the allotment – someone had left them unlocked, again – and walked through the grassy accessway that ran between the allotment land and the back of a row of terraced houses.

He passed a back gate with its old 'Beware of the Dog' sign. Instinctively he looked down and watched himself step on a dog turd. Typical. Cursing, he wiped his boot on some grass, then spotting another pile, he gathered some leaves, scooped it up and slung it over the small gate. Gathering up his basket of slug traps he noticed a smear on his hand. Cursing louder, he went to the allotment tap, and then proceeded to lay down the traps in Sylvia's greenhouse.

The dog's owner curled his bottom lip as he watched Clive stomp away from his back gate. He stood just a foot away from his top-floor window. From there he had a view of the whole allotment. He could see the vandals as they came and went. He could see the so-called respectable old gentleman slinging poo into his tidy garden.

He waited, he had little else to do these days, passing the time by looking out the window, catching glimpses of Clive as he shuffled around in the greenhouse, then to'd and fro'd with the watering can in the rain.

He watched Clive finish and trudge back past his gate again. And, after he heard the metal gates being pulled shut, he went downstairs, coaxed a reluctant dog out into the rain. He opened the garden gate, placed his foot under the dog's belly, half lifted it over the step, its short legs scrabbling in the air. Giving the animal a stern face, he shooed it onto the vegetable plots.

The dog, an unwell, uneven-tempered mongrel, whined for a while, then began sniffing about. It passed its own smells of shit and piss, some old, some recent, skirted the vegetables, cocked a hopeful ear for the frogs that lived near Sylvia's greenhouse. It went to the corner of the common lot, which the people from the terraced houses used for dumping things they were supposed to take to the tip. It rootled among the rubbish, the broken bits of plastic bottles and lager cans, wooden chairs missing legs or backs, some metal plates, parts of a fridge, the drum from a tumble dryer, then came upon a brown leather valise.

The dog nosed open its flap, sniffed at the paper and plastic smells inside. It smelled faintly of old peanuts, but the dog found nothing actually edible. Cocking an ear for sounds, the dog licked the raindrops off its own nose, yawned. Then it shuffled into position, crooked its back and strained. It did its business in the mouth of the open valise. Then the dog trotted back to the gate and whined till it was let back in.

In the evening, as the watery sun disappeared for the night, a hedgehog uncurled from under the valise flap, and emerged to look for a quieter bolthole. It had found a nice burrow under a pile of dried brambles before all the disturbances began, before the flap appeared to roof its new home. Its movement pushed the flap up and over, closing the valise again.

Not long after, a teenage gang convened at their usual spot, by the allotment gates, which as usual were open. So they went in to smoke spliffs by the unofficial tip. In the failing light, one of them noticed the brown bag. He eagerly picked up the bag and opened it. 'Eeow,' he said, turning his face away in disgust.

'Wassup, bruv?' said his friend.

'It stinks, man,' said the spiky youth and flung the bag as far as he could. By the time his brain registered the valise's heaviness, his arms were already sending it away into 2B's flower bed.

By Tuesday evening, the rain had eased off and Clive returned to the allotment, keen to see if his traps had worked. Indeed, they had; the smell far from pleasant, but gosh it felt satisfying. Decades of growing vegetables and Sylvia had never discovered this trick. Who would have thought slugs were mad for beer? Perhaps they weren't so different from humans, after all.

He gathered up all the containers into an old plastic tub and, hips aching, went over to the compost bins. Then he wondered about introducing a sudden glut of dead slugs steeped in stale beer into Sylvia's compost. Wasn't beer full of salt? No, he didn't think she'd approve. He cast his eyes about, unwilling to dispose of the stinky things anywhere on Sylvia's plot, briefly contemplated the dog gate, then settled on the common bit of land, used as a tip by the inhabitants of the terraced houses. He noticed new beer cans. He should write to the secretary about it. Take over the complaining from Sylvia.

He squinted in the failing light. Should have come a bit earlier. He put down the tray, and shook free a chair from the rubbish, startling a frog. No. Broken. He slung it back on the heap and emptied the slugs and beer. When he turned to go he spotted the shoe.

He bent, peered at it, picked it up, looked some more, trying to read without his glasses. 'Oh my,' he said out loud, when he made out the letters PRADA. His size too. The soles were a bit muddy but otherwise dry under the brambles.

He slipped off his welly, teetering a bit as he tried not to put his socked foot on the wet ground, slipped the shoe on. Perfect fit. He couldn't believe someone from the terraces could own, much less throw out an expensive, branded shoe. If people threw away this kind of stuff, he wouldn't complain about fly tipping. Wouldn't it be dandy if he had the pair? He began looking about in the failing light, wishing he could see better. He imagined the look on Sylvia's face when he walked into the house in his artfully scuffed Pradas.

Welly in one hand, slightly off balance, he poked around the rubbish. He had no luck, never had. His eyes roved over the rubbish as evening came on, and there, by the side of the broken wheelbarrow, in a tangle of brambles, was that it? Yes, the other shoe, sticking up out from the thorny sticks. He pulled the shoe from the brambles. Staggered back empty-handed. It wouldn't come off.

This shoe still clung to its owner's foot.

Chapter Two

Vijay Patel leaned forward in his seat at the Trent Bridge Cricket Ground, his heart for the first time in weeks experiencing a flutter of excitement. The Indian Captain, Virat Kohli, stepped forward to hit a cover-drive. Patel had a fine outfield view. This, the last in a four-test series, and England led 1–0. Patel sat in a box filled with the management team from Ageas Chemicals. He'd shaken hands with the five chemical execs, all of South Asian origin, had partaken of the complimentary nibbles and champagne, chatted, mostly about the weather, the pitch and India's bowling efforts, and let the small talk wind down as the wickets began to fall.

Holed up in his mother's house since his return from India, healing from wounds both mental and physical, Patel had been surprised by a call from his former cricket mentor, Sir Roger Wallace.

'Heard you were in Leicester,' said Sir Roger. 'Come to the match tomorrow. I'll send over a ticket.'

Patel had been too surprised to say no. He'd barely left the house since collecting his things from the London flat he'd shared with his ex-fiancée Sarah two weeks ago.

The ticket arrived and he'd wavered until his mother's incessant phone conversations, her voice penetrating brick and eardrum, had driven him out of the house at ten, and he'd boarded the train to Nottingham, then the bus to Trent Bridge. He'd arrived as the fifth over of the morning session ended at 11.30.

Kohli's partner Sharma blocked all six balls of the next over. One of the men behind him groaned. For weeks now, Patel had lurked in a pit of gloom back in his childhood home. An Indian son's rightful home was forever his parents' and Patel for once felt grateful for the unquestioning graciousness with which his mother took him in.

He'd already extended his sick leave twice. For a few days now he'd been working on two different email drafts saved in his police account. One, a letter extending his sick leave for the third time, the second, a letter accepting the Met's redundancy offer. The force was making cuts. Late last night his mother had found him in front of his laptop for the umpteenth time, head in his hands, and urged him to get some fresh air, go and meet people, do something, for heaven's sake.

Since his return from India he had endured endless debrief sessions, trauma counselling, treatments for his shattered elbow. The same GP who didn't give a monkey's about his three-month-long cough agreed to sign him off work for as long as he wanted after a two-minute conversation. This while going through the process of uncoupling from his fiancée. Then he extricated seven years' worth of accumulated stuff from what had been their flat and moved back to Leicester – temporarily.

Someone passed him a pair of binoculars. Patel adjusted the focus on Kohli's face. *Switched on.* Eyes wide, lips pursed. He fought the bowlers just as hard in every game of cricket, no matter the colours they wore, the continent they played in. In this case, of course, being a test match, they all wore white. The ball swung wildly. Overcast, damp in the air. Stuart Broad had a grin like the cat that got the cream. Three wickets in his bag already.

'Tough batting conditions,' commented the man beside him, compulsively crunching his way through a third packet of peanuts. They were all men, the chemical execs.

The Indians were struggling to adjust to English conditions. Each day a mystery, weather-wise. Test cricket in England, a game of weather-cat and weather-mouse. The clouds parted, the sun shone, the ball sliced the air, fast. The clouds loomed, and moisture in the air made the ball swing viciously. The Indian batsmen, supposedly the best in the world, tumbled. All but Kohli. A final, bright star in a fading sky. His fifth partnership. Short ball. He cut it beautifully between third slip and gully for four.

The Indians were now 148 for 7. *What*, thought Patel, *kept him going?* Kohli's fight in this patently losing battle felt to Patel like a physical assault on his own numb, gloom-filled body. It's just a game. No one's life is on the line.

Patel took his leave of the execs with a sense of relief. He made his way past the half-empty stands to the stairs that led down to Fox Road exit. As he rounded the top of the stairwell, he heard running steps behind and, for a moment, his heart thudded, remembering . . .

Just a gofer. 'Excuse me?' said the teenager with floppy, well-kempt hair, his all-access badge flapping on his chest. Did he leave his wallet on the seat?

'Sir, Mr Patel, you've been asked to come to the players' lounge.'

'Oh, who asked?'

'The chairman,' he said, breathlessly. 'They are all coming in now for tea.'

Patel had assumed Sir Roger was too busy to make time for his former protégé. Now Patel didn't think he had the stomach for socialising. But the boy waited, shifting on his feet. Patel didn't want him to get into trouble.

'OK,' he said. Just a quick hello.

The enclave underneath the home team's dressing room boasted very little of the sophistication promised by the seductive term 'members only'. Nothing fancy. Just tables and chairs and the brown carpeting ubiquitous of English clubs. Here the difference was usually the star quality of the players attracting hangers-on and superfans salivating at the fringes. Two security men stood by the entrances, hands together. The catering staff were laying out trestle tables. Hardly anyone there yet.

'Sir Roger won't be a minute,' said the gofer, and left the clubhouse on more errands.

With Indian and Pakistani cricket, usually a clutch of well-connected young women hung around the cricketers, dreams of eternal love and celebrity lifestyle alive in their over-mascaraed eyes. Today, for some reason, there was no gaggle of girls. Just one, drink in hand. She caught his eye, looked away and frowned.

He went to the bar, gave the hard liquor an old-fashioned stare, asked for a glass of orange juice.

The first players rolled in.

Turning with his glass, he noticed the woman, also holding an orange juice, accost Ryan Gonsalves, number six in the Indian batting line up. Ryan! Balding, sweaty and stout: hardly the man the girls usually went after.

Ryan seemed agitated. He said a few words, stepped back nervously. The girl, Patel now noted, did not have the iron-straight hair favoured by the typical groupie. Her hair curled and spiked, unkempt. She wore low-slung jeans and a crumpled, stained white top.

A rucksack hung from the crook of her index finger, behind her left leg, as though she was trying to hide it, as though she had turned up with her travel bag. Aware of eyes on her, she turned and caught Patel's gaze before turning back to Ryan.

Patel could not fathom what she wanted with Ryan. Perhaps a stalking fan? She didn't seem the type to be into cricket.

A security vassal turned up at Ryan's side, primed to nose out agitation and nip it in the bud. He escorted the woman from the clubhouse. The big-suited brute steered her by her elbow. And then it struck Patel. She was a reporter. Distaste soured his mouth. Reporters had hounded him on his return from India, so much so that he'd stopped going out at all and his mother had to go out through the neighbours' via a gap in the fence. He wondered what this one wanted from Ryan.

'Patel! Where have you been hiding?'

Sir Roger Wallace, chairman of the England Cricket Board. Grey hair and arched brows gave him a prematurely Gandalf quality. He'd taken Patel under his wing early in his cricket career, when he hadn't been *this* grand, though still fairly so. He'd been kind to Patel when he'd been green and skittish. Sought him out for chats, given him pointers about regulating nerves. Patel still did the breath counting.

'Holed up at home licking my wounds,' said Patel.

'Little birdie told me you were in Leicester. I thought you lived in London, being a hotshot policeman.'

'Not any more,' said Patel.

'They didn't send you here on a case?'

'No, sir. Just taking a breather after ... um, India.'

'I see ...'

People were coming in, greeting Sir Roger. While some showed deference in their attitude to him, there were also glances and smirks. Patel recalled a small item in the *Sun* a few months ago, scanned and emailed to him by a helpful cricket enthusiast uncle. Something personal, not to do with the cricket board. The usual sniggering gossip. He tried to remember the details. Family business? His stepson had filed a lawsuit, that was it.

Sir Roger gave him his attention once more.

'So, what's new with you, Patel?'

Patel rolled out the usual inanities, but Sir Roger didn't seem to be listening. He seemed a tad edgy.

'Well ...' Sir Roger paused as if, for once in his entire life, lost for words. Then someone waved him over. Sir Roger held up his hand in response, then said, 'Got to go. I thought I'd see if you needed, you know, any help or information, if you are ...'

Patel looked back at the older man, confused.

The sentence died on his lips. He suddenly leaned in close, whispered, 'You saw that girl ...'

'The reporter?'

'Yes.'

'Who is she?'

'Don't know. Probably press, yes. Likely nosing around about that dead actor.'

This surprised Patel. 'Majid Rahman?'

'Yes, he used to hang out with a couple of players. Indians, of course. Nothing to do with us. Are there suspicions about his death?'

'As far as I know, well, so my mother informs me, Majid Rahman's death was accidental overdose. She reads the tabloids. A drug addict, apparently.' He didn't add that his mother was secretary for the allotment grounds where Majid's body had been found.

'Is that so? I didn't know that. I need to find out how a journalist got through security. My own backyard.' He shook his head at the security staff standing at the door. 'Anyway, Freddie wants a word. Endless flimflam. See you in a minute.'

More men tracked in. Nursing his orange juice, Patel felt like a fish out of water. It'd been too long since his departure from cricket. He knew the coach, the physio, a couple of assistants,

but the players were all too young. Their presence, their mus-
cled, sweaty young men's bodies, induced a welter of envy in
him. His old acquaintances nodded, grinned, swapped hellos,
but conversation was limited to an exchange of banalities. He
needed to leave.

Waving a goodbye to Sir Roger who nodded absently, still
deep in a tête-à-tête with a suited board member, he left the
grounds. *You just can't go back*, he thought.

Walking down Radcliff Road, Patel passed a bunch of raucous
young men flinging beer cans into the grey water. Looking over
his shoulder, he noticed the reporter following a few paces
behind him. His hackles began to rise.

He couldn't be sure if she was following him or just going to
the station as well, along with a thousand other cricket fans. She
stood out, with her backpack, her short spiky hair, earrings, her
golden colouring, her rake-thin edginess.

What did she want from him? A titillating tell-all about
the case in India? He'd had every kind of approach from every
media outlet. Dignified to sleazy. One reporter even joined his
mother's Pilates class.

At a crossing, she came alongside to wait for the green man.
Patel tried not to study her from the corner of his eye. She didn't
seem to be looking at him.

She melted into the crowds as he made his way to the station.
He got a cuppa. Slipped into the WHSmith's. Avoided the crime
and thriller section. Picked up a book titled, *How to Organise
Your Socks for Success*. Lots of white spaces. Photos. Few words.
Red is for Power declared one chapter heading.

He killed twenty minutes and boarded the half-empty third
train of the hour. He found a window seat facing forward. He
settled with his new book. The one about socks.

The train's heaters were on, fogging up his window. He unfolded the small rectangular napkin that came with the take-away tea and cleaned the pane, which half reflected the inside of the carriage while also showing the view outside. Electric pylons straddled the Nottingham countryside.

In the half-mirror the reporter appeared and slid into the seat beside him.

'Wondering what I want with you, Mr Patel?'

The train shuddered over some track changes. She had a strong Indian accent. He turned slowly. 'I'm sure you'll tell me,' he said.

Among the medley of earrings, a diamond shone at him. She had a little nose that wrinkled as she smiled.

'Nothing. I'm just on the train to Leicester. I believe you live there?'

He did not answer.

'I'm looking into the death of Majid Rahman. Do you know south Leicester well?'

He didn't answer.

'I'm going there to see this allotment on ...' – she checked her phone – 'Kimberley Road.'

He wondered if she'd been in touch with his mother.

After a moment, she said, 'Don't you think there's something suspicious about his death?'

A death. A mystery. At least she wasn't interested in him.

Finally, he said, 'I've nothing to do with Leicester Homicide.'

She introduced herself as Neha Sinha.

His mother had been trying to get him interested in Majid Rahman's death for days. 'What's suspicious about his death?' he asked.

'For one, they found his body without shoes, among, what are they called ... brambles, in an informal, illegal rubbish tip. I'm quoting from the police report.'

He wondered how she'd got hold of that. Rather soon to release this information, surely.

'Those aren't grounds for suspicion. Given his history.'

'You mean the drug use.'

'I do.'

Neha raised her eyebrows. 'So what do you know about him?'

'I remember his films from the nineties.'

'Since then, he's been on a downward spiral. Film career stalled. Approaching fifty. Unlike the superstar Khans, Majid didn't keep in shape. Wrong sort of friends. Gambling addiction. Recreational drug use became occupational. Then he got swindled by his manager. Debts. Income couldn't keep up with his lifestyle.'

'Not unheard of, among ageing actors.'

'But Majid changed himself. He quit the drugs and the gambling. He's been clean for three months.'

'How do you know this?'

'I have my sources. What I haven't found out is how he suddenly became solvent, all the debts paid off. Where did the money come from?'

'Maybe he had rich friends.'

'He'd always been matey with cricketers, you know, Bollywood and cricketing celebrities hang out together, marry each other.'

Patel remembered his father talking about Tiger Pataudi marrying the actress Sharmila Tagore, fathering one of the now ageing Khans. Of course, Bollywood stars owned Indian Premier League teams nowadays.

Neha continued. 'Recently he's been seen a lot with his cricketing friends, especially Ryan Gonsalves and Ahmed Master. But two weeks ago, Majid disappeared from Mumbai. His sister rang the police to say he'd been kidnapped, only to call again half an hour later to say she'd been mistaken. No one knew his whereabouts. Then suddenly he appeared in Leicester in a Bollywood-style show. You know those?'

'Yeah, high culture in Leicester.' He knew family members who enjoyed the mindless spectacle of ageing Bollywood stars and teenage dancers cavorting on a garish stage.

'He wasn't even in the billing. Last-minute appearance. Then he disappears again for a couple of days. And turns up ... dead.'

She'd kept a straight face throughout her account, voice dry, but the last few words were forced out of her with emotion.

'I see.' Patel played noncommittal, but felt a flicker of interest.

'So you want to help me look into it?'

Patel gazed out the window. The train had slowed past Loughborough, now running a few minutes late. 'It's out of my jurisdiction.'

'Why did you come to the cricket match?'

'To watch the cricket.'

'Don't believe you.'

'Look. If there are suspicious circumstances, it's a case for East Midlands Special Crimes Unit. I'm with the Met. Scotland Yard. And I'm still on leave. Just about to extend it, in fact.' He didn't add, he wasn't in a fit state to investigate a missing cat.

She got out a notebook. 'Says here the contact for the allotment is a Padmini Patel. Is that a relative?'

He laughed. 'Leicester has thousands of Patels.' He had no desire to be embroiled in some Indian paparazzo's conspiracy theories.

'I've copied my notes. Will you read them?'

'No, thank you. I can't get involved, even if I wanted. It's forbidden in my job description.' Unsure about that edict, he said it with conviction just the same.

The train slowed, approaching Leicester.

'Ah, here we are.'

Nimbly he stepped over her legs and her half-open rucksack spilling notes and papers.

'Good luck with your story,' he said, as she hurriedly began gathering her things.

He leapt out of the train as soon as the doors opened and half jogged towards the taxi rank, lips set tight at the thought of how unready he felt even for a conversation about a case, let alone a full-blown investigation. The last person he'd collaborate with was a reporter with a crazed hankering for 'truth', whatever the cost. Some reporter; more like a conspiracy theorist.

A taxi pulled up. He would take the redundancy. Be done with it. He felt immediately better. He slid the door open and got in. 'Kimberley Road, please, mate.'

Chapter Three

Lawrence finished trimming his beard while his phone rang. Snapping the switch, he strode into the living room, where his daughter Chloe watched her morning cartoons. He picked up the phone before it went to voicemail. *I'll hop to it*, said Peter Rabbit on the telly, making his little Muffin laugh and repeat it, arm action and all.

'Yeah, sure,' Lawrence told the voice on the phone. He listened, checking his teeth in the hallway mirror. His wife Magdalena had left for work hours ago, so he didn't have to carry the phone into his attic office. 'Yep. Car ... OK ... Is it Ringo or Dingo? Right. Yeah, I know Saul's. Got it. And the job. You got a name and address? Good. Nah, I'll remember. Yeah. Yeah. OK, I'll keep you posted.'

Back in the bathroom, he checked his beard, rubbed a touch of grooming oil into the curls, checked the angles, was satisfied. He changed his clothes. He'd had a different kind of day planned before getting the call. Shedding the beige shorts and pink T-shirt, he dressed himself in black jeans, a navy shirt and a dark denim jacket, made big to comfortably hang from his hulking frame.

He dropped the Muffin at preschool, stopped off for a bagel and soy latte at the new deli. Nodded at another hipster with a nice little bun on top of his noggin. Sipping his latte from a reusable cup, he strolled down Queen's Road.

Saul's garage perched where the road rose and bent sharply, a silly place for a garage. Mayhem in a place like Leicester, where driving standards were abysmal. Lawrence finished the coffee, popped the flask into his bag. Went in past an old Renault Clio up on stakes, gliding a bit on the greasy floor. A skinny, scruffy man leaned against a new white hybrid, waiting for somebody or something.

'You Ringo?' Lawrence asked him.

The man held out his hand, and Lawrence clocked the handprint left on the gleaming car. Ignoring the offer, Lawrence said, 'This the car?'

'Our ride, man.'

'I expected something more ...' Lawrence made a gesture indicating oomph.

'The higher-ups are environmentally conscious, innit,' said Ringo.

Lawrence caught a whiff of Ringo's breath and noticed the brown stains on his teeth. He wondered why he had to babysit this creature. After all, it wasn't the kind of job that needed a buddy. Some nitwit the boss wanted to unload, he figured.

Lawrence got into the driver's seat. Ringo flopped in beside him, bringing his strong body odour. Lawrence turned the air con high. Sod the climate.

They headed out of the garage. Lawrence kept to twenty-eight miles an hour along London Road, letting a queue form behind him. He took the right onto Stanley Road.

'It's Dixon Drive and you've just passed it,' said Ringo.

'I thought he said Kimberley Road.'

'That's where the allotment entrance is. We need to go to Dixon Drive.'

Lawrence made a tight U-turn, slowing right down when an impatient Indian woman tried to edge past in her Audi. He gave her a calm, cool look till she relented, head shaking in disapproval.

'What number?' said Lawrence.

'Sixty-one.' They cruised past number sixty-one, a 1930s semi, the front garden all proudly done up, bursting with petunias and lavender bushes. The other semis had their front lawns paved over and turned into parking bays. Not a hint of green apart from plastic flowers here and there. Sixty-one was an oasis in a tarmac desert. Lawrence studied the front garden. If one were to be hyper critical, he thought, the holly hedge needed a trim.

They parked next to a builder's entrance, fifty yards away. Ringo's odour filled the car. Lawrence turned the engine off, rolled the windows down. He turned sideways and took in the oversize football T-shirt and the tracksuit bottoms on the scruffy eejit.

'Take a walk,' he told Ringo.

'A what?'

'Go walkabout. I'll watch.'

'But what if he comes out and hops in his car?'

'Stay close. I'll call you if he pops out.'

'When do I get back here?'

'Check with me in two hours.'

'What if I didn't want to go for no walk, man?'

'Take a walk. Go back to Queens Road. Get a coffee. Eat a pasty. You look half-starved. There's a charity shop down there. Get some clothes. Smart ones. A man only works as smart as he looks.'

'Man, you kidding me?'

Lawrence put his face right up close to Ringo's, glared into the depths of his pale, colourless eyes. 'I look like I'm kidding?'

Ringo got out. Lawrence opened the driver's door to let the

air circulate further. Then settled to watch number sixty-one's front door.

He knew other men in his profession – *or women*, he added with a mental chuckle – would have marched straight up and rung the doorbell. But Lawrence liked to watch first, make sense of the person, develop the right attitude before a confrontation. Temper was key. He watched the scumbag, for they mostly were scumbags, the men – *or women* – in his profession. In his study of them, he found them objectionable in all kinds of ways, and this was what got his temper up. Then he could do his job.

Two hours of nothing but the sky turning grey. Half a dozen dog-walkers. An old bird shuffling along with her shopping trolley. Students. Mothers with pushchairs. Number sixty-one's door didn't open.

Ringo arrived back in a new pair of jeans, two sizes too big for him and hanging off his waist, a T-shirt a tad small for him and a bit short, showing Lawrence the branded elastic of his boxer shorts.

'Look.' Ringo's eyes had strayed past Lawrence's face and widened.

Lawrence turned to see an old white man stepping out of the target's door.

'That him?'

'Fits the description, innit.'

'He's getting in the car.'

Ringo jumped in. They followed the Ford Focus to London Road, where it turned left. The old geezer drove like a bat out of hell. Lawrence wondered if he'd seen them watching. Though normally a cautious driver, when called for, he could improvise. He kept up with the target, never letting himself get too close, keeping two cars between them.

'What's the fella's name again?' Lawrence asked Ringo.

'Clive Atkins, innit?'

Clive did thirty-five in the thirty-mile zone. Lawrence had to hassle the cars between, driving too close to them and flashing his lights, to get them to move quicker. Then, on the approach to the Oadby roundabout, Clive pressed on the gas entering the forty-mile zone. Lawrence had to overtake the two cars in front to stay with their target. Horns blasted, drawing too much attention to the white hybrid; not at all a good thing. In fact, it defeated the purpose of staying two cars behind.

'Eff it,' he muttered, and just stuck right behind Clive, who didn't seem the type to bother with his mirrors in any case.

Clive slid sharply into the right-hand turn into the Sainsbury's.

'Indicate,' hissed Lawrence, as he swung sharply into the turn too, inviting another horn blast. He turned into the car park and slid the hybrid into a free slot two bays past Clive.

'Bloody 'ell,' remarked Ringo as he stumbled out of the car.

'Is right,' muttered Lawrence. He felt wobbly as he got out the car, and wondered at the irony of it. He, the tough guy, shaking like a wet leaf due to the antics of a pensioner. He took a moment to calm himself down, wipe his face and neaten his hair, before hitting the trolley park.

Inside the supermarket, they found Clive sauntering up an aisle with a trolley, all the time in the world. Lawrence followed with his trolley, pretended to mull over the fruit display.

'So what's he done, man?' said Ringo, fingering a box of strawberries.

'He stole something.'

'What?'

'A bag.'

'What's in the bag?'

'Not sure.'

'What sort of bag?'

'A case. Like a ...'

'Man bag?'

'Valise.'

'Valise?'

'Yes.'

'What's he, a ponce?'

'It's like a laptop bag.' Lawrence himself had one in nice, rugged leather.

'So, he stole a laptop?'

'No. Just the bag.'

'Right.'

Clive pottered about the meat aisle, picked up lamb chops. In the milk aisle, he picked up a bottle of vanilla milkshake, opened it and glugged it down. Lawrence thought perhaps he was diabetic, needed the sugar kick and couldn't wait. Clive pushed his trolley to the frozen foods aisle with one hand, shaking onto his tongue the last drops of the milkshake. The frozen foods aisle was devoid of people. He looked around, and almost caught Lawrence's eye as he rounded the yogurt display. Lawrence abruptly turned and picked up a six-pack of Yeo Valley.

'Doesn't look like a thief,' said Ringo, by his elbow, as he slurped from a bottle of Lucozade he'd picked up from a shelf.

'You can tell?'

'Come on. Look at him. Butter wouldn't melt in his mouth.'

When Lawrence turned back to sweep a look, he saw Clive sliding shut a freezer chest. The milkshake bottle had disappeared from his hand. Instead, he held a bag of peas and a family-size box of fish fingers. From the freezer aisle he made straight to the till. Lawrence went to the chest freezer and saw the empty milkshake bottle nestling among frozen broad beans.

'Son of a gun,' he said.

*

They were back in the car after Lawrence made Ringo pay for his Lucozade. Tailing Clive felt easier now he knew the guy drove like a bat out of hell. Ringo opened a packet of crisps and began crunching. Lawrence took his eyes off the road and looked at him. Ringo extended the packet. The smell of fried potatoes covered in a bacon flavouring and salt hit his nostrils.

'Thanks,' said Lawrence and helped himself. *If you can't beat the devil . . .*

Back at the house, parking four doors down, they waited. Some fifteen minutes after Clive had hefted the shopping in, time enough to put everything away and get changed, he came out with a trug, a trowel in it, wearing wellies and a scruffy coat.

''Ee's off to the lottie,' said Ringo.

Time to corner the bastard, thought Lawrence.

'This is the plan,' he told Ringo. 'You ask the questions. I'll stay a step behind you. Quiet-like. Let's see if he spills the beans. If he isn't buckling under the pressure you apply, then I step in.'

'Got it,' Ringo said with a wink.

They stepped up to Clive as he fiddled with the gates.

Ringo sang out: 'Yo, man, how's it hanging, bro?'

Clive frowned. 'Pardon?' he said.

'What you up to? Tending the veggies? Say,' Ringo paused dramatically, as though he'd twigged something. 'Ain't you the lucky guy?'

'Lucky?' Clive looked irritated, not scared. 'Who are you?'

'Never mind me, man. You. You're the dude who found the body? You was in the papers, man. Famous, are you, now?' Ringo chuckled.

Clive turned back to fiddling with the gates. 'Sorry, I've got to go.'

'Wait, man, talk to me. I need to ask you something.'

Clive gave a wave. 'Another time,' he said, got the gates open.

Lawrence decided he'd had enough. He stepped forward, put his hand on Ringo's shoulder to silence him. 'Clive,' he said. 'Look at me.'

Surprised, Clive turned to look at Lawrence.

'Did you take anything from the dead man? Something you may have forgotten to tell the coppers about?'

'Certainly not,' said Clive, his eyes darting to the right.

He's lying, thought Lawrence.

'I'll ask you again. Did you take anything off the body?'

Clive looked outraged. *Fake*, thought Lawrence. 'No, I'd never.'

'I don't believe you.'

'You're harassing me,' Clive cried, with a show of courage. 'Leave me alone or I'm calling the police.' He flourished his phone at them.

Lawrence had already seen in the supermarket what sticky fingers the pensioner had. His moral indignation was all fakery. He stepped around Ringo, curled his meaty fingers around Clive's shirt collar and pressed his head back against the metal gate. Clive's Adam's apple wobbled underneath the bunched collar, tickling Lawrence's knuckles.

'Tell you what, Clive,' he said, using his kind voice. 'Maybe your memory's a bit confused. Getting on a bit, aren't ya? Maybe there's some bits that ain't working like they ought to be, up there in the noggin. We'll give you till tomorrow morning. You bring what you took, alright?'

'Get off me,' shouted Clive. 'I'll call the police, I swear.'

Lawrence smiled. 'Here's what'll happen if you do.' Switching the hand on Clive's collar, he made a good fist with his right and rammed it into Clive's nose.

Clive stumbled to his knees, keened, clutching the edge of the gate.

'Come on,' Lawrence told Ringo.

They got in the car, waited to see Clive get back up, then shuffle off home on shaky legs, a handkerchief pressed to his bleeding nose.

'You think he's got it?' Ringo said.

'For sure,' Lawrence said.

'Ain't right, man,' Ringo said. 'Stealing from a dead person.' Ringo spat through the open window. 'Ethics, innit?'

Padmini Patel nodded at the big, angry-looking man driving a new white car, letting him past first. Best to avoid confrontation. A couple of weeks back, Wendy, who lived two streets away, had provoked some horrible man who got out and smashed her windscreen in. Padmini arrived in time for her Pilates class, did the crunches and planks without complaint, did the shopping, not forgetting Yakult for Vijay, then drove on straight to Helen's coffee morning.

There she sat among the eight or ten other women, too shy to talk to the shadow health minister, whom Helen had somehow managed to wrangle an appearance from. The woman always managed to surprise her. Padmini made chit-chat with one or two others. The minister looked enquiringly towards her, a slight smile on his face, but she felt tongue-tied. Padmini: the only Asian lady there, among a posset of white middle-aged women. The shadow health minister: in the pink, literally so. His nourished flesh a rosy, whitish hue, genetically inured to a good, golden tan. Padmini had nothing to say to him. In great health for her age, she didn't need the NHS like a lot of people did, not yet anyway.

She thought there'd be gossip about the murder, that they'd want to know about this famous actor. But no one did. Everyone was preoccupied with their own little world, no curiosity about anything outside it. But then, the same could be said of her own community. Perhaps she was the freak, to be the possessor of a lively mind.

Padmini had lived here since 1975. She still couldn't think of herself as British, or even Ugandan, though she had been born there and married a fellow Ugandan. What was she then? Indian, but what kind, thinking of the south Indians newly arrived, dotted about the place, always looking curiously at her, wondering if she had anything in common with them.

She called herself Gujarati, even though she'd only ever visited Gujarat twice in her life, and couldn't stand the spitting, the open drains and traffic chaos. And the curiosity above all, the prying. A wry smile appeared on her lips as she thought of how she didn't abide both the lack of curiosity from the English and the prying from the Gujaratis. Was there such a thing as a happy middle?

She lingered after the rest of them left. She said goodbye to Helen, then waited, giving her a meaningful look till Helen cracked and said, 'It's all finished with the police inquiry, isn't it?'

'Oh yes,' said Padmini. 'Either suicide or accidental overdose. The allotment's not a crime scene any more.'

'Hope it doesn't put people off.'

'Not a chance,' Padmini said. 'Climate change concerns mean more and more on the waiting list, dead Bollywood actors or no.'

Helen didn't crack a smile. Padmini had hoped for a chat about the murder of the man who used to be such a heart-throb, but Helen wasn't interested.

Hey ho, thought Padmini, and took her leave. She thirsted for a good gossip session. She would ring her daughter when she got back from work.

She hadn't been home for two minutes, just stowed away the shopping and put the kettle on, when the doorbell rang long and insistent. And you could have knocked her down with a feather when she saw Clive, Sylvia's husband, slumped at her doorstep with a bloodied nose, shaking.

'Sylvia thought it a good idea to come to you,' he said, his swollen nose thickening his voice.

'Her speech has returned?' she exclaimed. A miracle! But then ... Did Sylvia get up and biff him as well?

'Please,' said Clive, 'is your son here?'

'My son? Whatever for?'

'Let me get this straight,' said Patel. He sat on a sofa opposite the elderly man whom he only vaguely ever said hello to and never much more than *Nice day, isn't it*? He'd barely got his change from the taxi driver when he'd been set upon by his mother. This man needed his help, but what kind of help? Clive perched opposite, cowering, his eyes blue and black, fingering the tape on his nose. 'They think you took something from Majid Rahman before he died.'

'After,' said Clive. 'When I found his body.' The old man seemed so shaken he could barely lift his head up to look at Patel.

Patel frowned. 'Why haven't you gone to the police?'

The head rose an inch, but then slumped again. His mother came in with coffee and sat down beside Clive. Patel waited for Clive's answer.

'I can take you if you wish,' said Padmini.

'No,' said Clive, the 'No' bursting out of him, his fear writ large.

Padmini, after a beat, said, 'What did you take, Clive?'

'Tell us,' Patel said, keeping his voice soft.

Clive groaned, put his head in his hands, rubbed his face, winced. 'I don't know what came over me,' he said. 'I found one in the brambles, you see, and already in my head, finders keepers, all mine. And thinking, what a treat it would be to find the pair, and all my life, you know, wishing for this and that, and looking at the end of the tunnel, crummy old life, and wanting just a little treat, and I've always fancied the brand, you see, a nice, well-worn, scuffed pair, like a young man about town, and well, there it flashed at me, sticking out of the brambles, ice lolly on a stick.'

'What flashed?' said Patel, his mind conjuring up visions of rubies, diamonds, a maharaja's ransom.

'These,' said Clive, pointing at his feet.

'This old pair of shoes?' said Padmini. 'They are scuffed and dirty.'

'They are Pradas,' said Clive, and groaned again.

'They look cooler when they are scuffed, Ma,' said Patel.

She grunted, unladylike. 'Not worth the threat to life and limb, I can tell you that.'

Clive said, 'I didn't know anyone would come looking for them. They're only shoes.'

'Why did you come here?' said Patel.

'I came home after getting my nose fixed. Sat on the sofa, thinking. Half an hour it must've been. Sylvia having a nap. I'd just about decided to put the shoes in a bag and leave it outside, you know, so they could pick it up and I didn't have to see them again, have no more aggravation, when this smashed through the front room window. Cut my head, a piece of glass.' He pushed his hair back, showed a plaster stuck all awkward near his left earlobe.

'Can I see the note?' said Patel.

Clive reached into a bag and brought it out.

A half-brick. A piece of paper around it with a rubber band. Patel opened it: DONT THINK OF CALING THE POLICE. SEE YER TOMORO.

'They gave me till tomorrow morning,' said Clive. 'I thought I better bring you the shoes, so you can work out why they want them.'

Patel asked Clive to take off his shoes and inspected them. They were completely ordinary. Thin soles. Nothing seemed to be hidden.

'They can't be after the shoes,' said Patel.

'So what are they after?' said Clive.

'No idea. Might need an expert to find anything in these thin shoes. Here's my advice,' said Patel. 'Find someone to look after Sylvia. First thing tomorrow, go to the police and tell them everything. They might arrest you for obstruction of justice and for tampering with the crime scene, but I'll see about getting you out on bail ...'

'They'll arrest me?'

Patel continued as if Clive hadn't spoken. '... Or my mother will post a bond for you. Go home. Don't worry.'

Chapter Four

Patel waited for Detective Sergeant Keith Codman at the busy coffee shop outside the police building.

Codman was late. Patel had been surprised to get a call from him on the way, asking to meet in the coffee shop instead of his office. Ten minutes' waiting later, he turned up: skinny guy with a beaked nose below restless eyes.

After the preliminaries, Patel said, 'Wouldn't it be better to meet at your office? It's about a case, after all. Might need your computer.'

Codman shook his head. 'Computer went bust this morning. Some techie's in there now, fixing it.'

'That's quick,' said Patel. 'In London you have to wait for weeks to get your equipment fixed.'

'Yeah, same here. But she was already in the building sorting something else out. Got lucky, I guess, though who knows how long it'll take.' Codman looked around him. 'So where's the fella then?'

Clive hadn't turned up. Patel wished he'd listened to his mother who'd wanted Patel to escort Clive to Codman and explain the trouble he'd got into because of his 'harmless' pinching habits.

'I'll babysit him while he's at the copshop,' he'd told his mother, 'but I'm damned if I'm going to chauffeur him as well.'

'Potty-mouth,' Padmini had said, making him feel about twelve years old.

Now Patel wished he'd listened to her. He bought Codman a double espresso, and himself a single shot macchiato. Then he explained that he suspected Clive felt afraid, both of the police and the men hunting him.

Codman sipped his coffee and said, 'When you called, I thought, wow, a real-life celebrity, wanting to see me, a nobody.' He gave Patel the once-over, like he would some chick with a tight rack.

Patel smiled thinly.

'So what brings you to Leicester? A case?'

'No. Just spending time with family after, you know . . . '

'Oh yeah.' Codman sucked his cheeks with relish. 'I read about the India case. What a cluster fuck. Still, you can sell your memoirs now. You can name your price, I reckon.'

Patel felt his thin smile disappear.

'You know,' said Codman, 'I kinda fancy making a move myself. To the bright lights. You reckon you can put in a good word for me?'

'Ah no.' Patel felt embarrassed. 'I'm hardly someone who can recommend officers.' He didn't add that his word was mud to his nemesis of a boss, Superintendent Skinner.

Codman looked disappointed as he sipped his coffee.

'So you think you can reopen the Majid Rahman file?' said Patel.

Codman hissed between yellow teeth. 'This case has passed beyond my jurisdiction. I closed the case yesterday, the pathologist's report being conclusive. There isn't any need to get the East Midlands Special Crimes Unit involved. And this Clive Atkins, well, he hasn't turned up, has he? And even if he does, what of it? We need material evidence. Solid. To reopen a straightforward closed case. Accidental overdose. There are no witnesses to the contrary. The body's on its way to India, so there you go.'

'You think there's no foul play?'

'I think nothing. I just work on the evidence available. The only evidence we have is that Majid Rahman had a history of drug use. Three years ago, a police caution in Birmingham for drunk and disorderly, a couple of arrests and release without charge in India.'

'Isn't this a bit like bringing up a woman's sexual history in a rape conviction?'

Codman's eyes narrowed. 'Didn't I read you're on medical leave? Trauma after the event or something?'

Patel wouldn't rise to the bait. 'This isn't about me. I'm a concerned friend of Clive's. He's being hounded by some very dangerous people for missing evidence to do with a possible murder.'

'Look,' said Codman. 'I think we're done here, don't you? Even if this story is true, that this friend of yours is being harassed about something missing from the dead guy, it doesn't automatically tally that it's a murder, now does it?'

Patel controlled his anger and spoke as calmly as possible. 'Equally, the fact of drug-use history doesn't make Majid's death from a drug overdose accidental. Look at the circumstances of death. Midnight in a very secluded area. Not exactly in his own bed.'

'There's no motive that we can see. No suspects.'

'Well, that is part of your job, isn't it, to find the motive and the suspects?'

Codman's nose and the tops of his cheeks coloured. 'Are you telling me my job, Detective Patel?'

'Of course not.'

'Well, I'll be going then. Some of us have work to do.' He started getting up.

'Come on, this case looks suspicious as hell.'

'Isn't paranoia one of the side-effects of trauma?' Codman sneered.

Patel made a fist under the table. If he stayed a minute longer, Codman would end up in A&E. He brought his anger under control with some effort. It really had nothing to do with him. *What you can't control* ... Patel let it go with a breath. He held his hands up to show Codman he was done here. He'd tell his mother he'd tried his best to help Clive.

Codman walked out of the café and towards the police building. Patel hurriedly finished his coffee and followed, hoping to see if Clive had indeed turned up and waited at the reception, browsing the brochures like he should've been half an hour ago.

Nearing the entrance, Codman paused, addressed someone walking out of the building. 'Hey, is it all fixed then?'

A small woman in jeans and a tucked-in shirt a bit big on her small frame, a baseball cap half covering her face, mumbled something to Codman without looking up, head down staring at her phone.

'That's pretty quick for a chick,' Codman said, breaking out a leering smile, and the woman, glancing up, gave him a withering look. Then she noticed Patel, seemed taken aback. Without speaking, she turned from Codman and strode rather quickly away, hitching up her rucksack as she went.

'Thanks,' called Codman after her.

Patel forgot Clive entirely, staring after her. He didn't move until Codman went inside.

At the end of the street, he found her waiting.

'Neha,' he said. 'Doing a bit of sleuthing, are we?'

'Getting at the truth,' she said.

'You were just in Codman's office, posing as an IT technician?'

'Yep.'

'Why?'

'I'll show you.'

Patel watched for a moment as she began walking. He'd thought he'd got rid of her the previous evening. Apparently not.

She looked back when he didn't immediately follow. 'Coming?'

She took him around a corner into a café with free WiFi. They settled into a corner sofa, her laptop propped open between them. It seemed like one of those cannibalised, build-your-own machines that had a mind of its own.

Neha clicked open several windows, paused for a moment as if having second thoughts, then said, 'Look, I've done some investigative journalism in my life, so don't ask me how I got hold of this. This is the First Response report.'

Patel read through, sat back, frowning. Thoughtfully, he took a sip of his second macchiato of the morning, now cold, and grimaced.

'Well?' said Neha.

'It's a bit short.'

'That's an understatement. No one in the neighbourhood has been interviewed.'

'The cops did put up notices on a couple of lamp posts asking people to come forward with information.'

'Forensics never turned up.'

'For practical reasons. Because of all the rain that night.'

Neha minimised the report window. 'Here are a couple of emails, one to Codman's official account, and one from his personal account, which you may be interested to read.'

Despite himself, Patel leaned in. The first one was from a PC Seymour.

Sir, you asked for anything relevant to the suspected
murder reported today. Last night we got a report from
the manager of Best Buy store on London Road. An
Asian man, around 40–50 years old bought cigarettes
from the shop, stopped outside by two other men of
unclear ethnicity. They seemed to have an argument. He
offered CCTV footage from the store, which shows the
shop entrance.

Neha showed DS Codman's reply.

As no crime has been reported, there isn't any need to
view the CCTV footage.

Then Codman sent another email, an hour later, asking for
CCTV footage and copies if any. This one from his personal
email account to the PC's personal email account.

Patel found this very curious indeed. What was Codman
playing at?

He said, 'I wonder what he did with the CCTV footage?'

Neha said, 'He deleted it, and emptied the bin.'

'Ah. That's a shame.'

'You want to see it?'

'How . . . ?' Patel trailed off.

Neha smiled. Her fingers flew on the keyboard, and before he
knew it, Patel was watching grainy footage shot in streetlighting
on an immovable camera. A brown-skinned man with south-
Asian features came out of the store entrance. Two men spoke
to him, their backs to the camera, features indistinguishable.
One of the men pulled a sharp object out of his pocket and the
Asian man darted from view, the two men following. Around
11 p.m., store closing time.

'Does look suspicious,' Patel said.

She said, 'Does this mean you'll help me uncover the truth?'

Patel felt a headache coming on. Hadn't he just decided this wasn't anything to do with him? 'I can't get involved directly,' he said. 'I could ring my old boss at the Met and see what can be done.' *Not Skinner*, he thought. *Rima*. 'We need to find out who those two men are.' He bit the inside of his cheek, realising the slip. He'd said 'we'.

Neha said, 'I want to talk to the man who found the body. And see the allotment where Majid ended up.'

Patel sighed. It seemed he would be involved, whether he wanted to be or not. 'You better come with me.'

Chapter Five

Clive returned home from Mrs Patel's house with his finger-nails digging into his palms. His jaw ached and he realised he'd clamped his teeth tight.

'Get up. Get up, Sylvia,' he said, fearing, from the way she lay, so still, duvet over her face, that she had died. Turned over in bed while he'd been away and suffocated in her pillow. But as he pulled her duvet off, he could see she lay on her back, not her front, and that she still breathed.

'Surprise. We are going on holiday. A surprise holiday,' he said. He'd never so much as peekaboo-ed at her in all their years together. 'Aldeburgh. Remember, Syl?'

She looked at him with an expression that seemed to say: *When pigs fly.*

The last holiday they had before her stroke. If he'd known it was the last holiday she'd be able to enjoy, he'd have behaved differently. He'd been cross about the cost of the one-room barn conversion. She'd found it. All glass and exposed beams. Two months since he'd retired and he couldn't get used to a life of 'pottering'. He'd become sick of channel-surfing, looking for football games to watch. Suffocating in his own stink in the front room. Couldn't afford Sky Sports. And now, coming to this posh place on holiday. To do what?

The Suffolk coast seemed so dull. Benjamin Britten's former

home had been one of the few local attractions. But then, the sea got to him, and the pebble beach. He began to breathe more deeply, freely. He could sit at the beach for hours. What a place. The light. He read somewhere, on some leaflet, that artists loved the Aldeburgh coast because of the light. He could see what the fuss was about.

It had been unusually warm for October. Climate change, don't you know. Nevertheless. Warmed him right through to his soul. And the pebble beach.

'Come and sit yourself down,' she'd said to him.

He'd been walking back and forth, admiring the oil rigs parked way out, and ships or boats, he couldn't tell which, going to and fro. She folded her raincoat neatly on the pebbles, sat down. A smile lit her up, the glorious Suffolk light shining on her eyes.

'It's quite comfortable, really; surprisingly so,' she'd said to him. He'd just grumped at her, unwilling to admit he'd come around to the place.

Tears flowing freely now, he packed a suitcase for them both and emptied the snack cupboard into a couple of market bags. Then the thought occurred to him. 'Syl, I'm an old duffer,' he said. 'I've not booked anywhere.'

He could not, for the life of him, get on to the internet thingy and find a place. Sylvia had been the internet wiz. He wracked his brain for a minute, and more in desperation than hope, he trawled through his mobile phone and found the contact number of the woman, Marion, who ran a string of cottages in and around Aldeburgh, who'd been so nice to them when they couldn't work out the key lock system outside the house. She'd turned up within ten minutes to sort it out. Showed them how you put in the code and get the small box open, get the key out, and how to put it back in.

Sylvia sat with an expression of bewilderment on her face as he packed. When he returned from putting her wheelchair in the boot, he noticed her anxiety.

'What's that, dear?' he said. 'We have to go away for a week,' he said, holding himself low with his hands on the bed, his face in front of her face. She seemed puzzled.

'We are going on holiday, Syl,' he said, inserting an upbeat tone into his voice. 'Yay.'

She crinkled her eyes and smiled.

Clive had just gone past Kibworth, Sylvia staring at the traffic without comment, when the vehicle behind flashed its lights. Dread gripped his chest as he recognised the neat beard of the driver, and the mean little face in the front passenger seat. He pushed down on the accelerator and turned a sharp left. He found himself on a deserted country lane.

Nothing to do but speed on. Careening around a bend, a Land Rover blasted its horn as it passed him. Frantically he looked for a turn when he felt the great big whack in the back. His car was forced onto the left-hand verge.

Too dazed to move, Clive heard his door open and great big hands grabbed him by his collar and pulled him out.

In the quickly falling dark, he heard shuffling, a whimpering sound from Sylvia and the other man calling out, 'Come on, shift yer bottom, sister. I can see you ain't injured.'

'Leave her be,' said the hipster, and dragged Clive around the car, away from the road, further into the trees. Clive felt his senses fading.

'Remember us? Lawrence and Ringo.'

'Laurel and Hardy,' mumbled Clive.

'Hey,' said Lawrence, slapping Clive on the cheek. 'Where were you off to?'

Clive's brain scrambled back to speed. 'Just to Market Harborough, to visit friends.'

'Staying the night, are we?'

Clive realised his error. 'Oh no. Just a cuppa.'

'I saw you hefting luggage into the boot.'

'That's just some old clothes, for charity.'

'Where's the bag?'

'What bag?'

Lawrence nodded to the other man.

He went over and opened the boot. They waited as he rifled around, cursed. 'Fucking boxer shorts and bras, man.'

Lawrence said, 'You look in the car.'

Ringo searched the car and the big man, one hand holding Clive's collar, rifled in the luggage. The thin man came back around, shook his head. 'Nothing, man. I checked the seats, footwell, even under the old lady.'

Lawrence turned to Clive. 'Where's the bag?'

'That one?' Clive pointed to Sylvia's holdall.

'OK, not a bag, a man bag. Let's call it a satchel. A valise, if you will.'

'Honest to God, I didn't see one.'

'Listen, I know when a man lies to me. I know you took something.'

'It was just these shoes. I swear. I did not see a satchel.'

'Shoes?'

'Prada shoes.'

'You took a dead man's shoes?'

Clive felt the shame of it. 'Spur of the moment, and don't think I haven't regretted it every minute since.'

'These shoes on your feet?' Lawrence bent to peer at them. 'You're still wearing them.'

'I haven't had a chance to—'

'This afternoon you were wearing wellies. To the allotment. I was there. I saw. You went home, changed into these shoes. You are one sick old man.'

'I wasn't thinking, that's all.'

'We saw him, didn't we, bruv,' Ringo piped up. 'We saw him at the supermarket. He pinches stuff. He must have taken the bag.'

Lawrence looked speculatively at Clive. 'How do we get the truth out of you?' Lawrence grabbed Clive's ear. Twisted hard.

Clive yelled. 'Stop, I'm telling the truth. There might have been someone else there.'

'Who else was there? Did you see anybody?'

Then it occurred to Clive what should have been obvious from the outset. 'Yes. These young people who hang out there. They come to smoke and do drugs. It must have been them. They wouldn't care about stealing from a dead man.' Clive bit his tongue.

Lawrence twisted Clive's ear harder. Clive's head felt close to exploding.

'Hmmm,' Lawrence said. 'You might be telling the truth, or you might not. I don't believe you, or not fully, anyway. You are a real fuck-meister.'

A whimper slipped out of Clive.

Lawrence said, 'Here's what we do. You run on home.'

He eased up on the ear. Clive felt sweet relief.

'We go see these boys. How many are there?'

'Four. Usually four.'

'Do they come every night?'

'Most nights.'

'OK, if it's your lucky night, they'll be there. And we'll talk to them. If what you say is true, and they return the bag ...' Lawrence paused. 'But how do I know you won't try to run away again? Hmm?'

'I won't,' said Clive.

'I know. We keep your old woman. We have a nice comfy van she can sit in.'

'But ...'

'Off you toddle.'

Clive watched as they opened the passenger side of his battered old car, half lifted and half dragged Sylvia. She complied, head turned sideways towards him as if saying a half-hearted goodbye. They put her in the back of their van, a big black beast with a metal grille. It looked untouched.

Clive stared after the black van as it left with his wife inside. He roused himself and thought he'd better follow them. But his car wouldn't start. He called the garage and left a voicemail. He couldn't call the police for help. He'd have to admit he tried to run away after committing a crime, harmless pinching though it'd been. They'd arrest him on the spot and Sylvia would be lost. He wondered what to do. It was a long walk home. He couldn't afford a taxi that far, and who knew what buses plied at this hour. Even the holiday he'd booked on his credit card. Next April when the card needed renewing, he knew he wouldn't be able to. They didn't give credit to old-age pensioners, did they? Nothing for it now, but to walk.

He stuffed back all the clothes Ringo had pulled out of the suitcase, taking care to repack Sylvia's medication. He hefted the case down. Thankfully, he'd brought the good suitcase, with wheels still intact.

By the time he reached Oadby, he floated in a fatigue-fuelled trance. Passing the big poster of the Alsatian dog that had been killed trying to cross the road from Oadby Tennis Club, he felt utterly deflated. Not a bench in sight, so he sat on the pavement, the tarmac rough and cold against his buttocks, leaning a little on the suitcase, but not too much in case it slid away.

'What have I done?' he muttered to himself.

Lawrence experienced a moment of self-doubt. Ignoring Ringo's grunts as he slugged down a Red Bull, he considered the woman in the rear-view mirror, no more than a silhouette in the dark there. The steel-grey Caprice, people carrier par excellence, or so the advert claimed, had a back seat arrangement where the seats faced each other. He supposed so it resembled a mini lounge, for the family to sit together and bicker, while the dad, or mum, screened effectively from all that nonsense, concentrated on the road. Good idea. He liked this vehicle. Plus, of course, it served to keep old ladies strapped in while being interrogated.

'Right,' he heard Ringo mutter, crumpling the emptied can and chucking it out through the window. It landed on top of a bush, stayed there like an ugly Christmas ornament. 'What now, boss?'

'Let's talk to her,' said Lawrence, and got out of the van.

'Seriously?' Ringo said, following him out.

Lawrence prised open the door and got in the back.

'Hello,' said Lawrence.

She stared at him, her mouth working at something. A tear slid down her chin.

'Get a tissue,' he said to Ringo. 'Wipe her chin.'

Ringo began to object, till Lawrence gave him a look, then did as he'd been asked.

When he finished, Lawrence said to the woman, 'You can get home as soon as we find the bag. You understand?'

The woman didn't or couldn't reply.

'You know where he put the bag?'

No reply.

'You can't talk. Can you sign? Lift up your arm if you've seen it? Has he showed it to you?'

'Like this,' said Ringo, darting forward and wrenching her arm up. The woman's eyes widened in panic.

'Get out,' said Lawrence, mastering his instinct to put his fist through Ringo's face. Ringo opened his mouth, thought better of it, got out, shut the door.

'So,' he said to the woman, softly. 'Can you make a sign? What about with your eyes? Can you blink twice if you've seen the bag?'

He waited. The woman's eyes, still wide with panic, now turned red in her effort to keep them unblinking. She mewled so pitifully he had to look away.

Outside, Ringo systematically destroyed a bush with his kicks. Lawrence watched him for a moment, amazed.

'Yaagh, yaagh,' yelled Ringo, till a misjudged kick sent him sprawling. He got up spluttering and cursing, pulling out twigs from his hair.

'Karma.' Lawrence cracked a smile at the old woman. 'What do you know?'

Her eyes were still wide with panic, and he began to regret this. Having her here.

'Flipping heck,' he said. He hoped Clive hadn't done a runner. But where could he go? Surely he wouldn't abandon his missus.

Lawrence scratched his beard. He wouldn't get anything from Sylvia.

'Right,' he said, making up his mind, and opened the door.

Ringo stood there dusting himself off, his face scratched raw by the bush. He said to Lawrence, 'Yo, man, I think we should take the lady back home and dump her.'

'You read my mind,' said Lawrence.

*

Clive felt in the zone by the time he came to London Road. Just walking, one foot in front of the other. The suitcase dragging and rolling, going bumpity bump on the paving slabs in a kind of staccato rhythm to his thoughts. *What had he done?* Overcome by a moment of greed. So unlike him, really. He, an honest to God Englishman. Never so much as pinched a sugar cube in his life. What had come over him?

They weren't even new. That was the thing. He wouldn't have pinched them if they'd been new. That would've been proper stealing. Artfully scuffed they were, there for the taking. It had seemed easy and simple. He'd even felt he deserved it for having retired with barely a penny, what with all the pension funds crashing and being defrauded by his boss the Yellow Maggot. A small compensation for having, whilst still healthy and possessing a tip-top mind, nothing to look forward to all day except laying slug traps and harvesting cabbage, and watching the fucking telly till the end of days, not even Sky Sports.

And if he outlived Sylvia, how long would his health last? Who'd look after him? His sons were in Australia. Sylvia had laughed thinking Steven had just told a good joke when he informed them he was off to Australia to be a sheep farmer. But he went. All the way to Oz. Might as well be the moon. Then out of the blue, Peter left to join his brother. Sylvia cried for two days. Goddamn shoes. After all he'd been through, he'd deserved a treat.

By the time he turned onto the darkness of Elmfield Avenue, passing the cars with the engines running, nervous single men waiting inside for some panacea, definitely illegal, and there, around the Ashfield Road bend, some sort of shady transaction taking place, stuff changing hands. Not that Clive cared, he merely cast himself in a future film of lonesomeness. He didn't know if he'd see Sylvia alive again. Those guys looked capable of murder, and worse. A fist of fear clutched his heart.

He turned the corner onto his street, with barely energy left for his suitcase. He just left it there on the pavement. Sod it. All Sylvia's things. He felt weighed down in his bones even as the top of his skull seemed to have lifted off. He wondered if he was on the verge of passing out.

He saw his door, and the figure huddled on the step. Suddenly the energy came from nowhere and surged through him. He ran. Sylvia, sitting slumped, dumped, propped up against the door. He ran to her and crumpled down beside her, cradling her, showering her wet chin and eyes and forehead with kisses. Just thankful she was still alive and back in his life again.

Chapter Six

'Clive!'

Patel banged on the door, and heard no noises, no shuffling feet towards the door, nothing stirring, just silence on the inside.

'This is not good,' said Neha. 'Shall we see if the neighbour has a key?'

'Best not to get more people involved than strictly necessary.'

'Is there a back door?'

'Just an alleyway.'

'Too noisy to bust in?'

'Not to mention illegal.'

'Let me at the lock,' said Neha. She reached into her backpack.

'Seriously? You're going to use a hairpin?'

'Never go anywhere without these.' She took out a bunch of tiny skeleton keys, chose one, pulled to extend it, then pushed it into the lock.

'Stop. This is illegal.'

'Oh, how do we get in then?' She pulled the key out, chose another.

'We need to apply for a search warrant, which we can't because you're not a police officer, and I'm out of jurisdiction.'

The lock clicked open. 'Oops,' she said. 'How long till they grant us permission?'

He felt a grudging admiration despite himself. 'Twenty-four hours?'

'He could be in there, mortally wounded.'

Patel hesitated, looked at the unlocked door. Perhaps they could just take a quick peep.

With a low, long creak on hinges that need oiling, the door swung open to reveal a typical hallway. A rug for wiping your shoes, a little shoe rack with six pairs of shoes, neatly put away. A council-fitted rung for a stairlift by the stairs.

Carefully, they stepped into the house, passing prints of irises, photos of two young boys and younger selves of Clive and Sylvia, smiling with the air of people who didn't smile all that often.

Through to the living room. A couple of well-used but good-condition sofas, a little kitchen table, bare, a small kitchen with pots and pans all put away.

A calendar hung on the back door, the dates of the entire month unmarked except for three. Roughly ten days apart. *Hosp 11 a.m., hosp 2.30 p.m., physio 10 a.m. What a life*, he thought, but then his life was not considerably better. Just that he had more options. Not so much if he resigned.

'Upstairs, I guess,' said Neha.

They went up the stairs, Patel calling, 'Clive? Are you up there? We're coming up to see if you're OK,' but receiving no answer.

The stairlift was stationed upstairs. With a sense of foreboding, Patel opened the door to the room that seemed largest.

A double bed, a free-standing wardrobe and a side table were crammed into the room. In the bed lay two people, huddled together under covers, either unconscious or dead.

Patel flung the duvet off. He checked Sylvia's pulse. Definitely alive, but sleeping deeply.

Then he turned to the huddled figure of Clive, curled next to Sylvia. *How had the noise not woken him?* He pulled up a sleeve to feel his pulse. Definitely there and he definitely still breathed.

'I'm calling 999,' said Neha from the doorway, her phone clamped onto her ear.

'No, hang up,' said Patel.

'Why? Are they? Is he?'

'He's fine. I think.'

Clive, curled in a foetal position next to a sleeping Sylvia, held himself so tight it'd seemed to Patel like rigor mortis. Silent tears streaked his half-hidden face.

'Clive, before we talk just let me know if Sylvia's alright. What have you given her?'

Clive said something, but with his cheek pressed against the pillow, it came out garbled.

'Clive! What did you give Sylvia?'

Clive lifted his head slightly from the pillow, and mumbled through a stuffy nose, 'Just a sleeping pill. The usual dose. She's alright.'

A cup of tea, half-drunk in great gulps, and still steaming in his hand, Clive looked halfway to his usual self. Haltingly, eyes downcast, he told them what had happened.

Patel's anger towards Clive melted as Clive finished his tale, still trembling. But now he felt furious towards the scumbags who kidnapped and tormented a disabled woman to punish her helpless husband. A part of him wanted to teach them a lesson, the law be damned. Perhaps Chandra's philosophy had rubbed off on him. He thought of the Indian policewoman's Bollywood style of policing – thump first and ask questions later. He calmed himself down back to the reasonable, law-abiding, English police officer that he was.

Patel said, 'Clive, listen to me. You must go to the police right away. Tell them everything. Describe the men and their vehicle.'

'But you said they'll arrest me for ... the shoes.'

Patel noticed that Clive still had the shoes on. Clive noticed him noticing, and sheepishly pulled his feet back a bit. 'I keep forgetting,' he murmured.

'So, I'll take you to the cops?'

Clive said, 'If they arrest me, what happens to Sylvia?'

'Is there a relative or a friend who could look after her?'

'No one. I can't put her in a home either, not with such short notice. She'd get so stressed. She'd worry about what's happened to me. Oh no. I'm staying put. If it kills me ...'

'Which it might,' Patel said.

Clive washed his cup at the sink, while Neha fiddled with her laptop. Sylvia, awake, seated downstairs now, had her eyes fixed on the wall photos.

'Where are your sons?'

'Australia.' The way he said it, it may as well have been the moon.

Patel felt all of Clive's agonies. The slow, grinding poverty, the absence of his sons, the strain of being a carer and the desperate act of petty theft. He felt terribly sorry for Clive, and his anger against the two men for tormenting Sylvia and Clive for the sake of some drug money only increased.

'If he won't go to the cops,' whispered Neha, looking up from her laptop, 'then we can't force Codman to reopen the case.'

'Even if he does go, Codman insisted we need material evidence.'

'The bag's the material evidence, that's what the thugs are desperate to get hold of.'

'Then that's what *we* need to get hold of.'

'How do we do that?'

Of course. His mother had mentioned some young men who haunted the allotment at night-time. Perhaps they'd seen something.

He told Neha his plan to go talk to the youngsters.

'One of us has to stay here in case the thugs turn up to harass Clive and Sylvia.'

Patel wondered since when they'd become a team. 'I'll go. You two put your feet up. Watch telly.'

Neha turned to Clive. 'Movies or cricket?'

'Football,' said Clive.

'When in Rome ...' Neha sighed.

Patel perched on a rickety wooden chair beside Sylvia's shed, deliberating whether it felt warm enough to discard his jumper.

He tilted back the squeaking chair, looked up at the darkening sky. Here he lurked in a quintessentially English scene. The ol' lottie. Green everywhere he looked. Neat rows of vegetables and netting, flowers and beanpoles, sheds and greenhouses. How different from the dust and chaos of India. People milled everywhere in Bangalore, at all hours. What creep did Chandra hunt this very minute? He knew she'd returned to work, the fury within her couldn't be quelled by a mere knife to the stomach.

Did he hope there could be more between them, after the intense experience they'd shared? But her life, her passport, her career, were all Indian. And no matter the colour of his skin or his mother-tongue or his family's habits, his roots, branches or leaves, Patel would only be home in Britain.

He thought about Codman. Did he drift into his job too? When Codman got assigned a case, did he think, paperwork: *how little can I get away with?* Or did he think – *right, let's see about getting to the heart of the matter.*

He realised he was soul-searching. Did he even want to be a police detective?

A distant squeak. The gates opening. Shrill male voices, banter, friendly scuffles, swearing. Patel waited, tense, gripping his torch, a big one that took three fat batteries. His mother used it on her jaunts to the ol' lottie in the dark, especially after a good rain, slug- and snail-hunting.

Lights. Mobile phones, lit up like torches. He imagined the batteries on those phones were draining quickly. He waited. The screens of light, four of them, travelled, accompanied with banter, Leicesterese spoken at speed, incomprehensible from this distance.

He realised his error. He'd be a prize plum springing up from the dark with his torch to chat with these boys. They couldn't see his face. He couldn't see theirs. He should have waited on the street, under the street lamp. His unannounced presence would spook them. They'd freak out, scatter.

He should approach them once they were out on the street again. But they could be here for hours. He'd have to keep still. He imagined bugs and slugs crawling over him while the kids got high as kites, or blind drunk. Now was the moment, good or bad.

As if providing a cue, the moon came out from behind a cloud. He turned his torch on and walked towards them.

They were joshing each other, smoking spliffs; cans were being opened. Slowly, one by one, as he approached, they fell silent.

Patel took a breath, filled his lungs with the acrid skunk. 'Hey there.'

They stood as though carved from stone.

'Sorry to startle you,' said Patel in a cheery voice. 'I didn't realise it would be so dark here.' No one joined him in his little laugh.

'Just have a question for you lads about the other day. You know the body discovered here?'

After a longish pause, one of them said, 'Yeeaah?'

'Wassit to you, man?' said another.

'I'm investigating what happened.'

He felt, more than saw, a couple of the boys jerk back.

Patel said, 'I'm not with the police,' adding silently, *not officially, anyway.*

'Ssso,' said the chap who'd said 'Yeeaah' earlier, 'you're a PI?'

'What?'

'Private investigator?'

'Hey, what's that, yo?' said a chap who hadn't yet spoken. A note of fear in his voice. 'Who's that? Your mate?'

Neha? Patel turned to see a shadow shift in a sliver of moonlight, near the gate. Then the moon disappeared behind a cloud, and it was pitch-dark again. Patel thought he could see better if he turned the torch off, but he didn't want to spook the kids. He listened. Deadly quiet. They stood together like startled cows, stock-still, silently breathing. A swish of wind, something moving at pace, something large as a man in the darkness.

The figure loomed close, and a voice said in a twangy nasal Leicesterese, 'It's effing dark here. Can't you lads get the grannies to string up some lights?'

Patel realised the man could see them clearly in the light of the phones and his torch.

A shift of shadow within the shadow made Patel realise there were two men. One small and noisy, the other big and still. The chaps Clive had described.

The big man said in a low growl, 'I thought there were four of you. Brought a friend, did you?'

'What's going on?' said the one who'd said 'Yeeaah' and 'Ssso' earlier.

'What did you do with the bag, you little shits?' said the smaller man.

'What bag?' said another.

'Who are you?' said Patel.

'Your elders and betters,' said the large man in a growl. 'Now where's the satchel?'

'Satchel,' blurted a third youth, Patel knew that tone. He heard the drop of the invisible penny. The big guy knew too. But just then the little guy launched himself forward and tried to grab one of the young men. He leapt away. Something jangled as it fell. The small guy scrambled around, cursing. A phone fell, its glow diving to the floor like a little Tinker Bell and was snuffed. Patel quickly groped the ground where he heard the noise, grabbed hold of something long and metallic, a chain.

The big man cursed like a primary school mum. 'Flipping heck' and 'bugger'. It would've been amusing if all hell hadn't been breaking loose around him. The big man went after one of the young men.

Shoving the bit of jewellery into his pocket, Patel ran quickly behind him and brought the torch down (or up, in this case) on where he judged his head to be.

The torch clanged as though it had hit metal, the light went off.

'Fuck.' The big man cursed. This time, a real curse. He thrashed his arms around, catching Patel under the chin. Seeing stars, Patel scrambled away. They were now in a thick and impenetrable murk. The torch had only given a glancing blow to the big man, but slowed him just enough that his captive got away.

Patel kept low and ran in the opposite direction to the kids. Of course, they knew the lay of the allotment like the back of their hands. Unlike the new visitors. He could hear them stumbling around, cursing.

'Should have brought a fucking torch, man,' said the little man.

'Shut the heck up, Ringo,' said the big man. 'I can't hear.'

Ah, he's the clever one, thought Patel, keeping as quiet as possible. He decided to hide and listen, find out a bit more. He crept in their wake, within earshot.

'This is embarrassing, man,' said the little guy, and Patel thought *this* could mean any number of things, his whining attitude, his attack at an inopportune moment just as they were beginning to get the information they were after. Or he could be embarrassed by the fact that he failed to grab the guy and sprawled in the dirt instead.

'Shh,' said the big guy.

Patel, crouching behind a bush, saw the moon come out from behind the cloud again. The men scanned around as they walked towards the gates. He supposed the big man didn't want to turn his phone torch on, to avoid making them into targets, for an invisible assailant. Him.

The men spoke to each other, this time quietly, while scanning the surroundings. They knew what they took to be 'one of the youths', Patel, to have gone off deep into the allotments. Patel wondered why they weren't staying and searching for him. Perhaps it was too unfamiliar a territory for them. City folk. Vegetation made them nervous. As if proving his point, a wind shook the sisal leaves into a rustle and the two men whipped their necks around.

They walked quickly. When he felt the moon to be suitably obscured, he raced in their direction as swiftly as he could whilst keeping low and quiet. He heard their voices again, this time near the gates. They were pulling them shut behind them.

'What number is it, again?'

'Doesn't matter. It's the only house with a hedge in front of it.'

They were heading to Clive's house.

'Hey,' he shouted, 'I need to talk to you.'

They froze on the other side of the gates, silhouetted by very bright headlamps. He ran towards them. A van, parked half on the pavement, half turned around, its headlamps shining in through the allotment gates. The little guy in the process of lighting a cigarette. Patel couldn't see their faces, but to them, he was lit up like a model in a film shoot. They could see his face. Like thugs all over the world, they knew a copper when they saw one.

The big man clicked the lock. Just as Patel's hands grabbed the gate. Patel pulled. They didn't budge. Patel cursed, searched his pockets for the key his mother had given him, couldn't find it. How did the others get in and out? The men leapt into the van, doors slammed and they took off, even as Patel found his key. He undid the bottom latch, then pulled, the gates just came open, lock notwithstanding.

Quick though he'd been to get out of the gates, nevertheless the men had flown and Patel hadn't read the van's number plate. All the commotion hadn't brought a single person out of their houses. Typically Leicester, that 'live and let live' attitude.

He jogged down the road and around the bend to Clive's. He burst in on Clive, Sylvia and Neha, plus his mother, sitting in the front room watching Leicester City losing to Southend United.

Chapter Seven

Ringo slapped his thighs twice, guffawed. In the mirror, Lawrence saw the copper drag the gates apart and run out. He chased after them until Lawrence turned the corner. Lawrence put his foot down and sped across a pedestrian crossing turning from amber to red.

'Who the fuck was that?' said Ringo.

'Police.'

'But I thought . . .'

'Yeah, I know.'

'What do you know, man?'

'Hey?'

'I didn't finish speaking. I said, I thought . . . and you said, "I know." How do you know what I thought?'

'OK, joker. Tell me what you thought.'

'I thought the police closed the case, saying it weren't no murder.'

'I knew you thought that, and I agreed with you.'

'But I could have thought something else, man? You could've been agreeing with anything.'

'Ah, Christ.' Lawrence eased his foot off the accelerator.

'So what do we have?' Neha said. 'Two thugs who are after a bag, and four boys who know where it is. We need to find them.'

Patel felt vexed that he'd been so close to getting information from the boys before Laurel and Hardy turned up to wreck the situation.

They examined the gold chain Patel had found. Broken. The pendant had serious heft to it. Spelled, in what looked like eighteen-carat gold, the word 'LESTAH'.

'What is this word?' Neha asked.

'It's how young people like to write Leicester,' said Padmini. 'Like Gangsta.'

Patel smiled. His mum still managed to surprise him. Then he grew serious. He said: 'The men will prove slippery, now they've clocked me, but the boys, Clive can direct us to them, can't you, Clive?'

'What?' Clive hadn't been paying attention. He drooped in front of the post-match analysis.

Patel looked intently at Clive. 'How did those thugs know about the kids?'

Padmini, not getting the gist, said, 'Who could've told them?'

Neha looked at Clive too, expectantly. 'Tell us, Clive.' Her manner promised no judgement.

Clive squirmed for a moment, then said, 'Sorry. It slipped my mind. They had me cornered. Wrecked my car. Grabbed my wife. I blabbed.'

Patel studied Clive for a moment, clocking his unreliability and tendency to lie.

'Where do the boys live? Do you know their names?'

'No idea,' said Clive.

'They come after dark,' said Padmini, 'and we know they've been there only by the rubbish they leave behind. Cigarette butts, crushed beer cans, chip boxes. As long as they don't mess with the vegetables, eh, and ha ha, they don't, probably don't touch veggies with a bargepole, ha ha.'

'Mum,' said Patel, 'give it a rest.'

Neha said, 'So they could come from anywhere.'

Patel said, 'One or two could be from the terraced houses. Seems logical. We could knock on doors in the morning.'

'Good luck with that,' said Clive. 'I'm off to bed now.' He stood up expectantly, waiting for them to take their leave.

'I suppose we can't stay here all night,' said Patel. 'Doubt the men will be back before morning.'

'We'll be here first thing, Clive,' Neha said, and Clive nodded wearily.

'Don't go out looking for trouble,' Patel told him.

Lawrence said: 'We got to find those kids. And find out what that plainclothes at the allotment was doing.'

They were in his basement garage, which he had decked out with old leather sofas and a turntable. He hadn't been keen on bringing bloody Ringo here. It being the early hours, there had been nowhere else to park up for a think and discuss what to do next. They had moves to ponder, war plans to draw up. He heard a small child cry out in her sleep. His daughter. She did that sometimes, after a busy day at preschool. He missed her. Hadn't seen his Cupcake all day.

He sized up Ringo, who inspected his games collection like a kid in a candy store. Ringo reminded him of one of those whiny, wimpy kids in school with a cruel streak, all grown up. Why on earth did he let him into his house?

'Hey, Ringo?'

'Yeah?' Ringo's eyes were still on the games console.

'Is that really your name, Ringo?'

Ringo spun around, surprised. 'As a matter of fact, my name is Abdul Karim.'

Lawrence looked blankly at Ringo for a moment, then burst out laughing. He immediately shushed himself in case he disturbed the sleep of his wife and daughter. But the mirth still bubbled out of him. *The sap has a bit of a sense of humour, who knew?*

After a moment, Ringo said, 'Well, it's what my folk gave me.'

'I guess your mother was a Beatles fan,' he muttered.

Ringo chuckled. 'You guessed right. Before she became too tight to remember their names.'

Lawrence felt intrigued. Ringo wasn't what one would call a natural fit for his line of work. Contrary to popular ideas, a muscle man, an enforcer like him, needed to be the opposite of a jack-in-the-box psycho. He needed to exude menace with his physical presence, say the right things at the right time, and instigate fear that resulted in the punters being afraid enough that they bent over backwards to pay their dues. A shrill, screamy runt like Ringo panicked people into running or ended up with a broken neck.

Lawrence sighed. What did he care? Ringo was probably the nephew of someone who wanted him out of their hair. Lawrence suddenly felt sick of this whole business. He had never thought he'd stoop to threatening an old man and his disabled wife. What could he reply when his wife said, 'How was your day, hon?' in her quaint English.

Ringo turned away from the games at last and said, 'Do you wonder what happened to that actor, man?'

Lawrence felt relieved Ringo didn't ask to play games. He said, 'Who, Majid?'

'Yeah. Do you wonder, what did he do to get in that situation? Who had it in for him? And what do you think is in the mystery bag?'

'Money, what else?' said Lawrence. But he hadn't wondered. It hadn't occurred to him to wonder. Even when a child, it had been instilled in him by his father, mother, brothers, uncles, aunts, never to wonder, never to discuss. He'd had to cultivate a kind of tunnel vision for his job. And he'd been good at it. Until now. The Cupcake forced him to reassess his blinkers.

'The system is corrupt, man. Have you ever thought of that?'

'Huh?' What was Ringo on about?

Ringo came too close to him and even in the gloom, his eyes shone with intensity as he said, 'Sometimes there is a rage so great inside that I want to really destroy ... You know? Fuck something up good. You know what I mean.'

He didn't. For Lawrence, anger was a frame of mind. He got into it like he got into clothes. Purely for professional appearances. It didn't bubble out of him like a volcano. Something about Ringo made Lawrence uneasy. It felt as though, while Lawrence put on an act of toughness for the sake of his job, Ringo had, under the layers of sappy, weedy geek, a real intense fucker, someone who would snap and go apeshit on you.

Best not to get into this line of conversation with the little sprig, he thought. In fact, best not to converse with him at all.

'Listen,' he told Ringo, gruffly. 'Let's not discuss the whys and wherefores of our job, yeah? Majid was involved in some shit that bit him in the backside. All we need to do is find the bag, not embark on detective work. Get it?'

Back to his timid self, Ringo nodded. 'Good idea,' he said.

'Where d'you live?' he asked Ringo.

'Beaumont Leys, man.'

Lawrence said, 'I'll call you a taxi.'

'Can I meet Mr T with you, man?'

'OK,' said Lawrence. 'Come to my house early tomorrow. We'll go see him.'

*

Padmini Patel found herself knocking on doors with her son. Never in a million years did she imagine herself as a cop's sidekick in a murder mystery. She had to remind herself of the caveats, of course, that the cops officially on the case had pegged it as either suicide or accidental death, and that her son was officially on sick leave and not supposed to be meddling in this business in the first place.

Padmini, her ancestors and her offspring had always been law abiders. Was she, in fact, breaking the law? She felt far from ready to trust in her grown-up son's good sense over her own. Still, he'd been looking like he needed help since he got off the plane from India.

'You take this one,' Patel told her.

She knocked on the door, Patel staying a foot behind. The door opened a crack, on its chain. A woman's eyes and nose appeared.

'Hi,' Padmini said.

The woman nodded, didn't speak. The door remained on the chain, her eyes travelled to Patel's face and widened in alarm.

'We are helping with a police investigation,' said Padmini, a voice inside shouting, *Liar, liar, pants on fire*. 'We are looking for some young men who go to the allotment in the evenings. Have you got any teenagers in the house?'

The woman stared. Her expression was either one of incomprehension, or simply pig-ignorance, Padmini couldn't say which. The woman made a throaty noise, as if pondering. Then nodded her head sideways, and said, 'No, no one like that here.'

She began shutting the door.

'Wait, wait.' Padmini pulled out the gold chain. 'Have you seen—'

The woman had shut the door.

Padmini looked at her son. They were at the first house. There were at least fifty more.

'Trouble is,' she said, 'the boys probably come out there without the knowledge of their parents. They are mostly strict Asian families around here, after all.'

'They are not all strict and Asian,' said Patel. 'I think the young men were a mix.'

They knocked on more doors, taking turns. It turned out all sorts of people occupied the terraces edging the allotments, including: an eccentric old white Englishman who filled his front garden with plastic flowers arranged in used Coca-Cola bottles; a family with no English whose kids emerged from every crevice in their two rooms; a grumpy old single woman; some friendly young Asian families with two kids apiece; a house shared by European mature students from the university. But no one knew anything. No one knew their neighbours more than as passing acquaintances, and a surprising number didn't know there were allotments right behind their own back gardens.

An hour later, they reached the end of the row. Padmini needed a lie-down. *Police work*, she thought, *isn't for me*. She didn't want to say it aloud, but she worried for her son. Although she usually thought of him as the strong, silent type, she feared for what this kind of drudgery must do to his mental health. And he'd been a wreck since he'd come back from India.

Those bloody reporters, bloody Sarah, and bloody Skinner from Scotland Yard. The GP so readily writing him off work. So many counselling sessions but he wouldn't talk to his mother. Mental health a hot topic these days. Wasn't there a new minister for suicide prevention?

'Right,' said Patel, in his inscrutable way. She pondered the possibility that he enjoyed this drudgery. Or did Neha's arrival in their lives perk him up? Although a reporter, she seemed a breath of fresh air. So charming and guileless, if a bit fixated on her laptop.

'Let's go see Clive and Neha,' Patel said. 'We will have a look at the allotments, see if there are any clues on the ground. You can let us in. Although, Ma, those gates need a better lock.'

She couldn't get a sense of his feelings towards Neha. Padmini thought it curious that her own son should be inscrutable to her.

When they arrived back at Clive's house, they found Neha immersed in her laptop screen. Clive busied himself at the stove making porridge and Sylvia sat on the sofa with an interested expression. Her mouth began to work when she saw Patel and his mother enter, as though she wanted to greet them. Padmini felt a rush of affection for Sylvia, with whom she'd always been friendly. It must be so frustrating not to be able to communicate.

Neha said, 'How did it go?'

'Nothing,' said Patel. 'No one knows anything.'

'Ask me what I've got,' said Neha.

'What have you got?'

'I've got the name of one of the boys, and just waiting for his address.' The laptop pinged. 'And here it is.'

'How on earth?'

'Never underestimate the importance of the community Facebook page. Come and have a look.'

Patel looked at her laptop screen. He read Neha's message.

> Found: a gold chain, looks real, pendant,
> at the Kimberley Road allotments.
> Reply with the word on pendant.

The reply within half an hour.

Yes is mine. Only dropped it last
night. Word is Lestah. ☺

Come by library café this afty or I can
drop it on the way back at your house
if close by Stoneygate/Knighton?

Twisted my ankle. So plese yes drop
it off. Address: 234 Aber Road.

'Bingo,' said Patel. 'I'm impressed.'

Padmini said, 'You are a clever girl, Neha. You should run the country.'

'Which one, aunty?'

'Both!'

Neha looked ridiculously pleased. Padmini noticed Vijay looking at the young woman speculatively. *Aha*, she thought.

Chapter Eight

Lawrence woke to joyful sounds. Screams of delight, giggles. He put a hand out to the bedside table and groped around for the clock. Nearly dropped it. Brought it close to his face and forced an eyelid open. Nine a.m.

'Flip,' he said.

Throwing on some clothes, he nearly missed the note on the bedside table, pushed to the edge and about to fall under the bed. He grabbed it and read.

Gt an early call. Ring lookn aft Chloe till u wake. Drop her off preschool pls. No cheerios, weetabik. M x.

'Flippin H,' he said.

In the kitchen, Ringo and Chloe sat at opposite ends of the table with a bowl of Cheerios each. Milk slopped all over the place. They were entertaining each other by fishing out the soggy Cheerios and sticking them onto their foreheads, cheeks and eyelids. Lawrence felt the mother-hen anxiety that assailed him whenever he saw Chloe being friendly with another man. He wanted to shout and scream, snatch her up from the chair and run far from Ringo. Instead, he made a bright face and said, 'Cupcake!' and felt pleased to see his daughter jump out of her chair and bound into his arms.

*

Lawrence dropped Chloe off at preschool half an hour late, to frosty twitching from the preschool manager. He didn't say, 'Christ, it's preschool. It's not like she's late for a rocket ship launch.'

When he got back in the car, Ringo said, 'Nice family, man.'

Lawrence flinched. This was exactly the kind of conversation he did not want to have with Ringo. 'You want to catch a bus home or something?'

'Na, pardner. I want to meet the Mr T, man.'

Dinky little café. *Tea rooms*, Lawrence tried saying under his breath. Annabel's Tea Rooms run by real middle-aged white Englishwomen. Lawrence and Ringo squeezed into dinky little chairs around a wobbly table, laden with a fretwork tablecloth, a bowl of potpourri and a glass vase with a yellow rose. He glanced over at Ringo, frowning at the menu options, the ugly duckling turned up at a swan's bash.

Only one other punter there, it being ten in the morning. The breakfast rush was over and the ladies were having a breather before the elevenses and lunch crowd. One of the ladies, aproned and bunned, arranged a mountain of scones in a display case.

The other punter was in black with his hair also in a bun. A big, handsome guy, tap-tapping away at his laptop, frowning and pursing his lips. He hadn't looked up when they came in, so Lawrence had assumed he wasn't Mr T.

Lawrence ordered scones.

'Jam and cream, or cream and jam?' Ringo asked Lawrence.

'Somehow I never took you to be a person who appreciated scones,' Lawrence said.

'Me nan used to make 'em,' said Ringo.

'You have hidden depths, man,' said Lawrence.

Lawrence looked at his watch, glanced at the laptop guy

again, wondered if it was really Mr T playing coy. Then someone else came in.

A skinny guy, preppy, in glasses and a suit, slick and clean-shaven with a fifty-pound haircut, he made straight for their table.

'Sorry I'm late, traffic's murder.'

Lawrence and Ringo half rose and shook his hand.

'Scones? Oh, go on then,' he said. He clicked his fingers. 'Cup of tea, love,' he said, and the hostess flashed a special smile. Regular, Lawrence supposed.

Lawrence had already warned Ringo they weren't to ask any questions. He'd felt unsure about bringing Ringo, but there hadn't been any specific instruction not to, or to keep him out of the loop in any way. They were to state the facts of the case, and wait for instructions.

Mr T ate his scone, cream on jam. Lawrence and Ringo copied him. He was that kind of guy. The way he poured his tea, buttered his scone, you wanted to do it exactly like he did, for you knew it was the only way to do it.

Lawrence wondered about Mr T's age. He looked young. Late twenties, the hair swishy and fabulous, but when he smiled, a fine pattering of crow's feet appeared around his eyes, took him nearer forty. An enigma.

'Give us the facts then.'

Ringo opened his mouth, and Lawrence spoke over him. 'We went to see Clive Atkins, like you said.'

'The man who found the body?'

'He didn't have a clue about the bag.'

'We didn't believe him, though, did we?' interjected Ringo.

'Why not?' said Mr T.

'Because he looked all shifty-mgifty, man,' said Ringo.

Mr T's mouth turned down in distaste.

'Thank you, Ringo,' said Lawrence, raising a warning eyebrow. 'Yes, he seemed to be misleading us. So, we applied a bit of pressure.'

'How much pressure?'

'Nabbed his missus, innit?'

Lawrence quelled the urge to stamp on Ringo's foot.

'Seriously?' Mr T raised his eyebrows.

''Cept she were like too much hard work and we dumped her back.'

'Ah.' Mr T brushed some crumbs from his mouth with a paper napkin. Lawrence waited.

'Kidnapping not good,' Mr T addressed Ringo. 'Abduction with intent to harm. Plus a witness to your mugs.'

'She veggie man. She won't speak to no one. Can't speak, period.'

'Did this kidnapping produce results?'

'Yes,' said Lawrence. 'Clive told us there were some youths at the allotment. They come every night. So we went looking for them.'

'Find them?'

'Yes. We know they took the bag, but we lost them again.'

'We don't know who they are,' Ringo pitched in again, irritating Lawrence.

Mr T pursed his lips. 'Where do they come from? Local boys?'

'Probably, but it was too dark to see their faces.'

'So you have nothing.'

'Doubt they'll come back, man.'

Mr T sat back and gave Lawrence a level look, waiting.

'The reason we're here,' said Lawrence. 'We saw a bloke also talking to the youths. He tried to come after us. Asian guy, early mid-thirties. Copper written all over him.'

Mr T frowned. 'You sure?'

'Definitely a copper,' Ringo said.

'I thought the cops had closed the case,' Lawrence said.

'I'll look into this. Asian, you say?' Lawrence nodded. 'I'll ring you in an hour.'

Mr T got up, threw down a twenty on the table. 'Ta, love,' he said to the hostess watching from the cake counter.

Lawrence glanced over at the laptop guy who'd been oblivious to their whole existence. He hadn't looked up at all. *Must be some engrossing work*, Lawrence thought, with a touch of envy.

His phone rang after Lawrence had dropped Ringo back in Beaumont Leys and was on the way back home. He took his time finding a safe spot. The phone stopped ringing. He parked and then picked up the phone. Mr T. He didn't leave a voicemail. He rang him back.

'Patel from Scotland Yard. Leicester's own Sherlock Holmes,' he said.

'Who?' Lawrence said.

'Patel or Holmes?'

'Patel.'

'Follow cricket?'

'Naa, man.'

'Read the news?'

'Sure.'

'Which papers?'

'*Guardian*. Sometimes *The Times*.'

'Patel is the cricketer turned homicide detective. Real hotshot. He's just come back from India after nabbing a serial killer. Front page of the *Sun* and the *Mail On Sunday* back in January. Paparazzi photos at Heathrow. His girlfriend nearly a victim of the Indian Ripper. No idea why he's involved in our little Leicester bag theft. Find out. Go and watch him.

When he finds the bag, you find it. Go and stake out his house. Take Ringo.'

'Is he a local then?'

'310 Kimberley Road. Across the road from the allotment.'

Lawrence went home and sprawled on his Chesterfield. He had a think. Things were getting riskier. He hadn't signed up to grapple with some big-shit cop. He googled Patel on his phone, and his eyebrows rose. He'd missed all the tabloid frenzy over this man. The paps had done a real number on him.

Shots of the girlfriend moving house. Shots of Patel moving his things. RIPPER COP RIPS RELATIONSHIP. Shots of a woman in a wetsuit by a river. PATEL'S MISSUS ON DEATHWISH, screamed a headline. Coldest day of the year apparently, and she was out swimming. Patel crossing the road.

Hey, was that Knighton Road? Looked like he'd come from the Co-op round the corner. He held a shopping bag. PATEL SHOPPING WITHOUT A CARE, opined this headline. And more in the same vein.

Lawrence put his phone down. Whattdaya know. Local chap and all. Lawrence always said Leicester had unrecognised potential. A real man, got things done in the world. Not like Clive; his sort were weak, weasely. Patel was more his heft. He'd feel good putting his fist through that handsome face. For the first time in months, he didn't feel sick of his job. He'd been toying with the idea of how to get paid enough to quit the business once and for all. This job was OK. But he couldn't quit with what he made from it. A few more like this, then, yes. Then he'd properly inhabit the hipster shell he'd built for himself.

But he kidded himself. Lawrence was no middle-class hipster. Just pretending to be one. Like those role-play nerds playing at being knights in Bradgate Park. Just the same, didn't he read somewhere that you are what you do, not what you think? The moment he'd met Magdalena at some party, a light in his head had switched on. He'd presented himself to her as a chap who did some harmless wheeling and dealing.

She wasn't the curious type so he'd stepped into this new persona like stepping into new clothes. He'd even abandoned his family and old friends. His whole life had turned like a penny on its head. Any doubts he had about the morality of his actions disappeared the second he laid eyes on his little Muffin. He'd never taken her to meet his family, although, well, they all still lived only a couple of miles away. But Lawrence just cut them dead when he saw them about town. Only, from time to time, the old temptations visited him. He'd been doing well controlling the urge to put a fist through a man's face, to break bones. Just two in the last six months, not counting Mr Prada Pincher.

He wondered if Patel would be good in a fight. Do they do some boxing in police training? Lawrence shivered himself out from thoughts of violence directed at Patel's handsome features. Really he wanted to be a dad they invited for school talks. He could be a businessman. Why not? He could open a café. He'd be good at it. He would take a few tips from Annabel's Tea Rooms. Doilies, no; potpourri, maybe; scones, yes, a definite yes to scones. And not tiny little plastic packets of butter and jam. He'd dole them out in tasteful pots.

But enough daydreaming. First he needed to track Patel down, find the bag. Got to get the job done. After all, in freelance, you were only as good as your last job.

He got up, went to phone Ringo.

Chapter Nine

Patel and Neha walked to Aber Road, eyes all the while scanning passengers and drivers of passing cars, looking for the two men Clive had done his best to describe, of whom Patel had made out only silhouettes in the lamplit darkness.

'This route takes me back,' Patel said.

'How so?'

'My best friend used to live on Aber Road.'

'Maybe he's still there,' said Neha, 'in his mum's house.'

'Oi,' said Patel, perceiving the insult, but Neha looked innocently at him, and he realised she wasn't cocking a snook at him. An Indian son's rightful place, after all, was in his mother's house.

'Aren't you in touch any more?' she said.

'Naah. We kind of fell out.'

'Over what?'

'Long story.'

'We have a few minutes.'

'OK.' Patel told her. The two of them used to smoke dope behind the shed at the end of the long garden. You needed binoculars to see anything compromising from the house. Which was exactly what Iphraim's mother bought herself to spy on them. Boy did they get into trouble. It led to Patel being cast out of his friend's life, as though Iphraim was all innocence and it was purely Patel's influence that so corrupted their son.

A few months later, Iphraim was mugged, beaten up in the alleyway that led to Allandale Road. Cut, bleeding, dazed, Iphraim walked all the way to Patel's house instead of going home, which was a mere twenty yards away. Patel's mother rang Iphraim's, despite Patel begging her not to. Iphraim's parents arrived in a fury. They ignored their son, didn't even check his wounds, a cut on his chin and an ugly bruise on his head. While the father stood mutely glowering, the mother rained abuse on Patel and his mother for corrupting their son, turning his head to vice.

'They had this big black Range Rover,' Patel said. 'The whole time they were in our house, ranting, it spewed black smoke, like poison. Some exhaust fault, probably.'

The final image of Iphraim, seared on Patel's mind: tail between his legs, throwing Patel a last look as he climbed into the back of the car. He remembered thinking, *your fucking car is half as big as your house, you fucking twerps.*

'I heard later they'd moved away to the countryside.'

'Stoneygate too edgy for them?' Neha said.

'It is infested by middle-class ganja-smoking teenagers.'

Neha laughed. Patel felt as though he'd had the first real conversation in a long time. He realised he'd not ever mentioned Iphraim to Sarah. Perhaps he'd been ashamed of how it ended.

'It must have hurt you that they insulted your mother,' Neha said.

Bingo. She understood. It was an Indian-son thing. He hadn't been able to defend his mother against vile insults. It had cut him deep.

Neha shrugged, looking sad. 'We all have these stories.'

'So what is your family like?' he said, realising he knew nothing at all about her.

'Oh, you know, just the usual,' she said.

She seemed tense all of a sudden. Patel wondered if family wasn't a good topic with her. God knows he was sympathetic. He resolved to stick to work.

'You're very dedicated to finding the truth of the matter, aren't you? You aren't sleeping at night.'

She looked startled. 'Why do you say that?'

'Dark circles.' He indicated her eyes. 'Your job's keeping you up?'

Neha looked strangely guilty. She shrugged off the compliment with a murmur, then gazed at the house numbers.

'Here we are,' Neha said, stopping in front of number 234.

Patel found the front door and façade so familiar, he almost felt Iphraim would emerge when Neha knocked. The latch rattled, and Patel held his breath as a boy just like his old mate hobbled out.

'Hassan,' he said, and shook Neha's hand after a second's hesitation.

'This yours?' Neha reached into a pocket and brought out the chain, the pendant dangling heavy from it.

'Thanks,' said Hassan and reached out. But Neha whisked it away and put it back into her pocket.

'First, we need a couple of questions answered.'

'Hey, what?'

'Can we come in?'

'No, what the— Gimme my chain, bitch.'

'Language,' said Patel, taking a step forward, crowding Hassan against his front door. Hassan scrambled back, unsteady on his injured ankle, and struck the wood.

Mustering a teacherly voice, Patel said, 'Looks like you need to sit down and reflect on your behaviour.'

Patel and Neha pressed forward, forcing Hassan back into his own house. In the living room, they made themselves comfortable on a sofa, invited Hassan to sit down too. Before they could talk a woman walked in from the kitchen.

'Hello?' she said, hospitable, if bewildered. Patel supposed they weren't the usual sort of friends and acquaintances Hassan brought home.

'Hello, aunty,' said Neha. Patel threw her a look. Surely, Hassan's mum wasn't old enough to merit an 'aunty' suffix. Mid-forties, at the most.

'You are?' she said, still puzzled.

'Tell them, Hassan,' Patel said.

'They found my chain, Ammi, one I lost yesterday. Told you, no?'

'I'm pretty sure you didn't tell me, Hassan. When did you lose it?'

'On the way back from college, na. On the road. Must have split and fell. This lady found it.'

The woman blossomed with kindliness and gratitude, all suspicion forgotten. 'In this day and age. Such kindness. Can I get you something? Coffee? Tea?'

'Love a cuppa,' said Patel.

'How do you take it?'

'Strong, no sugar.'

'Two sugars for me, please,' said Neha. Mum bustled off.

'She's nice,' Neha told him, sweetly. 'You call her bitch too?' Hassan glowered.

Patel stage-whispered, 'She knows you hang out at the allotment smoking dope?'

The boy flinched visibly, his eyes darting towards the kitchen.

'Tell us the truth and we'll go away,' said Neha.

'I don't know anything,' said Hassan.

'The bag you found? Where is it?'

The boy froze. 'It was you, yesterday,' he said.

'Where is the bag?'

Hassan shook his head. 'Sammy picked up this bag, man. Good quality leather. When he opened it, a funky smell came from it. Like maybe some shit in it, you know, not shit shit, the foxes and dogs, whatnot, they shit everywhere, don't they? Anyway, he flung it away into the bushes. That's all I know, man.'

'Sammy say what was in it, besides shit?'

Hassan shook his head after a moment.

Patel wasn't convinced. 'We'll stick around till you remember something useful to us.' He leaned back on the sofa, put his hands behind his head.

The sound of the kettle coming to a boil seemed to suddenly jog Hassan's memory. 'Yeah, I 'member. Sammy, he felt something heavy in it, tight plastic bag or something. Probably bricks, a prank or something, you know. That's what we told him. But he didn't think so. Should've checked, man, he said a couple of times, but by then it was quite dark anyway. We went early the next day and it was all like, vegetation everywhere, flowers, brambles and shit.'

'So, it's still at the allotment,' said Neha.

Before Hassan could answer, his mum came in with the mugs. 'What's this?' she said.

'I was just saying, your son of course is too young to remember, did you have a neighbour with a son called Iphraim? My age.'

'Ah, let me think.' She got comfortable – she seemed the type to take time with her thoughts.

They all waited companionably. Hassan looked as though he was about to pass out. Neha winked at him.

Half an hour later, Neha said, 'Do you believe him?'

They were at the allotment gates. Patel watched his mother

struggle with the rusty lock. He said, 'Hassan isn't exactly a model youth. But, yes, I do.'

'He seems a congenital liar,' said Neha.

Patel said, 'His description of events was convincing, if somewhat graphic.'

Padmini Patel finally got the lock open and let them in through the squeaky gates.

'Council inspection,' Padmini told the plotholders as they passed them. Some of the old-timers gave her the inscrutable look they'd practised all their working lives and mastered in retirement. Patel and Neha were no councillors, and they'd seen a few in their lives; some of them had held their plot for thirty-five years.

Rows of potatoes were being earthed. Strawberries mulched and purple broccoli harvested. Someone teetered on a rickety wooden ladder, fixing a shed roof. The air breezy and balmy, unusual in the turgid bowl that was more usually Leicester.

They came to the unofficial tip. A swathe of brambles growing over uncompostable household rubbish.

'The people who live along the accessway nip out their back garden gates and come through here to dump unwanted stuff. Too lazy to drive to the tip.'

Patel hadn't paid attention to the tip area on his earlier jaunt. Great arcing whips studded with vicious thorns draped over broken chairs and mattresses. Cigarette butts in beer cans.

'This must be where the kids hang out.'

Neha said, 'He could have thrown the bag anywhere. Hundred different places.'

'We could search in a rough circle around the beer cans. Bag-throwing distance being the radius.'

'He said it disappeared into the bushes.'

'It's been three days,' said Padmini. 'I see some of the plots have been tidied up since.'

Patel went and stood in a patch that looked trodden down. Close by was Sylvia's plot, with its neat chicken-wire fence going around, a home-made but effective gate that had a piece of wire as a makeshift latch, to keep out foxes, he supposed. Across was a plot that was neat and tidy, covered over almost entirely in black plastic. Only a little corner of it had been lifted and something green and healthy-looking (spinach, Padmini informed him), was planted.

'Betty's. Probably too busy to grow vegetables. Too busy to cook. What's the point?'

'What about the plot next to it?'

'Belongs to Linda. Bit eccentric. Doesn't get on with most people, especially Clive. Looks like she's come and tidied her plot.'

Patel, Neha and Padmini searched among all the bushes in the throwing circumference from where the youths hung out. It wasn't an easy job wading through brambles and nettles, all kinds of plastic rubbish, broken glass. Padmini said it was good for sheltering wildlife, so the association encouraged people to leave weedy overgrown bits in their plots.

'What wildlife?' said Neha, looking apprehensive.

'Foxes, hedgehogs, bugs and beetles, frogs, snakes even.'

'She's kidding,' said Patel. 'No snakes in Britain.'

'Yes, there are,' said Padmini. 'Non-poisonous though. Mostly.'

'Hmm,' said Neha, and didn't delve too deeply into the bushes from then on.

Half an hour later, they'd found nothing. Patel walked further up the plot, came upon a seating area by a large pond. His hairs on the back of his neck prickled. He turned and looked at the top-floor window of a house, whose back gate had a sign, 'Beware of the Dog'. He thought he saw movement there. As if someone had been standing watching him from the window, and decided to move back when he looked up.

Neha came up. 'See anything?'

'No,' he said.

Padmini joined them. 'Steve won best plot in the competition twice. Only thing is, he does the same thing every year so they've asked me not to enter it again, as it never changes. You can imagine that bit of news went down like a ton of bricks. Made Linda happy though. One person she hates more than Clive is Steve.'

'Ah. The politics among recreational vegetable growers, eh?'

'Oh yes, cut-throat. Did you see the news in London? Disturbed man murdered allotment secretary for trying to throw him off the plot.' Padmini fake-shuddered. 'You can't tell with most of these people. Supressing a hell of a lot of rage under all that chit-chat about weather and dwarf beans' watering needs.'

'Vicious,' said Neha.

'Hello there,' boomed a voice. A man, early sixties, approached with a broad smile. 'Admiring my pond, are you?'

'Hello, Steve,' said Padmini. 'Have you seen either Betty or Linda lately?'

'Oh, don't talk to me about Linda. The woman makes me mad.'

'What's happened now?'

'She's been moaning that I've chucked rubbish on her plot.'

Patel perked up. 'What sort?'

'As if I would bring rubbish all the way from my house to the lottie to chuck it specifically onto her plot. The woman's mad. Last time it was a fake bearskin rug with dog poo on it. Can you imagine? I said to her someone walking along the accessway must have thrown it, seeing as her plot's close to the path. But no, she says she's logically worked out it could only have been me.'

'When was this?' Patel asked.

'Oh. Six months ago.'

'Nothing more recently then,' Patel muttered, and began to move away.

'Two days ago she had another blazing row with me about some rubbish.'

Patel's heart beat faster again. 'Did she say what you'd thrown on her plot?'

'Nothing, that's what I'd thrown onto her plot,' said Steve, now all heated up. 'Why on earth would I do that, I ask you?'

'But what did she say got thrown onto her plot?'

'That's what I wanted to know. Soon as I asked her to produce this piece of rubbish, she suddenly went shtum. Tried to change the topic. Got rid of it, she claimed. I tell you, the woman's lost her marbles.'

'She didn't mention what it was?'

'She did, but you know how she speaks, half shouts, half mumbles.' Steve turned away, as if he'd had enough of airing his grievances and had more important things to do. He picked up his watering can.

'What could it have been?' Patel said.

Steve paused, cocked his head as if listening to a song in his head. 'Oh, I remember now. She said *leather bag.*'

Chapter Ten

Clive put the phone down with a trembling hand and gasped for air. He'd been holding his breath, his chest tight as Padmini explained how they'd worked out Linda had the bag.

'Did you get it off her?' he asked.

'The moment I mentioned the bag, she hung up on me. Wouldn't pick up again.'

Clive swore. Padmini said, 'I only have Linda's old address on the rental form. I'll ring around to see if anyone knows where she lives.'

Clive had to sit down to digest this information, struggling for breath, his heart hammering, all his anxiety of the past days churning up into something hot within.

After the Patels and Neha left his home the previous night, he'd taken paracetamol, ibuprofen, then some of Sylvia's codeine, trying to numb the panic. But it didn't work. He'd barely slept. Threw up twice.

Sylvia sat in front of the telly. A World War II movie began. Bombs dropped and he thought of Linda holding the bag. Was she even still in town? Had she flown off to Spain, to spend whatever fortune she'd found? Linda had what those men wanted and they were making Clive suffer for it. He veered between despair and fury.

He couldn't look at Sylvia. She sat opposite him, her mouth

working words that couldn't escape, her hands trembling in her lap. She began making a sound of stress. He tried looking away. It kept getting louder, till he could bear it no longer.

He leapt to his feet and brayed at Sylvia. 'Stop it, stop it, stop it!' His voice rose in volume, a rage mingled with a desperate plea.

She stopped.

He felt a rush of relief for an instant, then a black pit of despair engulfed him. He dropped before her, howled. Pressed his head to her legs. When he looked up at last, 'I don't know, I don't know,' was all he could say.

Sylvia had closed her eyes.

'Come on, babe, look at me. Open your eyes. I won't shout at you again. I promise. I won't ...'

His voice broke. He sobbed afresh. Ah, heck. He left her on the sofa, eyes still closed and shaking, came back with her pills. She had her eyes shut tight, but accepted them into her mouth. He held her jaw and felt her swallow. Then he got her into the stairlift.

'Oh, come on, love,' he said to her. 'I've said sorry, haven't I?' But she wouldn't open her eyes, or maybe couldn't.

He heaved her onto the bed and pulled the covers over her. She trembled, still with eyes closed.

He watched her for a few more moments, then went down the stairs and sat on the sofa again, and this time, unwatched by Sylvia, he gave in to the grief life pressed upon him.

He thought of the strangers trying to help him. These ... these educated foreigners whose manners felt strange to him but who were also Leicester folk. He'd had interactions with them all his life, of course, being Leicester born and bred. South Leicester was a vibrant place. There's a good word, he thought. How many of his own kind were left in his life, the old white folk like himself?

Linda was one. Nasty piece of work. His blood began to boil at the thought of Linda holding on to the suitcase or satchel or whatever those bastards were looking for. It had to be her to come and ruin his life like this. Those big flower bushes along the border between hers and the one next door to hers, the one covered in black plastic.

She'd razed the bushes two days ago. Was it there she found the bag? Where was it? In her house. Had she taken it anywhere? No. She didn't drive, did she? Didn't have a car. Probably sitting at her kitchen table, counting the cash. Cleaner, wasn't she? Yes, a cleaner at the university. Didn't he see her once, in a blue uniform, on some pavement? On Herschell Street. Going in a front door!

The revelation made him snort. Yes, he knew where Linda lived.

Before he knew what he was doing, he had his mac and wellies on, as though he were off to the allotment. With no plan more than a vague urgency, he went straight up Kimberley Road, turned left and found himself on Herschell Street.

He remembered being startled at seeing the woman in an unexpected place. They weren't exactly friends, were they? Her face like a stone, that bloody madam cut him dead.

In disbelief at this rudeness, he'd turned around to give her a hateful look and saw her taking her key out and going up to a red door. She went in and a light came on, a reddish glow spilled out the glass, which had puzzled him for a moment till he realised it was frosted red.

There. That door. She was probably in there now, behind that red-frosted glass, counting the cash. Cow. While the thugs murdered him over a pair of scuffed Pradas.

He rang the bell. No answer. She could be at work, he thought, slightly relieved. Really he wasn't up for a showdown with the foul-mouthed old curmudgeon.

The door opened as he turned to leave. Linda stood there wiping her eyes. Sniffing. Took her a few moments to blink her eyes clear so she could have a proper look. All she could say, upon clocking who stood in front of her, was, 'Ugh?'

'We need to speak,' he said.

She just blew her nose on a hankie and stood by to let him in.

Thick dust on everything. Piles of junk everywhere. Some professional cleaner, he thought, her own house a tip. To add to the irony, how neat and tidy her allotment had always been. Top notch, completely weed free. Many a time, he'd come across her on her knees, old bit of card or plastic under them, pulling up iffy little tendrils of newly emerged weeds. His Sylvia only noticed them when they were a foot high, apologised to them sweetly as she dug them out with a fork. He missed that. He pushed the thought away.

'Put the kettle on, shall I?' said Linda, dripping sarcasm. And then, to his amazement, she did go off into the kitchen to put the kettle on. She made the tea, sniffling and blowing her nose and wiping her hands on a dress with a pattern that looked much too cheerful for Linda, a riot of yellow and red and blue roses against her sallow skin and spirit.

Clive sat at the dining table and looked at the heaps of half-open cans and spices on the counter, a lot of Indian ones. Linda, as far as he knew, was a racist old bird, and he didn't think she went in for 'foreign food'. Now she loomed with the mugs of tea, sneezing and sniffing, breathing heavily.

He said, 'You not well or something?'

She handed him a filthy mug with the weakest tea imaginable, then heaved onto a chair, wheezing. 'What's this, a social call?'

'Listen, I see you cleared those flower bushes of yours.'

'What's it to you? Not your plot, is it?'

'I'm just . . . it's just that some chaps have been around looking for something.'

'What chaps?'

Clive's antennae quivered. He thought, she didn't say what *something*. She said what *chaps*.

'Linda,' he tried to keep the pleading out of his voice, gripping the hot mug, too hot, the heat searing the skin of his palm. 'Did you find something?'

'What you talking about?' Her voice husky, out of breath. She wheezed, he could hear every laboured breath.

'Linda,' he said, getting angry. 'Where's the bag?'

Her eyes widened. She knew what he was talking about. Her expression turned cagey. 'No idea.'

'You cow,' he said. 'You bitch.'

'Get out of my house,' she said.

A switch flipped in Clive's head.

He screamed at the old ill bird, her heart a lump of coal. He opened and closed cupboards, drawers, upending chairs with piles of stuff. She just sat there, wheezing.

He stormed up the stairs, tore bed covers off, flipped over mattresses, ripped pillows from their cases. He broke things, threw things down the stairs. It would help, he thought, if he knew what the bag looked like. He went through the three or four small to medium bags he found, but they were all women's bags. Purple and lilac, only one of them brown, and that was some cheap moth-eaten thing with half a packet of Opal Fruits from the 1970s. All the while he raged and searched, he didn't hear a peep from Linda.

He found a hatch in the ceiling that came down with a ladder, and heaved his dodgy knees up it, found himself in a little squirrel warren stacked full of goodness knew what shit. Cobwebs and filth, knick-knacks and photos. Generations of them. Linda's ancestors, he presumed. White as paper and dressed up stiff and staring at the photographer, proper Victoriana. He recognised the old Leicester shoe factory. One of them ancestors, he supposed, stitched soles to the boots of men that went to the trenches in the Great War.

He broke down again, clutching this photo. He went down on his knees and wept, but quietly. He didn't want Linda to hear him crying. He wanted her to see him furious. He didn't have the heart to search any more. He put the photos back carefully, ironic considering he'd ripped through everything else in the house. He lumbered down the spindly attic stairs. As he stepped off the last rung he was almost disappointed that he hadn't fallen from the top rung and broken his neck. Can't blame him for theft if he lay there with a broken neck, now could they?

Then, as he sent the ladder back up and the hatch closed, he wondered why Linda was still sitting quietly on her kitchen chair all this time while he ransacked her house.

Chapter Eleven

'Trouble,' Patel said to Neha when he saw the squad car parked up as they turned into Herschell Street.

It had taken Padmini a while to do a circuit of all the plot-holders. No one knew where Linda lived. Then someone rang her to say Linda worked at the university. This was promising. Except, the university had no details of its cleaning staff, just the name of the company contracted to do the work. After a few fruitless phone calls, Patel had driven over to the Humberstone office, pulled out his ID to get Linda's address.

Herschell Street was cordoned off. A uniformed officer waited by the cordon, directing traffic. People were looking out of houses up and down the street.

'Vijay,' she called, as they approached.

'Jess,' Patel said. 'Community officer now, then?'

'Guess so.'

He introduced her to Neha. 'School mate,' he said. Jess gave Neha the once-over, twice. Neha looked nervous under Jess's scrutiny, but then, thought Patel, Jess'd made everyone nervous on the primary school playground.

'So what's going on?' Patel asked Jess.

'Dead body.'

Patel's heart sank. 'Not Linda, is it?'

'You knew her?'

'Is Codman in there?'

'Sure is.'

'Can I talk to him?'

'What about her?' Jess indicated Neha.

'She's with me.'

Jess pursed her lips, then lifted the police tape.

He peeped through the window, saw Codman amidst what looked like the aftermath of a tsunami. Neha began clicking photos through the glass. When he saw Patel through the window, Codman came outside.

'Do you know anything about this?' he asked Patel, giving Neha a suspicious squint. She'd put her phone away before he spotted her.

'Well, well. Bit of a rum coincidence, you being here. Didn't you mention a pensioner' – Codman consulted his notes – 'white, male, late sixties, five foot seven, five foot eight, as having stolen a pair of shoes from Majid Rahman?'

'Linda is an allotment holder,' said Patel. 'We believe that Majid Rahman's bag ended up with her. We came here to ask her about it. Too late, looks like.'

'Is Linda's death suspicious?' Neha asked.

'A neighbour heard shouting, saw a man leave Linda's house, got twitchy, then decided to check on Linda. Found the door open, house ransacked, Linda dead.'

'Description?' Patel said.

'Just told you. White male, about five foot seven, grey-white hair, dressed in a khaki mac and green wellies.' Codman grinned with relish.

Patel and Neha looked at each other.

Codman said, 'It would be quicker if you gave me his address.'

Patel sighed. 'Sixty-one Oakfield Road.'

'Right. Be seeing you.'

'Can I come?' said Patel.

'No.'

'It's not likely Clive committed a murder.'

'We'll see about that, won't we?'

'Let me talk to him.'

'Not your case, mate. Go back to London and your fancy murders. If I see you digging around here any more, I'll make an official complaint.'

Neha burst in. 'But we've been telling you all this while to treat Majid Rahman's death as suspicious. Now will you re-open the case?'

'Who's she?' Codman asked Patel.

'I'm a journalist from India,' Neha said.

Codman turned his cold eyes on Neha. 'Should you even be here? You have permission?'

'I've got a visa. I don't need permission. It's a free country, yours, isn't it?'

'We'll see about that,' said Codman, turning from her.

'See about what?' Neha stepped towards him. 'Are you going off to check your rulebook to see whether it says yours is a free country?'

Patel gripped Neha's elbow.

'Right,' Codman snapped. 'Here's what's about to happen. We're opening a murder investigation into the death of Linda Botham. Prime suspect: Clive Atkins. I'll also re-open the case of Majid Rahman. Suspected murder. Prime suspect: Clive Atkins. He found the body, after all. Maybe there's a poisonous nettle he knows about, maybe the old bird saw him do it, and he followed her home, put the nettle in her tea.' Patel glanced through the window at the kitchen table, saw the two mugs, with what looked like remnants of tea.

Codman lifted a stern finger, as if to halt the interruptions of Patel and Neha. 'And, if I see you anywhere near either the allotment crime scene, or Clive's house or here, I'll arrest you for interfering with police business with the intention to obstruct justice. Are we clear?'

'Crystal,' Patel said.

'Bloody buffoon,' muttered Neha.

Back home, Neha continued to fume, while Patel remained thoughtful. The circumstances surrounding Linda's death did not bode well for Clive. Padmini, after fruitless attempts to contact Clive, had gone over to his house. He doubted she would find him on the sofa watching telly.

He thought about Codman warning him off the case. At least now there was a case. Both deaths, Majid's and Linda's, would now be properly investigated by the East Midlands Crimes Unit. It was out of Codman's hands. A good thing.

Patel said to Neha, 'Looks like we're done, don't you think?'

'But you are the police.'

'In London. I'm just another Joe on the street here. Shouldn't you be getting back to India?'

'Are you kidding? No chance.'

'If Codman arrests you for obstruction, you'll be in all sorts of trouble, Neha.'

'I'll take the risk.'

Patel frowned. 'Is it worth it? It's just some has-been actor, and it looks like, at best, some dodgy drug business.'

Neha opened her mouth, but couldn't speak. Her eyes began watering. She hid her face behind her sleeve, drawing big gulps of air, sniffing. Patel found a clean tissue in his pocket and handed it to her.

'Sorry,' said Neha. 'I get these sudden attacks of hayfever.' She laughed, sniffed, blew her nose again.

'So, you'll go back?'

'Certainly not.'

'You still want to be involved?'

'Of course I want to be involved. I don't trust Codman at all. You saw how he tried to cover up the case, right?'

Again, Patel wondered how she had access to his files. He said, 'He'll have to hand this over to the Specialist Crime Unit.'

'They could be his friends.'

'Is getting a scoop that important?'

'Yeah,' said Neha. 'Imagine the feature I'll be able to write.' Her voice sounded brittle. 'All of India will love the fact that I've disobeyed cops' orders and stayed on "undercover"' – she used finger quotes – 'to root out the murderer of a beloved of the people. They'll have forgotten by now, of course, that he long since ceased to be a media darling, and was used as a symbol of moral corruption with his wayward behaviour for so long.'

Patel raised an eyebrow. 'Was he now?'

'Oh yeah. He was often photographed cigarette in hand, arm around some starlet or other.' She used air quotes again. '"Separated from wife", "child living with mother", "oh the shame", and all that. Thing is, they twist everything. The poor starlet was probably being polite, you know, just posing for the photographers. The reporters goading him, *Come on, Majid, yaar, put an arm around Dolly or Bunty or whoever, give her smooch, na?*'

Patel imagined these jolly, lewd people, in diaphanous gold-flecked pyjama-suits, extravagantly coiffured and perfumed and bejewelled . . .

Neha mumbled, half to herself . . . 'I don't think *he* would have given in to the photographer cajoling him though, why was Majid whispering in his ear; they weren't even looking at the camera . . .'

'Who?'

'Oh, sorry, thinking aloud. This fellow ...' She sat up abruptly.

'Who?'

'Zakir. There was a picture. It got buried quite quickly. Furore for fifteen minutes, nothing before, nothing after.' Neha leapt up from her chair and clapped her hands together. 'Yes,' she said, 'we need to look into this.'

'Goodness, who is this guy?'

'He's completely under the radar, but my friends who do undercover stuff, they think he's got sticky fingers in all kinds of pies, though they can't get anything on him. That's why I noticed the picture.'

'Back it up a little,' Patel said, exasperated.

'OK, let's sit down.'

Patel, already seated, waited. Neha flopped back into the chair, gathered her thoughts, then began. 'About a year ago, I bumped into a friend, and she couldn't talk about what she was up to, just that it was some big fish who was pretending to be small fry, and very smart and quick. Then this in the paper, with a curious caption from the photographer, "murky musings" or "tricksy tête-à-tête", something along those lines, and it clicked that she was investigating this chap, his name floats across the media from time to time, just a presence, you know, and what attracted me is the absence of anything around it. A name in a vacuum, unconnected to anything, the name Sharjah cropping up in one remove, like he meets someone who's just been to Sharjah, and you know what that is all about ... right?'

'Mmm, no ...' said Patel.

Neha rolled her eyes. 'You Brits don't know anything about anywhere that isn't America, do you?'

Patel shrugged.

'Right, this is what intrigued me. The name in a vacuum, as if all the connections have been erased, the names and context hoovered away. The name echoing through its own power in the shadows. Then this truly incongruous photo, the two men in the shadows, Majid whispering into Zakir's ear.'

'Zakir the tabla player?'

'Zakir Bai. The mafia guy.'

'Ah.'

'The bag isn't important,' said Neha.

'No?'

'It has one of two things. Money or information. Money we don't care about. Even if it's fifty million, it's not ours, so who cares? Let the bastards tear chunks off each other looking for it. Information. That's what we need. But now the police and Laurel and Hardy are looking for the bag. Majid's supposed to have overdosed, so nobody is looking at Majid himself. We need to know who he was meeting.'

'I can't go sleuthing around Leicester. Scotland Yard will have my scalp.'

'Well, there's the other option,' said Neha.

'Which is?'

'Go to India, use my connections, find out who Majid was fraternising with.'

'Can't we do that from here?'

'Ah, no. We might have to hassle people to get information.'

'Hassle?'

'Time is of the essence when it comes to hassling. If I ring around, email and WhatsApp, that'd be stirring the pond. All the little fishes will go and hide. If we get in people's faces, they feel more pressured, will be more forthcoming.'

'I see.'

'So come on then, pack your bag.'

Patel laughed. 'No chance.'

'I need you.'

'What use am I in India? You can use your connections there without my involvement.'

'I can be the brain, you be the brawn. In case of trouble.'

'No chance. I'm Sherlock Holmes. I solve cases from my armchair, me.'

'Holmes was a man of action when the situation required. And in this case, we might well be entering a den of gangsters. You are needed.'

'No, I'm not.'

'Of course you must go with Neha,' said Padmini. She seemed irritated that Patel wouldn't do the obvious. She'd had a tough time explaining to Sylvia that Clive was away on an unexpected visit and to get any clue out of her as to where he might be, without alarming her.

Patel said, 'You want me to go to India, grapple with gangsters? I've barely unpacked from the last trip.'

'You must find out what happened to Majid. I don't trust the British police. Only ticking boxes.'

'But *I am* British police!'

'I've just been in touch with my contacts,' Neha piped up from her laptop. 'I know who we must see first thing.'

'But why must I go?' said Patel. 'It's East Midlands homicide's case. They have a strong track record.'

'I don't like that Codman. Twitchy.' Padmini looked at Neha. 'I always thought Majid had a good soul.'

'Ma!' Patel shook his head. 'Majid is not the hero of a Bollywood movie in real life. At the time of his death, he was bankrupt, owed all over the place. He was a known drug user, and an infamous sex pest.'

'Good father, according to *Bollywood Times*,' said his mother firmly.

Neha launched herself at Padmini, hugging her tight. 'Thank you, aunty,' she said.

His mother caught Patel's eyes over Neha's shoulders, and raised her eyebrows. He wasn't the only one flummoxed by Neha's mercurial behaviour.

'You're going,' she said to him.

Patel thought of going once more to India, on such short notice. He felt the air being sucked out of his lungs, but at the same time, he felt the pull. It surprised him. Mumbai crooked a finger beckoning him, its mysteries unfathomable.

'My own mother wants me dead,' he said.

'Don't be so melodramatic,' she told him.

Chapter Twelve

Here we go again, thought Patel, butting the fellow behind him in the Immigration queue with his overnight bag to keep him from breathing on his neck. He was called forth by a somnolent lady who wanted to know everything about the relatives he was in Mumbai to visit. Neha had given him some names and addresses to put in the forms. Then he was sent to another cubicle.

He could see Neha under a sign marked Exit, nervously jiggling up and down, trying to communicate with him through a form of mime and head waggle. Even if he understood her question, *Why the delay?*, he was unable to answer, for he stood in front of an Immigration clerk with muttonchop moustache who, in true Indian bureaucratic style, studied Patel's passport and his forms with a look of relish on his face.

Finally, the clerk noticed Patel glancing once too often at Neha, swivelled around to study her, and said to him, *'Beti hai kya?'*

Patel nodded sagely. He'd no idea what the man said.

The man gave him a cheeky grin. 'Alright, alright, getting impatient?' He stamped Patel's passport with benevolent violence and let him go.

With a sigh of relief Patel emerged into the Santacruz Road, only to wilt by the time they got to the taxi rank. Summer in India, with stifling coastal humidity thrown in.

'Where to, now?'

'Basanti Chawl.'

All through the taxi ride, Patel battled his need to throw up. Car rides weren't different from rollercoaster rides in India. He knew Neha noticed his confusion, his struggle to adjust to the assault of sounds, smells and colours, the heat and the humidity, the traffic.

To take his mind off the agitations in his body, he asked, 'So who are we going to see?'

'A man who was in touch with Majid regularly until three months ago. Then suddenly dropped all contact. This man used a burner phone to make a series of phone calls six months ago, to a number that was flagged up as a potential mafia phone. But he's just a tiny cog in the wheel.'

Patel wondered how she found this out. Who her contacts were.

'How—' he began, when the taxi violently swerved around a pedestrian in the middle of the road, making Patel's stomach jump to his throat. Patel cursed.

She smirked. 'Come to think of it, why did I need you here?'

'You wanted muscle.'

'You don't know the language, the people. Have you ever been to Mumbai?'

'No.'

'Speak Hindi or Marathi?'

'No.'

She shook her head. 'Useless.'

'I can speak cricket.'

'Ah yes, there's that.'

They entered a dizzying maze of old high-rise apartment buildings east of Worli.

Basanti Chawl was a decrepit building ten floors high. Neha explained that the apartments were long ago cannibalised into 'portions', meaning a room with a corner for cooking. Whole families lived in each 'portion'. They shared one bathroom and toilet per floor.

'How many families on each floor?'

'Fifteen, twenty,' said Neha.

'Blimey,' he said. It'd be a scandal in the UK.

It wouldn't be so bad, he thought, climbing the scrupulously clean stairs, if the sea breeze wasn't cut off by a gleaming new skyscraper right next door. Looming over it like the dark tower of Sauron, ugly black glass and phallic smooth white concrete. It looked freshly smartened up, smirking next to the dilapidated chawl which hadn't seen a lick of paint in years.

The men and women who hung around the building seemed relatively peaceful, rather jolly. They chatted with great animation on the little balconies, on doorsteps, stairwells and corners. No one gave Patel or Neha a second glance. They went up a winding staircase of four floors and passed several doorways. Family life requiring space had spilled out into doorways and the little porch areas. They climbed to the top floor. They knocked and waited.

'Is he out?' Patel said.

Neha knocked again, got no answer.

Patel put his ear on the door. Eventually they heard the creak of a mattress. A leaden thump. The door opened.

'Yeah?' A chubby man, eyes full of sleep.

'Rakesh Katare?' said Neha. 'Can we talk to you?'

'Come in, come in,' he said, not particularly surprised or bothered by their presence.

'Just going to wash,' he said, and left the room.

They sat side by side on the bed. A man's whole existence in an eight-by-eight room. Thin hard mattress two and a half feet wide. A blanket and pillow. A small stove in the corner. A plate and a spoon. Saucepan. Frying pan. A mug. A mirror on the wall you could just about see your face in. On a little shelf a bar of soap, a toothbrush and a travel-size tube of toothpaste. A ceiling fan that revolved slowly, stirring the humid air. This, Patel knew, was an absolute luxury in Mumbai, a single-occupancy room.

Rakesh reappeared, drying his hands with his handkerchief.

Neha said, 'Do you know why we're here?'

Rakesh nodded, still seemingly sanguine. He sat on a small, low stool.

Neha said, 'Did you know Majid Rahman?'

'Yes.'

'How?'

'Work with him. Colleagues.'

'In the film industry?'

'No, no,' he said. 'Cricket industry.'

'Sorry?' said Patel.

'Why you sorry?'

'I mean, can you explain?'

'Sure, sure. We run betting. Majid help by going to players and telling them what to do.'

It dawned on Patel what Rakesh meant. 'Match fixing?'

'Not fix whole match. Just small bets.'

This is India, thought Patel, *where cricket was religion.*

Rakesh explained the scheme. He hired a room in Gorai with computers and phone connections. There were different areas run by different operators. Rakesh was in charge of the central hub. The technicalities were dealt with by students of computer engineering from the nearby Jawahar Institute of Technology. Rakesh contacted Majid after collating bets from all territories and consulted on the outcomes desired by his bosses.

'So what was Majid's role?' Neha asked. 'He was an actor, not a cricketer.'

'He acted as a go-between. He was a friend to us and the cricketers. He could go and see them during matches, in the dressing room, at teatime.'

'What are some of the bets?' Patel asked.

'Little bets. How many runs in an over. Or if the third ball in the twenty-seventh over will be a dot ball. How many run-outs.'

'Bets that don't affect the outcome of the match.'

'That is very difficult.' Rakesh shook his head. 'That is high level. But we have done it. Not for every match. The biggest one we ever did was India–Pakistan at World Cup 2011.'

Patel couldn't believe it. There was no way a match of that profile could be fixed. Was Rakesh exaggerating a tad?

'Big patriotic money that time. Dropped catches, sitters, you English-wallas call them. Two leg before wickets. LBW sometimes hard to control, sometimes easy.'

'You talk rot,' Patel said. 'I bet you don't play any cricket.'

'LBW difficult to fix?' He gave Patel a keen look. 'We still doing business, you know. Need replacement for Majid. We like English county cricket. All on ESPN. Easy to fix.'

Patel was too appalled to speak.

Rakesh narrowed his eyes at Patel, his jaw working. 'Ah. Patel. Vijay Patel, slow seam spin. I thought you familiar. Maybe look like one of my cousins, I am thinking, but you are famous cricketer.'

Rakesh sprang up from his stool, fished out a notepad and pen from somewhere and held it out to Patel. 'Autograph, place there.'

Patel signed his name with a lack of flourish as Neha looked on, a tad archly.

'What was Majid fixing in the UK last week?' Neha asked.

'Nothing,' said Rakesh. 'He is not fixing anything. I not speaking to him in three months.'

Neha said, 'He was at a cricket match last week, talking to Ryan Gonsalves.'

'Oh, Ryan, he is one of ours.'

'Then Majid must have been fixing something.'

Rakesh shook his head. 'No, no. Only we, that is, I, do cricket talk with Indian team.'

'So Majid was doing what?'

'Majid quitting cricket business three months ago, when he sided with the wrong brother.'

'What brother?' said Patel.

'Zakir or Akbar?' she asked.

'Majid went with Zakir, that maderchod. Sorry, sister.'

'Hang on,' Patel said. 'Slow down a bit. So Majid was involved with the Indian mafia? Who are these brothers?'

'Excuse me,' Rakesh said, waving his phone at them. 'You explain, sister, I need to making phone call. To mother.'

Rakesh left the room, carefully closing it behind him.

'Can you give me some background, then?' he asked Neha.

'Gladly,' said Neha.

Patel learned that Akbar and Zakir were Mumbai-based gangster brothers. Akbar, the older, was a loyal patriot. Zakir, increasingly disenchanted with the Hindutva spiel of the current party in power, was believed to have been courted by 'forces from abroad'. Neha used this term with a special emphasis. *Pakistan*, thought Patel. Was it an extremist group or Pakistani intelligence?

The cricket betting business was conducted by Akbar, the elder. Majid was the key when it came to the Indian team. He had friends among the middle- and lower-order batsmen. But the brothers' battle became so acrimonious they split territories, the cricket betting going solely to Akbar.

'Majid choosing to side with Zakir.' Neha shook her head.

Despite the splitting of the businesses going smoothly, within a few months the small skirmishes between the two sides escalated into all-out war. They had stopped short of contracting out each other's murders, but Zakir began laying low, in fear for his life.

No one knew where he now was, or even if he remained in Mumbai.

Patel was about to ask about Akbar's whereabouts when two men burst into the little room. Before Patel could react, he found himself pinned to the floor, hands bound. A rag was stuffed into his mouth and a bag thrown over his head.

He heard Rakesh's voice, soft and cheerful near him. 'Sorry, Mr Patel,' he said. 'Job, you understand?'

Chapter Thirteen

I'm like one of those movie characters, thought Clive. *A fugitive!* He looked about him, his hands on the steering wheel had just stopped trembling. He'd been hours on the road. Out of habit, he'd parked in the disabled bay. Halfway to Anglesey. Service station, car park concrete, the razoring cars on the motorway, the faux cheery red and yellow of KFC and McDonald's.

As far from the romantic images he had possessed of fugitives from American movies, wiry young men who spanned brooks and bridges, jumped in rivers to be plunged down waterfalls. Him, little old codger in a Renault van. Sitting in a service station car park. He took out his wallet, counted out the notes he had withdrawn back at the Evington Road Co-op cash machine.

After looking about him for any spying eyes, Clive stuffed some notes under the seat cover. Sylvia. He wouldn't think of her yet. What would happen to her? Who would look after her between the six-hourly visits of the carers. The council will have to do something. Mrs Patel wouldn't neglect her. He couldn't go back yet. He just couldn't. No, he wouldn't think about it. He'd go into the Services, order a hamburger. Hadn't eaten one of those in years.

He stepped out of the car.

Dear, dear, Sylvia. The last person he knew who'd ever have wanted to become a burden on anyone. Least of all Clive. It could have easily been the other way around. Him – part-paralysed, stuck in a wheelchair. She – driving and pushing. Without the strength to pick him up or move him in case he fell. Better this way around. He'd go back soon as he decided on a course of action. It was an accident, Linda's death. He didn't kill her. He was going on holiday, wasn't he? He'd told Sylvia. He didn't want to abandon her. Just having a bit of a break. Everything had been very stressful lately.

'Sir, you want to order?' Grease-shiny face of the young person in front of him came into view.

'Oh.'

A couple of angry tuts behind him. A queue had formed while he'd been standing in front of the till, lost in reverie.

'A double cheeseburger and a side of fries.'

The boy pressed buttons, paused, waiting.

'Diet Coke,' Clive added, peeling out a note.

Clive sat in the car eating the burger, tears streaming down his face. He tried to justify his actions over and over, tried to get the images of Linda from out of his head.

He'd run out of steam up there in Linda's attic. He'd gone downstairs, sapped utterly, half his mind on staggering out and lying on the pavement with a bin bag over his head till the rubbish truck came and chucked him in the crusher. That'd be a fitting end for someone like him.

He nearly tripped over some pillows he'd thrown down the stairs, stepped over boxes of mouldy cereal on the floor and a cat litter tray. Linda's chair was empty.

He found her on the floor, by a corner cabinet, asleep. He aimed a good kick at her shin with his Prada-shod foot. *That'd wake her up alright*, he thought. But it didn't.

He fetched some water from the sink and sprinkled it on her

face. Sylvia knew some woman who fainted a lot. When younger she was part of a mummies clique. One lady didn't quite fit in, who had all sorts going on in her life. In the middle of a birthday party, she'd faint out of the blue. To get attention, Sylvia used to say. They stopped being friends when the lady found out everyone thought she faked her faints.

'You are getting enough attention from me, love, don't have to pretend to faint for it,' said Clive.

Linda stayed crumpled on her side, one arm extended towards her little under-the-counter fridge. He stepped across her arm and opened the fridge. The bottom edge of the door snagged against Linda's fingers. Clive pushed her hand away with his foot, unable to bring himself to touch her.

In the fridge, there was a half-pint of milk, a family-size packet of KitKats, a half-open can of cat food, tuna, going by the smell. *Did she want to feed the cat?* he wondered. Then he saw, tucked away in the door, next to an open packet of cheese drying and curling at the edges, the blue inhaler.

'Christ,' he said. He grabbed the inhaler, shut the fridge, shook it.

He hooked one arm around Linda's head, hefted her over his knee. He inserted the inhaler into her mouth and squeezed the trigger.

'Ah fuck.'

Her head rolled off his knee, limp as a sausage-end.

He'd been shocked. Trembling, he'd sat in the car for over half an hour, the visions of police and arrest and the shame of it. But *he* didn't kill her. It was an accident. He'd trashed Linda's house. He'd raged, shouted. The whole neighbourhood must have heard.

Everyone at the allotment knew he hated Linda. Some joker had chucked a fake bearskin rug onto Linda's flower bed. It had dog poo on it. Linda had chucked it on top of Sylvia's cabbages. Sylvia had cried. Clive had stormed over in a rage. Late autumn, wasn't it? Everyone had been there. Sylvia in tears. Clive, newly retired and looking for a barney. He had cursed and shouted at Linda who hadn't held back either. The mouth on that woman. Shameful it had been. He crowed in victory after Linda was forced to remove the rug herself.

'Bitch,' he'd muttered, and everyone heard, he'd made sure. Sylvia didn't speak to him for the rest of the day, although it was on her account he had got into a rage with Linda. Early the next morning she'd suffered the stroke that put her in a wheelchair. He hadn't spoken to Linda since, nor her to him.

Now he had just been in her house, ranting and raging. And Linda was dead, stretched across the kitchen floor. Horror-frozen face he'd never be able to get out of his head.

Clive reached the campsite late evening, when the setting sun streaked the sky in pink and blue striations, like something out of a David Hockney painting. Garish and not something out of nature. But there it was, the sky above. As drawn on an iPad with fingers, in lurid colours.

Wheels sunk in the mud as he parked. The caravan looked intact, if old and weather-worn. A rotten panel here or there that he could see. The rusty lock wouldn't open. He rootled around in the car and found some WD-40. Sprayed it on the lock, then sat in the car eating chips, cold by now, and wishing for a cup of tea. He listened to the racket on Radio 1 for a bit, then inclined the seat and dozed fitfully.

He woke with the birds, at a ridiculously early hour. In the morning light, the sight of the caravan sunk his heart. He tried the lock again and it opened. Some floorboards had rotted over the year and a half of neglect, and his foot went through.

The low field was muddy from rain overnight. Pools and puddles of water. His caravan stood in a depression. Water came up to the first step.

There was only one other caravan in the field. Ten years ago there had been dozens. Sylvia and him used to come with the kids at first, then by themselves. The steps got too much for Sylvia's knees so they stopped coming around the time the incessant rains flooded the field.

The Co-op lost insurance cover and most owners took their caravans elsewhere. There were other uphill places one could park. But Clive didn't entertain the notion. Even if Sylvia were able to come. He'd loved this position. He still did. He could hear the sea. The estuary had untold treasures. He could potter here all day, every day, eat a meal of fish and chips. And if his wallet complained, just chips and a pickled onion.

He took out his phone and stared at the blank dead screen. He had turned it off as soon as he'd decided to flee Leicester. He itched to turn it on but resisted. He was sure they had the means of tracking his whereabouts through his phone GPS. He did not have the wherewithal to disable the GPS on it and still be able to use it for its primary function, to make calls. In any case, he had no one to call for help with Sylvia.

He'd not made the effort with his neighbours or Sylvia's two friends in all these years. He did not want to call Mrs Patel, for he felt he'd let her down. No doubt the police had already been and searched his house, but no one would know where he was now. Sylvia couldn't tell them. His sons were AWOL in the back of beyond. He could rot here, with only his dead phone for company. And no one would miss him. No one would know. He looked out over the landscape. The field ran on and into the estuary at Toch. Nobody but a dog-walker in the distance.

Seconds, minutes, hours. He sat roiling in his own thoughts. These dark emotions sucked at him like darkness sucks the corners of a twilight. He felt utterly alone. Did he actually escape jail? At least there were people to talk to in there, a variety in food. Here, with the collapse of the campsite, there was only the fish and chip stall in town. In fact, the whole area was condemned as a flood-risk zone. The people who lived here year-round, already poor to begin with, were now treading water, so to speak. Scratching a livelihood doing fuck knows what.

Saturday night at the chip shop, 10:00 p.m., and it was only him and two other customers. Full twenty minutes she took to fry the fish, but it was good. He was thankful for this single good thing that had happened to him all week. Nobody to give Sylvia fish and chips. The thought turned off his appetite. He mechanically ate the rest of it and threw the paper away for seagulls to fight over.

The night in eerie gloom. Clive was really starting to feel like he was living out a jail sentence. The irony of it killed him. How was it possible that this was the same place he and Sylvia came year after year? The boys kicking a ball in the sand endlessly, happy as muck, him and Sylvia just staring at the water, drinking beer, popping sausages on the camp stove to sizzle, feeling really like they were escaping drudgery, feeling free and nurtured. Now the same sky became a lid on his misery. The same water seemed an endless expanse. Some illusionist's trick.

The only human establishment other than his clapped-out caravan, as far as the eye could see, was the other clapped-out caravan. He walked out to it. If possible it seemed in a worse state of repair to his. Even the graffiti on the paintwork was fading. The rough salt air and winds eroded the juice from the paint. He put his face up to a broken bit of glass. An awful smell. Some animal, a badger, a fox, a cat, a bird must have got in, couldn't get out. Stuck, starved to death, started to putrefy. Or perhaps it was the caravan's owner. An old codger like himself. No one had come up to look for him. No one cared.

He banged on the door and it fell apart. Broken things so mangled he couldn't tell individual objects in it. A clump of plastic, metal and rotting wood. Damn soggy. Must be a leak in the roof or the joining seals. A prickle of horror at the possibility of a human corpse under the mangle of rubbish. One corpse was enough for anyone in a lifetime. Clive had two corpses in one week. He backed away from the caravan gasping a little for breath even though there was nothing blocking his airways or suffocating him, except perhaps his own thoughts.

Chapter Fourteen

For what felt like hours, Patel bumped around in the boot of a car, blind, trussed up, unable to shout. When eventually the sack on his head was lifted, and his eyes adjusted and he found himself in a vast, gloomy basement car park, he glanced at one of the men's watches and realised they'd been driving only for an hour.

Five men in uniforms, some kind of black commando jobs, complete with baseball caps and leather belts, surrounded him. They had guns. Some sort of long-nozzled, fat, submachine guns.

Another car pulled up, and to his relief they pulled Neha out, similarly trussed up and bag-headed. Once she could see him, he nodded at her, she nodded back. *Alright? Guess so.*

Still nobody spoke. One of the men gestured for Patel and Neha to follow. They walked, the gesturing man ahead, one on either side, Neha in front of Patel, three men covering the rear, towards a set of doors. On the way, they passed several very expensive cars with personalised number plates. 'Jeez'. 'Rak'. 'Godbless'. 'Shiva99'. 'Megladon'.

Megladon, a silver Lamborghini, had marigold garlands piled on it, with generous smears of turmeric and vermilion on the windshield.

Through the double doors and down a corridor, their hands still tied behind their backs, Patel and Neha were led. Patel could not for the life of him fathom where they were. Nobody around. A whole empty floor except for the five gunmen with them. They came to a door where their rags were removed from their mouths. Patel's throat felt dry and parched. He cleared his throat. The lead man gestured for him to open the door and go in.

Patel pushed the door open and blinked into the darkness.

'Hello,' he said, waiting for his eyes to adjust. He saw a fat man in an office chair. A state-of-the-art computer slumbered in front of him, the CCTV monitors above switched off. Neha went over to the equipment, as though drawn by a magnet. Patel heard her sigh. *Strange woman*, he thought.

The seated man chuckled and said, 'I am Vashist. I hear the two of you are interested in matters that are hundred per cent no concern of yours.'

He could well chuckle, thought Patel. The five men with the submachine guns had followed them in and were lining up by the wall to make sure Patel behaved himself.

Abruptly Neha said in Hindi, 'I'm Neha Sinha, a journalist. We have met before.'

The man frowned, as though trying to recall this meeting.

Patel said in English, 'Miss Neha and I are looking into Majid Rahman's death. I'm a police officer in London.'

The man cast his cold-fish eyes on Patel. Still staring, he reached into a bowl on the desk and popped a couple of spiced peanuts into his mouth. He said, 'I do not like policemen.'

That's a bummer, thought Patel. He looked to Neha, who was studying the switched-off security equipment. 'If it helps, I'm not on official duty,' he said to Vashist. 'I'm just helping Neha, as a friend.'

'What security system do you use?' said Neha, abruptly.

The man's face lit up. 'You know security systems?'

'Just interested. There were some problems with Aeneas, no?'

'We had Aeneas. Now changed to Achilles.'

'Ah.' She nodded. 'That's good. New.'

'Best in the world,' Vashist said.

Their branding's off, thought Patel. *Achilles had a fatal weakness in his heel.*

'About Majid,' he said, 'can you—?'

Neha interrupted, 'You are the head of security here?'

'Yes,' said Vashist.

'Family out of town?' She gestured to the switched-off systems.

'How many families live here?' Patel said, seeing as they were into the small talk.

Neha and Vashist looked at him speechlessly, in wonder.

'What did I say?'

'You don't know?' Neha said.

'What?'

'World's richest man. Sitaram. It is his house. We are next door to Basanti Chawl. They must have been driving around in circles. We could have walked here.'

'Ah' – Vashist held up a finger – 'that wouldn't have created the correct expectation.'

'Funny guy,' said Patel. He began to smile, and felt a guard step in and press his gun nozzle into the small of his back. The smile disappeared.

Vashist beamed at Neha. 'You are a clever girl.'

A knock on the door, and a woman brought a tray of food.

Vashist's eyes goggled in delight and he said in Hindi, 'Mmm, come, because you are clever girl, I will let you have a golgappa.'

Vashist gestured for their bonds to be undone. With relief, Patel rubbed his sore arms.

From the tray in front of him, Vashist prepared the golgappas, puffed round balls. He pierced each with his thumb and inserted a bit of spiced potato and onion, and a bit of green chutney, then filled it with spiced tamarind water.

He handed one to Patel first, who looked at it with suspicion.

'Put it whole into your mouth,' said Neha.

'Why?'

'Like this.' She took the next golgappa prepared by Vashist and popped it into her mouth.

Patel crammed the round snack into his mouth the best he could. A combination of sweet and tart and hot sensations exploded in the back of his head. A potent hit. He'd tried other kinds of chaat in Leicester but this here was the real deal. The puffs crisp, the water cold but not too cold , the flavours heightened by the humid, sweltering weather. The pleasure-pain of the experience invigorated him. Even Neha looked discombobulated, her eyes red and watering.

'Enjoying?' She grinned through her tears.

Vashist swallowed one and shook himself like a buffalo. 'Nice? Good enough for your last supper?'

Patel nearly choked on the golgappa he'd just stuffed into his mouth. Sharp hot pain seared up to his nose, and he grabbed a plastic cup of water from the tray and gulped it down.

'What are you?' said Vashist. 'A man or a mouse?'

'Listen,' said Neha. 'We have no fight with Akbar. We have no fight with anyone, we just want to find out what happened to Majid.'

'Last I hear Zakir and Majid were thick as thieves, plotting something big.'

'Do you know what they were plotting?'

'Not me,' Vashist said. 'Because you are nice girl, I'll give you his phone number, you find out?'

'You have Zakir's phone number?'

'Yes, he changes every few days, but I have the latest one, from a mutual acquaintance.' He rubbed his nose suggestively. 'The trick is to get him to answer the phone. He won't pick up unless he knows who it is.'

'So where do you come in, in all this? Did you quit working for the brothers?'

'I run security for richest man on the planet.'

'That's Jeff or Elon, not Sitaram.'

Vashist laughed. 'Hey, it is not white money, is it, that Forbes can count. Some people don't want to be in Forbes.'

'So you are a security expert?' Neha asked. 'Is that why Sitaram hired you?'

Vashist said, 'I'm Hindu. Sitaram not hire Muslim for security. All my boys outside, inside everywhere in building, all Hindu. See all this, all this. Zeus, Achilles, all this nonsense, any sixteen-year-old hacker can break, but people, loyal people, very hard. That is why Sitaram hire me.'

Patel felt he could almost understand what he said, but not quite. Why was he emphasising their religion?

Vashist grinned. 'Now you go, find out what happen to Majid,' he said.

Feeling utterly bewildered, Patel followed Neha out of the claustrophobic room, into the cloistering heat of Mumbai. Once outside, his knees nearly collapsed in relief. Neha, however, looked like she'd just gone out for a coffee with a friend.

'It worked out in the end,' she said, smoothing her hair which had been mussed up by the gunny sack.

'What did?' Patel asked.

'Our being kidnapped and intimidated. Now we have a lead.'

Patel shook his head. 'Couldn't he just have asked to meet us instead of the guns and hoods drama?'

Neha grinned. 'They got to have some fun, I guess. Maybe they watch too many American shows.'

They had rooms booked at an airport hotel. While Neha pre-occupied herself with her cannibalised laptop, Patel looked up Akbar on his.

Akbar Bai appeared to be a private man. He'd done a very small interview with an obscure local paper, where he'd declared death to all foreign agents who tried to incite terror in India. Otherwise, absolutely no information at all about his activities or whereabouts, except in a general asinine article about Mumbai businessmen's ethical values. The article was dated two months ago, and contained a single line about Akbar, that he'd newly started a security business.

'Get this,' he told Neha. 'Akbar must own the security firm that runs Sitaram's security.' Now he understood Vashist's digressions about Hindu security, the irony Patel had patently missed.

Neha said, 'Mmm hmm.' She wasn't paying attention. After a minute, she said, 'I know what to do. We need to download a new messaging app. Zulekha. It has very good encryption. So even Pegasus cannot penetrate.'

'What's Pegasus?' It sounded vaguely familiar.

'The Indian government is using Pegasus to spy on everyone.'

'Everyone?'

'Yeah, literally everyone. Environment activists, students, terrorists, its own government ministers. Even the minister in charge of security. Now anyone with a reason to be secretive is on high alert. Zulekha is the messaging service of the day.'

Again, he thought it incongruous that she knew all this in a line of work that involved writing about Salman Khan's latest poodle and Shilpa Shetty's top five savoury snacks for when she felt peckish.

Neha burst into action. She disappeared into the bathroom for ten minutes, then reappeared looking serious and made-up.

'What's the make-up for?' he said. He hadn't seen her in make-up before.

'I need a photo for the Zulekha profile. You've seen my WhatsApp photo, no?' She showed him. Her WhatsApp profile photo was that of a coffin. Something a goth teenager might appreciate, he thought.

She got him to take a mid-shot photo of her and used it to create her profile on Zulekha. Then she sent a message to Zakir's phone number. Zakir, your brother Akbar has given an exclusive interview that will be printed in the Sunday Times. He talks a lot about you, opens his heart about his disappointments in you. I'd like to give you a chance to respond. Please call me. Neha Sinha.

Five minutes of waiting after sending the message, Neha said, 'I don't know if he'll get in touch, or even if this is his number. We need a plan B.'

'We could find some other people to talk to,' he said.

'He had a couple of friends, good ones. I could go talk to them but you cannot come.'

'Why not?'

'They don't like cricket.'

'That's impossible.'

'They'll feel nervous about your presence, like we're playing good cop, bad cop.'

'We just met two men up to their necks in illegal activities. They liked me. I'm a cop and yet they talked to me, told me stuff that'd get them into trouble with Indian authorities. So why wouldn't Majid's friends want to see me? It's you who they'd want to avoid. The gossip journalist. I'm a cop. If they really want the best for Majid, they'd want justice for his death, and I can help – an actual homicide detective.'

'Oh,' said Neha, looking nonplussed by his logic. 'There is a good reason why you cannot come.'

'And what is it?'

'I can't tell you.'

He began laughing, then stopped when he saw that she looked close to breaking into tears. He felt anger rising in him. What was going on with her? What was the meaning of the communication between Vashist and her? Why didn't she want him to meet Majid's friends?

Her phone rang. A look of astonishment on her face. She said, 'Zakir.'

'Bingo,' he said, impressed with her despite his anger.

Neha accepted the call and put him on speaker phone.

Without any preamble, Zakir said to Neha, 'I don't believe you. My brother would never talk about me.'

She said, 'He's given me an exclusive interview. It's all about you.'

'Tell me what he said.'

'I will show you the draft of the interview after you give me some information.'

'You're bluffing.'

'Am I?'

'Tell me one detail he gave you that's personal.'

'I'll give you a taste. You had a dog called Tiger who died. You went to Goa Anjuna beach to scatter its ashes in the sea because Tigey loved jumping in the waves. All alone, without any protection. No one knows because you thought it would make you look too soft. Only Akbar knew.'

Silence.

'Now all of India will,' said Neha. Rather dramatic, thought Patel, but effective.

When he finally spoke, his voice sounded eerily calm. 'Well, then I'll have to tell you about his little habits, don't I?'

'There's one thing I want to know now. Nothing to do with your brother.'

Silence.

'Majid Rahman. You were friends with him?'

A sighing sound. 'He died. Accident in England.'

'Tell me what you were working on.'

'Working on? *Mera dost tha*. Who is he to you?'

Neha, her confident veneer cracking a bit, caught Patel's eyes again. He could see over her shoulder the dark screen. Zakir had blocked his video feed.

'I'll give you a centre spread,' she said. 'Cover feature in the Sunday magazine.'

Silence.

Patel thought he'd hung up. Neha began to expel a great big breath. She'd been a touch too desperate, and now—

'Is that the England bowler, Vijay Patel?'

Patel was startled to hear his name. Neha had turned around whilst nervously improvising, and Patel hadn't ducked out of view. He realised he'd made the foolish mistake of thinking that just because he couldn't see Zakir, Zakir couldn't see him.

'Yes,' Neha said. 'He works with me.'

She looked at Patel, raised her eyebrows.

The distinct tune came of Zakir requesting video feed. Neha swiped. Patel stepped over. Zakir looked to be in his early thirties, handsome, bearded. He bellowed, as if to an old friend: 'Patel! How is your wrist?'

Patel grimaced. He hated being asked about his wrist.

'Still a bit sore,' he said.

'And too old to take up baseball,' laughed Zakir. 'Big fan. Big fan. What are you doing with journalists, yaar?'

'Oh, you know . . . ' said Patel.

'Alright then, you two come and see me. I'll text you the

address. Tomorrow, eight p.m. Gives you twenty-four hours to get sorted.'

With that he went offline.

'Why can't we see him now?' Patel said.

Her phone pinged. Neha studied the message. 'His address is why,' she said.

Chapter Fifteen

All the way from hotel to airport, Patel quelled niggling suspicions about the wisdom in their course of action. His hairs had pricked up right from the moment Rakesh Katare had obligingly let them into his room to disrupt his sleep. Why were the two 'ex-colleagues' of Majid so forthcoming with information? Why were they eager for him and Neha to meet Zakir? Was it from a willingness to see justice done about Majid's death? Or did they have another purpose?

He could not broach his fears with Neha. Raring to get to Dubai, she ordered flight tickets and a taxi to the airport minutes after receiving Zakir's address for their rendezvous. Patel spent a sleepless night at the airport hotel mulling over the puzzle of Neha's motivations, as well as those of Rakesh and Vashist.

Mumbai Airport was a scene of organised chaos. They joined a snaking queue to the check-in desk. Neha, as ever, on her phone. No one paid them any attention. Patel was used to be being ignored in the subcontinent. After all, he looked like any one of them. Only the white-skinned Brits got stared at. But as he crept up the queue, he realised he was the object of an unusual level of scrutiny from a couple of men, who were at times behind him in the queue, and at times by the ATM or a coffee dispensary.

He tapped Neha on the shoulder. 'See those two men by the Café Coffee Day?'

'Yes,' said Neha. 'Romeos, staring at me. Downside of being female in a certain age bracket.'

'How do you know they aren't staring at me?'

'Oh.' Neha looked him up and down. 'Well,' she said, not looking convinced.

He had to smile. 'Perhaps they recognise me. Unlikely as that seems, what with my clever stubble since we met Rakesh and Vashist.'

'Possibly,' she said. 'I'm the one who gets stared at, normally, but I suppose, like Zakir ... well, everyone is a cricket fanatic.' She rolled her eyes.

'What about the third possibility?'

'Which is what? That they want to proposition you, both of them?'

'Ah, well. The fourth possibility then, that they are following us after getting a tip-off from Rakesh?'

'Or it could be Zakir's men, babysitting us?'

'I don't trust them.'

The queue suddenly began to move at speed, as was the Indian way. Patel couldn't quite keep track of the men, who seemed to melt away. Perhaps they sensed they had been spotted.

It was a smallish plane with uncomfortable-looking seats but they had been lucky to get tickets at such short notice. Patel decided to broach his concerns to Neha once more as they found their seats, but as soon as she sat down, Neha blinked out. Patel, on the verge of prodding her awake to discuss his fears, decided to let her sleep. All the accumulated tiredness of the last few days must have felled her.

The plane stayed in the hangar for a while, waiting for a

runway space. After some thought, Patel made two phone calls. The first one was very brief. The second one lasted longer. He explained his situation and asked for what he required.

He hung up, pleased, glanced over at Neha who hadn't heard a word of the content of his calls. The sleep-fairy had whisked her away to la-la-land. He asked the stewardess for a blanket and tucked her in.

Patel mulled over his apprehensions over stale airplane coffee with a dried-out cheese sandwich, the bread like polystyrene. Watching Neha's sleeping face, her mouth slightly open, he realised they had to get each other's back. True, she had secrets, and he found her mixture of strong will and petulance infuriating, but it seemed her heart was in the right place.

He looked at her face in repose, sharp features framed by hair the darkest shade of brown. He felt afraid for what was coming. They'd known each other for such a little time, yet now they were in the deep end together. So many entangled lives. His mother's Bollywood dreamboat murdered at her own allotment, Clive and Sylvia with absolutely no one to help them when they were at such peril from dangerous men, and this Neha, quixotic journalist, with her raging thirst for truth and her secrets.

He wished he had her clear-cut passions. But, he supposed, he did feel passion to do the right thing, to do right by people, to the best of his ability. He wondered if he willingly let himself be swept up into events? Much as he fancied himself a good person who liked to keep his nose clean, perhaps in actual fact he was a fucker who liked to get fucked up? Smash things up, ruffle feathers?

Then he reminded himself, his mother had made him go. So much for taking charge of his own life.

*

Padmini Patel made a cup of tea. She stood at the unfamiliar sink and twisted the unfamiliar tap, filled the ancient kettle crusted with limescale, popped into an old stained mug an own-brand teabag. As she stirred the brown sludge, she turned to offer a smile to Sylvia, who stared, face frozen, at Padmini's chest, her mouth giving just a hint of a smile back.

'I'm sure he'll be back,' said Padmini, not for the first or even the tenth time. She'd cut the 'soon' from her profession of hope though. It'd been over twenty-four hours since Clive disappeared. If he was going to return at all, it wouldn't be 'soon'. Maybe 'eventually'. She chased away the morbid thought and poured in the milk.

'What does Clive normally do for you, now?' she asked.

She sat near Sylvia, showed her the current psychological thriller she was reading.

'Shall I read to you? Haven't read a story to someone since Vijay was a young boy. He used to be obsessed with *Where the Wild Things Are.*'

She took a sip of the tea, grimaced at the taste, and began reading her book to Sylvia. From the first page, although she'd already read a third of it. After a little while, her voice attained a nice even cadence. It pleased her to see that Sylvia's face looked relaxed, and the way her hands and feet were still, she could tell that she listened deeply.

Padmini felt some cheer after a gloomy day and a half. She hadn't heard from Vijay. He'd said he'd only be in touch when there was anything to say. She had nothing new to tell him either. She'd put out word on the local social media, and had gone to see in person every member of the allotment society who couldn't be reached by phone. She even got a Radio Leicester announcer (a niece once removed) to ask if anyone knew the whereabouts of Clive Atkins, white male, sixty-seven, needed for a family emergency.

Nothing so far. No sign of the men who'd persecuted Clive and kidnapped Sylvia. Not that she knew what they looked like. At least she hadn't seen anyone around who looked 'thuggish'. DS Codman had spent a very short time talking to plotholders, just the ones who'd been there when the police taped off the area where Majid Rahman had been found. He hadn't been interested in finding the bag at all. Which was odd. She tried to tell him the bag might hold important clues as to the ID of Majid's killer, but Codman pretended he couldn't hear her.

In the afternoon, Padmini brought over a tin of her own teabags, and a bottle of her milkman's organic milk, new mugs, muscovado sugar and fresh digestives. She made Sylvia a cup and spooned the tea into Sylvia's mouth. Half of it spilled onto her bib but Sylvia seemed to enjoy the taste. She remembered how Sylvia had always sparked up at the first taste of good, strong tea.

Halfway through, a knock sounded on the door. Sylvia's eyes flew up in hope but it was only a council woman, who let herself in with a key. At first, the woman wouldn't discuss Sylvia's care with Padmini. 'Are you entitled to even be here? You are not mentioned in the papers. The husband, and two sons, are the only names.'

'Well, they aren't here, are they?' Padmini tried not show exasperation. 'The two sons are in Australia and her husband is missing, wanted by the police in connection to a suspicious death.' *Two deaths, in fact*, she thought, but didn't say. 'I'm here, looking after her. Looks like I'm her only friend at the moment. I was a council woman myself. But now I'm glad you are here. I do have my own house to run.'

The woman opened a folder and read from a printed-out A4 paper. 'In the event of the carer' – she spoke as though revising for an exam – 'being absent, and the vulnerable person being unable to complete basic tasks herself, she will need round-the-clock care and so will have to be moved into a residential facility. 'Now' – she consulted her paper – 'the only space available at the moment is a facility in Coalville, the Rotherman House.'

'It was in the news last month,' exclaimed Padmini. 'The staff were abusing the residents. Too many unexplained deaths. The manager was arrested.'

The woman looked flustered. Clearly she hadn't been prepared for anybody to state objections or even care about Sylvia. 'The home is under extra scrutiny now. Daily inspections, new board of executives. It's improving, I can assure you.'

'Anything closer to here? So I can pop by regularly to visit?'

She consulted her paper again. 'This is the closest, I'm afraid. I have staff standing by to move Sylvia within the hour.' She made to move, impatiently, as though this was the first in a long line of older people in need of care that she needed to cart from their homes and into the state's care.

A small sound of whimpering from behind. Padmini turned to see that Sylvia had been paying attention to all that was transpiring, and her face looked intensely agitated.

Before she could think twice on the matter and talk herself out of it, Padmini raised her voice to the woman already halfway out the door. 'I'll tell you what? I'll look after Sylvia until a space opens in a nice facility close by. Temporarily, of course. Her husband, Clive, I'm sure, will return, s-soon.' Her tongue tripped over the word 'soon'.

The council woman looked sour. Padmini had interrupted her best-laid plans. Well, they weren't best-laid plans from Sylvia's point of view, Padmini thought, crossly. The woman hadn't looked at Sylvia once since she entered the house. Padmini held the woman's eye and dared her to object.

'Let me have a think,' said the woman.

Padmini could see the wheels turning. The balance between convenience and inconvenience, of moving and setting up Sylvia in a new home. The cost saving to be made if she stayed where she was. To be sure, Padmini's offer meant less effort and resources from the council.

'Oh well,' said the woman, 'have it your way. Give me a call if you change your mind. People start off with good intentions . . .' She stopped, thought better of continuing her speech, nodded and left, without a goodbye for Sylvia.

A small sigh escaped Sylvia, although her expression was still that of frozen alarm. Padmini wondered whether the prospect of being looked after by her was welcome at all to Sylvia.

What a mess, thought Padmini, and switched on the TV.

'I have to pop home now,' she told Sylvia. 'The carers will be here in one hour.'

Sylvia stared at the telly, as though engrossed.

Vetri Gopal, freelance entertainment reporter who sold his gleanings to the highest bidder, waited at the little grassy knoll at the end of a long, as yet fruitless day. The Dubai heat was killing. He had a wet handkerchief tied to the back of the neck to keep himself cool. They'd been tipped off about Shah Rukh appearing for a little afternoon party but that didn't pan out. There were only two journos remaining now.

For a week now there'd been a sense of something brewing. The paps like him who'd bribed the domestic staff to be their eyes and ears, they smelled something in the air. A something burning. What was going on? Just hushed whispers and eye movements.

Burj Dubai. The playground of the rich and the famous from parts of the world that expected a certain norm of behaviour from them. Indian celebrities who had a pious reputation at home, members of a certain political party that promoted clean living, they escaped to Dubai, escaped Indian scrutiny in order to let go, relax, be recreated. Sometimes this resulted in bad behaviour. A keen journalist, a hound on the scent, a truth-sayer, you could even say, if he was lucky, not only caught a glimpse of the idols frolicking, he could also snap photos to publish the event. The photos ruptured the ridiculous rapture in which these idols were held by mindless devotees. The money the photos fetched was a bonus.

Vetri loved his job. It was 'moral and monetary' at the same time, as he liked to tell his friends. His great regret was that he hadn't been the one to snap those bathtub photos of the bloated Shumi, dead of a drug overdose in this very same hotel. The erstwhile superstar had played ten different goddesses in mythological films.

So paps like him turned up to these places, long lens in hand, wads of twenty-dollar bills in trouser pockets and handbags. Vetri had a nose for news. A scent for a scoop. He'd been in the biz long enough to trust himself when his antennae quivered. He noted the twitching behind the security guard's solid demeanour. He saw the old-time waiter glancing cagily when a new car pulled up.

Nothing so far. The other guy seemed in no hurry to go home. Vetri, who had only ever nodded to him, wondered if he had some information. Never make eye contact with fellow hyenas. Career suicide to be pally with the other journalists to the extent of sharing leads with them.

The weather, a dry thirty degrees. Vetri did not mind the heat. He used his long lens to cover the entrance. He had a good angle on the doors of the limousines that were opened by the porters, from whence spilled the rich and the famous. No one important so far. He had already bribed the receptionist to get tip-offs on who stayed the night. The restaurant-cum-bar was a hot ticket. Celebrities liked to go there because other celebrities did, proven by paparazzi photos. Of course, they came here to be photographed. Vetri and his ilk obliged.

The other guy, Joseph, looked ready to pack up.

A limousine pulled up. Vetri bent his head to the camera. But it delivered nonentities, probably some lottery winners. He almost missed the couple walking up to reception behind it. But as the limo pulled away, he saw them. Both slim. He couldn't see the woman's face, but recognised the man straight away. Vijay Patel.

He could sense Joseph looking over, curious now about what Vetri had found. As far as Vetri knew, Patel had returned to being a plodding PC back in London after the craziness of the tabloid murders in Bangalore. What on earth was he doing in Dubai? Vetri feverishly refocused the camera lens on them. Very pally they seemed. Heads bent together, intensely whispering, looking around, walking into the hotel reception. Joseph stopped packing up. Sensing, like a Rottweiler, Vetri's sudden sighting of quarry, he screwed on an even better lens on his camera and began scanning around.

Vetri knew the layout of the hotel like the back of his hand. The restaurant had a window that he could bribe the waiter to open. Convenient height to prop up the camera. He wondered if it might be worth borrowing Joseph's lens. But he did not want to share the credit.

Vetri wracked his brain about what could bring Patel to Burj Dubai. They must be meeting someone here. They looked travel worn. The woman's hair had that distinctive aeroplane frizz. He scurried around to the front of the man-made knoll, where strictly he was forbidden from as the guests could see him from the billiards room on the second floor and apparently this ruined their game. Well, fuck them. He could see into the restaurant. Patel and the woman chatted to the maître d' at his desk, who consulted an old-fashioned leather-bound diary.

Who were they meeting? No one interesting had come through so far that evening. He scanned some fresh arrivals. Then his blood froze. At the same time, Joseph let out a yelp of excitement.

Zakir Bai, one of the Bombay brothers, the tall one, the younger of the two. He got out of a taxi. *Aha*, but the taxi driver was a known mobster and he'd come packing. The second chap with the brother also looked armed. Another car stopped and four serious-looking men got out. Zakir nodded to them. Head waggle to each other. Indian version of 'wassup, bro?' Vetri's excitement frothed over.

He took his phone out and rang his pet waiter.

Vetri had a foothold on the trellis, but he dared not lift his other foot off the ground and onto it. He wasn't at all sure that it could hold his weight. He looked up at the skinny Joseph who had shimmied up the flimsy trellis like the teenage Spider-Man, and was now perched eight feet high at the window which Vetri's waiter promised had a good view of Zakir, Patel and the woman. Regrettably, they'd chosen to sit near the entrance of the restaurant, in plain view of everyone. The usual window didn't have a good angle on this table.

His spirits had sunk when he saw the trellis, so Vetri decided to swallow his pride and get Joseph's help. He had no head for heights. With Joseph's fancy lens, he'd have good photos, he hoped. They'd share the spoils. A fleeting thought occurred to him. What price would Zakir's older brother pay for this information? Vetri had the feeling this was important. He won-dered if Zakir was meeting Patel in the open because they didn't trust each other. But then, Zakir was a show-off.

Joseph took his face out of the lens's butt and looked down to whisper. 'Can't make out much, to be honest. I can see them at the table, but can't hear a thing.'

Vetri said, 'Crack the window open and extend the lens inside. You can use my dongle, see if you can pick up sounds.'

After a few minutes, Joseph looked down and shook his head. 'Another table in the way, group of Americans.'

'Ah damn.'

Joseph said, 'My legs are going numb. I've taken the photos, plenty of them. Shall I get down now?'

Vetri mulled. 'Just a few more minutes. See if anyone else turns up.'

Vetri wished he could have been in Joseph's place. He looked up, his neck cricking. He felt Joseph go quiet, concentrating, muttering. Vetri couldn't catch the words.

'No need to whisper,' he said, 'no one can hear us.'

Vetri gazed at Joseph's bent arse getting stiff with excitement when Joseph shouted, 'Oh fuck,' and fell out of the trellis right on top of him.

Popping sounds, loud. A fireworks party, he thought. That's what the whispering had been about all week. For someone famous? Then why was Joseph yelling, 'Run, man, run ...'?

Vetri snapped out of his daze. He scrambled out from the bush into which Joseph and he had plunged. They grabbed their equipment, ran to the grassy knoll, scooped the rest of their stuff, ran to their separate cars. As he squeezed inside, it dawned on Vetri that the people in the restaurant were possibly dead. Even the gobby Americans. And he had Joseph's camera. In the scramble to skedaddle, the lens had come off. Joseph had the lens. Vetri had the camera body. Perfect. He'd download the photos first. They would be the making of him.

Vetri sagged in the driver's seat. He should have been elated. Instead, he felt numb. A prickle of cold sweat at the thought that Patel, the woman and Zakir were dead. Did he snap their last images? He had to make sure. What would they fetch? They might be still alive. Should he check? No, he couldn't get involved, couldn't come forward as a witness. He didn't know anything anyway. Who were the assassins? Some sort of terrorist? No clue. He'd be useless to the Dubai police force, if they bothered at all with investigating a shooting concerning mostly foreigners. There weren't many Emiratis inside.

Vetri started his car, looked around. Joseph had legged it. The idiot hadn't even asked for his camera. Vetri drove out through the long drive, emerged onto the highway. He passed the speeding police cars and ambulances. But a minute later, as he neared the Caucaucus junction, he said, 'Fuck,' released his foot from the accelerator, and made a screeching, illegal U-turn. He had to see if any of them were still alive. Oddly, he felt responsible.

Chapter Sixteen

'Simon!' A rush of joy suffused Patel when he saw the floppy-haired, tanned and fit bull of a man take huge strides with his long legs across the marble floor of the Dubai Arrivals building.

He introduced Neha. 'Simon and I were in cop school together. Signed up to MI6 training together. Simon was a natural.'

'Vijay lasted a month,' said Simon, staring at Neha. 'How do you do?' For such a big, tough-looking guy, he was extremely soft-spoken. Cat-Catcher, his nickname among the MI6 brethren, Patel remembered.

'Why did you not stay on?' Neha asked Patel.

'You're assuming it was my choice,' laughed Patel.

'And while we walk to the waiting car,' said Simon, taking Neha's arm, 'tell me how such a bright lady like you came to be sharing aeroplane peanuts with this young scoundrel.'

Patel followed, clutching Neha's overnight bag, grinning.

Dubai's arid concrete-and-glass environment was a stark contrast to India's sweaty, boisterous bustle. Patel found himself looking at faces of people around, a mixture of men and women gliding on cooled marble, in suits, dresses, robes, burkhas.

'I found it extremely serendipitous when you called,' said Simon. 'Or it would have been two weeks ago.'

'How so?'

'We were tipped off about Zakir Bai and his UK activities. We took a good look. Couldn't find anything.'

'Is this about cricket betting?'

'Cricket? No, no. Something more serious. Anyway, he looks scrupulously clean in the area we're interested in. So, we've had to stop concerning ourselves with him.'

'You cannot talk about your area of interest?'

'Well, I can only say there's more concerning stuff we're looking into, in Pakistan, which may or may not have fringe involvement from Zakir.'

'Do you live here, Simon?' asked Neha.

'I have a base here,' he said. 'I wouldn't say I live anywhere, really. Perhaps when I retire, I'll live somewhere.'

'What's going on in Dubai?' asked Patel.

'Nothing and everything. It's a useful base, not just because the booze flows freely here. All the movers and shakers tend to congregate here for RNR.'

'Like us,' said Patel.

'Right,' said Simon, looking at his watch. 'We have six hours till your meeting. I shall fetch your requirements.'

They had booked a hotel room halfway between the airport and the venue of the meeting in Burj Dubai. Patel lay on the bed, slowly breathing in and out, whilst Neha stood at the windows, marvelling at the dizzyingly tall buildings. Every construction in Dubai seemed phallic. To show off the Emirati men's money, virility. Glass and concrete, ridiculously manicured lawns and palm trees, their pointy brown leaves and dry khaki trunks, instead of providing greenery to parched eyes, only accentuated the feeling of being desert-bound. As a Little Englander used to vast swathes of dewy green expanses, this palm tree and dust-brown citadel unnerved Patel.

The door opened.

'I'm back. Gather around, kids.'

Simon produced a little gunmetal case with a flourish. He went through two sets of combination locks to open it, before holding up a tiny nub, flesh-coloured, although the skin tone was more pink than brown.

'You put it into your ear.'

'That's it?' Patel said. 'Does it not connect to some battery – or do I wear the recorder on my legs?'

Neha guffawed. 'It's not the eighties, you know?'

Simon shook his head, smirked. 'See? You coppers miss out on all the cool gear which us spooks come to take for granted,' he said. 'This is it, my friend. Welcome to the world of nano engineering. This thing listens and records everything. You can play it back, separate out background noise, even pick up frequencies only a dog would normally hear. It's as high tech as it gets.'

'Israeli,' said Neha, offhandedly, suppressing a yawn.

'Yes, Mossad. But highly classified.' Simon's eyebrows were touching the perfect swell of well-groomed hair atop his forehead.

Neha waved away the implied compliment, muttering, 'Just came across it on the internet, yaar.' Simon and Patel exchanged glances.

'And this,' Simon said to Patel, 'you will completely be unfamiliar with. Being a regular detective without a license to kill.'

Patel raised his eyebrows, did not take the object Simon held out to him.

'I have no idea how to use one of these.'

'It's a gun,' said Neha. 'Just point and shoot.'

'You take it,' Patel told her. 'If that's OK with you, Simon. It makes me nervous. You know the statistics on accidental shooting.'

Simon and Neha exchanged glances, much to Patel's chagrin.

'Now you know why MI6 wouldn't take him on. He said he didn't want a gun.'

'Hey, you know it's true. Guns don't really protect people.'

'Well, this is strictly off the books,' said Simon. 'Clean, can't be traced.'

Patel shook his head.

Simon turned to Neha. 'You carry it in your handbag. I don't want you both going in to meet this guy unprotected. I don't trust them at all.'

'Can't you come,' Neha said, 'hide in a bush nearby?'

'Sadly, I can't.'

'Why not?' said Neha.

'Flying out at twenty-one hundred,' said Simon. 'I can't spare any other man either, or woman,' he said, unconvincingly, grinning at Patel. 'They all have their assignments. But we'd like a copy of whatever you hear. See what you can get out of him.'

'I'll sort a copy for you, Simon,' said Neha.

'I'll give you my number in case you need it,' Simon told Neha.

'I have it already,' Patel said.

'Not that number, my direct line.' Simon looked at Neha. 'But you can't put it into your phone, in case it gets hacked.'

'Oh right.' Patel hunted around for a piece of paper.

Neha pulled up her sleeve, smiling. 'Here,' she said.

Simon scribbled his number on her forearm.

Patel also pulled his sleeve up, and said to Simon, 'Here, dahlink,' and pursed his lips, affecting flirtation.

Simon scribbled his top-secret phone number on Patel's forearm with unnecessary pressure. 'Just make sure you wear long sleeves so it doesn't show.'

*

Before they left for the hotel, during Neha's bathroom sojourn, Patel quietly asked Simon about his mission.

'There's been a break-in at an MOD warehouse in Pakistan,' he said, looking grim.

Patel said, 'You have a Ministry of Defence warehouse in Pakistan?'

'Several. The Pakistanis are allies, after all. Our supplies, everything from combat fatigues to cigarettes, biscuits to army tanks, get stored there.'

'And what's been taken?'

'No idea. Big operation. Lots of casualties. We're hoping a swift response with the help of the Pakistani army has prevented the worst. Initial reports suggest there's nothing concerning.'

Patel could tell from Simon's attitude that he did not believe these initial reports. Otherwise he wouldn't be headed there.

The taxi dropped them off a few hundred yards from the Burj Dubai Hotel. Patel and Neha walked up the drive to the restaurant. Neha had dressed carefully for the meeting. She'd applied black eye shadow and lipstick, and donned a pair of jeans torn in a hundred places, like deep knife slashes, and a blouse like a postage stamp. When she'd emerged like this, Patel had been taken aback. She'd said, rather unconvincingly, 'Sorry, leaky water bottle. All my smart clothes got soaked.'

He wondered where she stowed this outfit and why. Perhaps it was undercover kit, along with the black make-up. It looked like she'd added a few more ear and nose rings too.

'Looks like a haunt for celebrities, this place,' Patel said to Neha. 'Why d'you think Zakir wants to meet us here?'

'Perhaps he wants to show you off?'

Patel noticed a paparazzo behind a sort of small hill, but

thought it unlikely that Zakir would want to be in the tabloids, hanging out with Patel.

Patel and Neha were discreetly escorted by the maître d' to a corner table, commanding the view of the main entrance as well as the doors to the kitchen and restrooms. Zakir Bai sat at the table, glued to his phone. They waited. Zakir, after a minute, handed the phone to a henchman waiting for it, got up, and booming, grabbed Patel in a bear hug, gave him a couple of thumps on the shoulder. He ignored Neha completely.

After the cricket chit-chat, Zakir leaned in, still all bonhomie, grinning, and said, 'Yaar, do you know how long my brother's been waiting to put his hands on me?'

Patel thought he detected in Zakir's eyes a glint of that ego of gangsters, the megalomania, that tinge of insanity, the willingness to risk lives – his own as well as of those around him – to satisfy a whim.

Pushing his whiskey away, Patel said, 'We're not interested in your feud with your brother. We want to know what Majid was involved in, and why he died.'

'You don't understand,' said Zakir. 'Majid has everything to do with our *feud*, as you put it. Majid split with the old man, the old ways. This sports betting. Cheap shit, man. Immoral, to toy with the hopes of millions of cricket fans, the *aam junta*.'

Neha interrupted, 'But the end result is often not affected, no?'

A henchman tensed, stepped a foot closer. They didn't like some young bird interrupting their little god.

Zakir looked annoyed by this unwanted bit of truth rupturing his cricket sentimentality, but let it pass. He said, 'Anyway, I said to Majid, no more of this betting. Come with me, and we will play big-boy games.'

The hairs on the back of Patel's neck pricked up. He waited.

Zakir smiled. 'But I'm not going to tell you about that. Forget it.' He slurped his drink through a straw.

'Then why did you agree to meet us?' Neha exclaimed. Again the thugs stepped closer, riled by her perceived insolence.

'I wanted to meet him.' Zakir pointed at Patel. 'I have a three-year-old boy.' He clicked his fingers and a smiley-faced henchman, who had the phone ready for just this moment, leaned in to show Patel pictures of a pudgy blob of a child sucking on his thumb.

'Here.' He held out his hand without glancing up and a stiff-faced henchman handed him a white T20 cricket ball. 'Sign,' said Zakir, flourishing a marker pen from his own pocket.

'I never played T20,' muttered Patel as he signed.

Patel was uneasy – what were they doing here? Here sat India's 'Most Wanted', having a tête-à-tête with a gossip journalist and high-profile cop. This wasn't right. Something smelled. What was Zakir playing at? He realised Zakir's henchmen weren't being cross-patches on purpose. They were super-keyed up and super-tense.

They were waiting for something. Suddenly, Vashist's slight grin, the twist to the corners of his mouth, pinged at Patel. *I'll get you Zakir's phone number, no problem.* He worked for Big Brother. Big Brother and Little Brother were at war. Patel and Neha were bait.

As casually as possible Patel handed the ball back to the smiley-faced henchman, who carefully placed it in a plastic Tupperware box and put it in his pocket.

'Well,' Patel said to Zakir, 'if that's all you wanted, we'd better scoot, catch an early flight back to London, maybe even make *Strictly*.'

Neha said, 'Hold on, we're not done yet. What was Majid involved in? Why was he killed?'

'No idea what you're talking about,' Zakir said.

'He's right,' Patel said, keeping his voice casual. 'Let's go, Neha.'

Patel stood. The stiff-faced henchman stepped forward and pushed Patel back into his seat.

Zakir said, 'You know you never said how you got hold of my phone number.'

Patel said, 'Your brother gave it to us. Then he had us followed. Now he knows where you are. But you know that already, don't you?'

Zakir looked up. Patel followed his gaze and noticed a third henchman press a finger to his earpiece, then nod at Zakir.

Zakir stood up. A smile like a gash appeared on his face. Patel noticed he had yellow incisors. 'Right, it's been nice knowing you both. Oh, I'm sorry, I meant, meeting you both. Now I must sayonara *auf wiedersehen*.'

He turned and walked to a door marked Service, which the stiff-faced henchman opened.

Through the door came forth four big fellas with pistols. They pointed at the entrance and took aim. The diners still dined; the waiters still hovered. No one seemed to have noticed anything. Patel turned to see two big Range Rovers pull up at the entrance. He heard a small scream from the far end of the restaurant. A waiter dropped a tray and ran into a trolley.

Patel leapt out of his chair, pulling Neha down. 'Fire,' he yelled. 'Everyone get out, quick.' He'd been trained to yell 'fire', in such a situation. Statistically, fire was what got people out of a building the quickest.

He heard a popping sound. 'Duck,' he yelled at Neha.

Neha dived down and half the glassware on the trolley behind her blew out. Glass sprayed over them like confetti.

Gunshots popping above their heads, Patel and Neha rolled

away from the table. Patel looked at Neha and pointed to the door where Zakir had escaped. She nodded. Staying low, they crept past Zakir's henchman firing towards the entrance and the maître d' table. Turning, Patel saw the maître d' himself ensconced inside the open back with the napkins and spare wine glasses, his eyes shut tight.

Patel reached up to turn the door handle. They got inside and scurried away from the door. Patel looked around. All the staff had either fled or were hiding. A second look showed most of them still there, hiding where they could. A closet marked 'Uniforms' was half ajar, a hand holding it that way. Chefs had stuffed themselves under metal tables that groaned with half-chopped vegetables and partly sliced meats; on the hobs pots of soups and sauces still simmered. The dishwasher pinged four times.

A scared-looking woman crawled towards them on her hands and knees, her hair wisping out of her chef's hat. Panting, she said, 'The back door is useless. Two men waiting outside with guns.'

Neha silently opened her bag, took out the gun.

'Are you going to use it?' Patel said.

'No. You use it.' She held it out to him.

'No way. You took the gun, not me.'

'You're the cop, aren't you?'

'I'm not American. We don't use guns in Britain.'

'Just take it,' said Neha, and threw the gun to him.

Patel caught it, eyes closed, terrified it would explode in his hands. It didn't. The safety was on. Thank fuck. 'Idiot,' he muttered at Neha.

Patel watched the Service door, tense, as the gunshots rose in crescendo, then tapered off. Patel had no idea how long they'd been there. *Could be an hour, or a minute*, he thought. How long had he been pointing the gun at the Service door? His arms ached. His wrists ached, especially the injured one. His finger trembled on the trigger.

The gunshots died down entirely. He heard a shuffling behind the door. His whole being tensed. He fought the urge to close his eyes and fire.

The door opened slowly, squeaking. A diner nervously stepped in.

Patel hurriedly lowered the gun, breathed in relief.

'They've all gone,' said the woman with an American accent, and burst into sobs. The chef put her arms around the woman, saying, 'There, there.'

Patel ran to the back door, saw two men jumping into one of the Range Rovers.

He heard several kinds of sirens begin afar, getting louder as the Range Rover screamed itself away into a puff of smoke.

He quickly got back to the Service door, stopped, turned to the closet, pulled it away from the fingers, rustled behind the terrified master-chef and sous-chef, and took out two sets of uniforms.

He threw one of them to Neha. 'Here, put this on.'

Parked up well out of the way, his best lens screwed onto Joseph's camera, Vetri saw the police officers go in and prepared for a long wait. He did not think he'd be able to get any information out of the medical staff or the cops but he wanted to see who emerged alive, and on their feet. Within minutes, the cops had shepherded the staff and brought them out. In gold- and silver-edged pantsuits, they looked utterly freaked out. Vetri felt glad there were so many of them. Another group came out, hands in the air. The diners. Again, this pleased him.

They were corralled together in a bunch, guarded by two

officers. No doubt, questions would be asked of them. Vetri focused on the faces. He saw the waiter who opened the window for them, fidgeting, whispering. They slowly began talking to each other, swapping notes presumably. *Did you see it? Where were you?*

Vetri's lens focused on two of the waiting staff slightly apart from the rest. Not talking. They looked at each other, began edging out of the core group further, then when the two cops began paying attention to their radios at the same time, they began walking away from the group. Something familiar about the taller one's walk. The shorter one swung his hips like a girl. Snug cap covering his hair completely. Vetri followed with his camera lens as far as he could. They were moving in the opposite direction to him and the cops. They would be away in seconds. Vetri made no move to follow them.

He reached for another lens – his longest range and best, usually used on golf courses and yachts. He trained the lens on the man's retreating head and waited patiently, whispering, 'Come on, come on ...' Thoughts of Shumi flitted through his brain. His favourite heroine of all time. If he'd come across her dead bloated body in a tub, he'd have clicked photos. No question.

The man turned and looked straight in the direction of Vetri and his camera. Vetri took at least twenty crisp photos of his famous face.

Chapter Seventeen

Lawrence swore, using the worst words he could think of, but in his head. He had been parked outside Patel's house for twelve hours straight. No sign of Patel, Clive or the bag. The previous day, he'd had Ringo wait at Patel's house while he trailed the mother all over town: she shopped, went to Pilates and yoga classes, volunteered at the library, inspected the allotment, dug and weeded, and spent hours with Sylvia.

There was a warrant out for Clive Atkins, his connection at the local cop house called to tell him. Wanted as prime suspect in two possible murders; an ex-actor and an old woman. At first, Lawrence had assumed it was Sylvia. But no. Another one. Perhaps he was having an affair. Lost his cool. Under pressure about the bag from Lawrence and Ringo. He couldn't fathom it out. No sign of Patel. Ringo had done the night shift. Lawrence rang him.

'Are you sure you didn't see Patel leave the house?'

'Absolutely damn right sure. I had my eyes peeled and all. Every second of every minute of every hour.'

Not bloody likely, thought Lawrence. He himself nearly missed Mrs Patel's comings and going once or twice, even though she bustled about as subtly as a baby elephant.

'Did anyone come to the house?'

'No, man. Oh yeah, there was this taxi. Victoria cabs. Came and waited two doors down but I didn't see anyone getting in.'

'How do you know it waited? Maybe the cabbie lives on the road.'

'Na, man. The engine was running. Lights on.'

'No one got in?'

'Don't think so.'

'You saw him drive off?'

'Sure.'

'Which direction?'

'Up the road. May have turned around.'

'May have?'

'Yeah, not sure, man.'

Lawrence swore under his breath.

Clive was AWOL. Patel was AWOL. Perhaps the bag was travelling too. What was in it? Cash, probably. How much cash could there be for his client to throw so much cash at retrieving it? A million? Ten million? Would that kind of cash fit into such a small bag? Not much bigger than a laptop bag, Mr T said. How many bundles of fifty-pound notes would fit into a bag not much bigger than a laptop case? It didn't compute. Who used cash nowadays anyway? Wasn't it all numbered accounts? Of course, it being Leicester, and— He sat up, the drowsiness suddenly disappearing. Gold! It had to be. That was why this was so important. Heavy, to be sure, but a couple of bricks of gold worth ... what? He had no idea.

Mrs Patel left her house on foot. He left his car and followed. She went to Clive's house. Do-gooder. Lawrence ducked behind a hedge when he saw a carer emerge. Mrs Patel chatted to her at the door. He couldn't hear them. An old man with a small dog – the ubiquitous cockapoo – gave him an incurious glance and walked on. The hedge belonged to a house that was, in Leicester-fashion, heavily curtained. They would be able to see Lawrence lurking behind the hedge.

The carer left. Mrs Patel went inside. He waited by the hedge for ten minutes. No one gave him any grief. People rarely did. But he didn't want to stay too long in someone's front garden. They might call the cops.

Then Lawrence had an idea. He got out the high-viz jacket he kept scrunched up in his cargo pockets, put it on and crouched in front of an electricity box opposite Sylvia's house. Twenty minutes later – his knee by then killing him – Mrs Patel emerged, letting the door shut behind her, and walked in the direction of her house. He went to the front door. Yale lock. He went to the side gate, reached over the top with his long arms and unlatched it.

Swiftly and quietly he entered, latched the side gate behind him. He came to the kitchen door. It had a cheap plastic handle that doubled as a lock. He tugged at it, and it came away in his hand. He pushed the door open and entered. Inside he let the door shut as silently as possible, slipped his shoes off. No one in the living room or kitchen. He glanced at the stairs. The stairlift was at the top. Was she taking a nap? Possibly. But even if she had heard him, she might think it was Clive. Good reason to grab a shotgun from under the bed. Lawrence chuckled.

He went past the kitchen and into the living room. Sofa. TV with a big screen. He looked around. Family photos on the bookshelves. He looked in the drawers under the TV console. Papers. Receipts kept for tax purposes. Clive was retired, wasn't he? Did retired people pay tax? He glanced at the receipts. Car MOT, wheelchair repair, council tax bills. A photo album. He heard a small scuffling sound.

Hairs on end, he froze. Did they have a cat? He hated cats. Couldn't see a pet bowl. Seemed unlikely, Sylvia being the way she was. It must be her – shuffling around in the bedroom. Surely she wasn't going to walk down the stairs. A thud. Suddenly he felt afraid. A grown man like him, afraid of phantom noises. He shook himself. Nervous, legs reluctant on the stairs, he tiptoed up, quiet as a mouse. And peeked around the bedroom door jamb. She was awake. Her hands twitched over the bed covers. The radio, a vintage Roberts, on the floor. The thud, explained. He hadn't heard it coming into the house.

Before he could ponder the advisability of such an action, Lawrence walked into the room, held Sylvia's frightened gaze with his own. He stood and looked at the woman on the bed. And she looked at him. He thought he could see the spark of awareness in her wrinkle-wreathed eyes. Damn, the woman knew everything. His heartbeat eased.

'Hey, lady,' he said to her. Funny he should have been spooked by such a helpless creature. He picked up the fallen radio. Switched it on, no sound. Gave it a couple of thumps and it came back to life. Radio 2. Some heated debate about the latest moronic chuntering from BOJO the clown. Oh, sorry, statement made by the prime minister. He laughed, and imagined Sylvia felt the same way.

'So, where is he then, your old man?' he asked her. Her eyes widened, as though defiant. As if refusing to give the goods away. There was a sense also of the great injustice being done to her. Lawrence finally admitted to a sense of shame in having kidnapped this helpless woman.

'Alright, lady,' he said. 'I'm sorry.'

Instantly, her eyes changed expression. Was it surprise?

'I'll be damned,' he said. 'You're alright up there, aren't you?' He tapped a finger on his skull. 'It's just your body . . .'

He saw a cup with a metal straw. A couple of cushions wedged onto a small chair by the window. He brought the cushions over and hefted her forward. So she could sit up and look out the window. Gave her a sip of water. Turned the volume on Radio 2 up a notch. A song from the Raven Sisters came on.

Humming along, he went downstairs to continue his search for clues. Another twenty fruitless minutes. He thought he was pushing his luck now, that one of the carers or Mrs Patel could barge in any second and he'd have to have a hell of an explanation for his presence.

Desultory now, his good mood from helping Sylvia deteriorating, he began putting the papers away. There was nothing on the laptop. An ancient Dell. Didn't look like it had ever been used, just a Google document with the title 'Thoughts of a man once young.' Blank inside. Perhaps Clive probed the depths of his mind and actually found nothing there to express.

He shut the laptop. His eyes fastened on the photo of Clive and Sylvia. Young and stiff. With the two boys, beside a caravan. He fingered the frame. Anglesey framers. Could it be that simple? Then in a flash the unexplainable receipts became explainable. Petrol receipts from an M5 service station from two years ago. Flood-warning notices for some unpronounceable area. Sounded Scandinavian, he'd told himself. A Welsh name of course. *Aha.* He marched upstairs. The noise woke Sylvia, who'd been nodding off.

'Is he at the caravan?' he asked her, watched as the frozen expression of fear in her eyes betrayed Clive.

Padmini let herself into Sylvia's house. Something odd in the air – a hint of something more masculine. Some kind of deodorant. Perhaps the carer who'd come for the afternoon shift was male, unlikely as that seemed. They were due an hour ago. And yet, the chair was upstairs. Usually by now Sylvia was seated in front of the telly. The carers brought her down and settled her in front of *Countdown*. Perhaps they hadn't come yet. Perhaps a new carer had his wires crossed and left her in bed. She made a cup of tea and took it upstairs. Sylvia was in bed. Staring at her in alarm.

'What's wrong?' said Padmini. 'Did the carers not take you downstairs?' She would leave a note for them tomorrow.

Sylvia made sounds. Padmini tried her best to decipher them. Nodded along.

'Hang on, love. Let me see what's happening.'

She rang the company number. The company gave her the carers' mobile number. She rang the number, and was assured by the girls that they were only a few minutes away. She wondered who'd look after her when it was her turn to be helpless. She couldn't see Vijay ministering to her. Or, in fact, her daughter, who had her hands full as it was. Just shove me in any old care home, she'd tell them when the time came.

She waited with Sylvia till the doorbell rang. With great relief, she let the carers in and sat on the sofa. She put the TV on. *A Place in the Sun*; *Countdown* long finished. Sylvia's TV only had the free-to-view terrestrial channels, no facilities to record or catch up. How all TV sets used to be not long ago. She wished Clive would come back. Sylvia must be wondering what the heck was going on. No one told her anything.

She looked at the pictures on the mantlepiece. She wished there was a way of communicating with her sons. If they knew, they'd come back to look after their mother. She couldn't imagine that Sylvia had been so awful a mother, that they'd rather not. Padmini hadn't a clue if Sylvia had sisters, brothers. She felt frustrated at not being able to do more.

Padmini got up and walked about the little room. Next time a carer failed to turn up at the scheduled time, who would notice? Padmini couldn't always be there. What should she do? Thoughtfully, she pushed a photo of the four of them – Clive,

Sylvia plus two kids on a beach – more in line with the photo next to it.

She took out her phone and rang Clive's number once more. Still no joy. She left yet another message asking him to call her back. She studied more pictures of Sylvia and her kids. By a beach; on the living-room sofa, same sofa but looking newer, brighter. In some field near a pond. Maybe it was their garden before they downsized. A huge, beautiful pond filled with flowers.

She googled a few carer agencies, carefully read through their reviews, and rang one. She couldn't look after Sylvia herself the way she needed to be looked after. She couldn't bring back her husband or sons. What she could do: pay for some extra care from a professional. She hired a lady to take Sylvia for daily trips to the park, to fix her lunch and feed her. And then to take her out for fresh air before bed. Three hours of care a day. She'd take it out of Vijay's inheritance, that her husband had specifically told her not to squander. Vijay wouldn't mind.

Chapter Eighteen

Patel and Neha barely spoke on the flight to East Midlands Airport. The plane shook for the entire duration of the flight. The captain's constant apologising only interrupted any attempt at rest.

Patel felt the outer turbulence matched his inner turmoil. He felt like he'd been put into a rattle and shaken. He had never seen Neha so quiet either. When the plane finally landed, the moment the engine switched off, the whole of the aeroplane breathed an audible sigh of relief. Taking that as his cue, Patel said to her, 'That's it, I'm done.'

'What do you mean?' she said.

'I'm done hunting a phantom pheasant in the woods. I'm a homicide detective, not a private investigator. Besides, no client has hired me.'

'I'm your client,' said Neha. 'You can help me by continuing to look for the reason behind P-p— Majid's death.'

Patel gave a dry chuckle. 'You're not a client. You're carrion. A reporter after a story, no matter the human cost. Well, in this case I'm feeling absolutely not up to carrying on. I never met Majid. I honestly don't care if he was killed by a drug overdose or if a pusher killed him in a freak accident.'

'I'm telling you Majid was clean for at least a year when he died. And the tox report from the deleted police files corroborated. Remember?'

He wondered again why she seemed so desperate to find Majid's killers.

'Thing is,' said Patel, 'I got into this trying to help Clive, who, frankly, is a bit of a git. And now he's disappeared. He's left his helpless wife without a word of farewell, abandoned her to the government's mercy. And Lord knows what he did to the other poor woman who is now dead. The police are looking for him. And if I continue on this, well, *quest*, I'll be aiding and abetting a felon. I'll be done for obstruction of justice, lose my job and worse. Can you imagine the trouble if Scotland Yard finds out I've been in Dubai in the crossfire between two criminal gangs at war?'

Neha had her lips set in petulant defiance. She wasn't going to gratify him by responding.

Sulky as a child now, he thought. 'Codman also ordered you to leave the country,' he told her, and finally provoked a response.

'No, I'm going to find out what happened to P— Majid.'

He shrugged, walked towards the Immigration for UK Citizens sign, joined a short queue. Neha went over to the other side of the hall to join the 'Aliens' queue.

Patel puzzled over why Neha stumbled over Majid's name twice during their conversation. At the desk he produced his passport expecting to be whisked through. His phone buzzed, his mother calling.

He answered. 'Hey, Ma, I'll call you in a minute.'

'Vijay,' screeched Padmini. 'You won't believe it, but I—'

'I'll call you in a minute,' he said, and hung up while she still prattled on. Preparing to move off, he held his hand out for his passport, already looking to the exit where Neha waited, her queue surprisingly quicker than his. Instead of handing back his passport, the border official spoke into a lapel microphone quietly. Patel's heart sank. He knew this procedure well.

Wraith-like in their quickness, but all too real, two armed G4S men appeared. 'If you would please step this way, sir.'

His phone buzzed. He lifted it and one of the men pointed his gun straight at Patel's chest and said, 'Please hand me your phone, sir.'

Patel raised his hands to indicate he was harmless and his phone was plucked from him. Neha, clever girl, had inched closer to the door marked 'Security'.

As he passed her, he muttered, 'Call Simon.' She heard him, nodded.

Padmini popped over at lunchtime to see how the new carer was getting on. Even as she stepped through the front door, she was reassured by the smell of something cooking. Hot and delicious. Local fresh bread on the counter. A chubby, jolly, booming woman with the delightful name, Habibi.

A hearty 'Hullo there!' made Padmini feel content that she had done the right thing. Sylvia had on her face a look of keen interest, her eyes following Habibi around the kitchen. Padmini stayed to watch Habibi blend Sylvia's lunch, then feed her with superb efficiency, never rushing, never flagging, ready with wipes and water. She swiftly washed up, dried and put away the pots, pans and cutlery. Then she settled Sylvia with a blanket on her knees in front of the telly and was off.

Padmini sat doing the sudoku, but her mind ran on. She counted how many days it had been since Clive disappeared and wondered again where he had gone. She wondered how long she should wait for Clive to return because really Sylvia needed full-time care. She mulled over these thoughts, torn this way and that, thinking how her own parents and her husband had died quickly with almost no time to say goodbye.

From leading full lives to dead in a matter of days, it still surprised her that her husband was dead. Lifted his arm up to serve in a tennis match at his club and fell down. He died instantly. Just like that. An A&E nurse playing on the next court had rushed up and done CPR. The ambulance arrived within minutes. No use. Sportsman's heart attack, they called it. Blessed way to go, someone said to her face. They were right in a way, she supposed. She wondered how Sylvia felt.

The sudoku numbers just swirled around on the paper in front of her. Pen poised to write in a box, forgotten, the tip staining the paper. The stain spread from a point to a pea shape. Padmini looked up to see that Sylvia too could not focus on her golden-oldie afternoon movie.

'Sylvia,' Padmini said softly, 'you must be so worried about Clive.'

Sylvia appeared not to be listening. Her eyes slightly widened, as if an important thought had just occurred to her. Padmini followed Sylvia's gaze to the photographs. The ones Padmini thought had been moved by a carer.

'Are they not in the right place?' Padmini asked. She couldn't tell what was wrong with the arrangement. Three photo frames leaned on their own stands. They were of Clive, Sylvia and the two boys. One on a sandy beach, one by a garden pond, one at some wedding.

Sylvia seemed to be staring at a particular photo fixedly. The younger boy was laughing in it, one foot in the air, balancing on the edge of the pond. On top of a brick. No, an ornamental stone.

Sylvia's eyes widened slightly, as though on the verge of great emotion. The pond was new. The stones were new. Sylvia teared up. Did she miss her old home and garden pond?

Padmini put the newspaper aside, got up. She went over to the photo and picked it up.

'Is it this one?' she asked Sylvia, bringing it close so she could look at it properly. An expression of almost feverish excitement on Sylvia's face. Her lips trembled. A sound came out of her. Anguish. Padmini drew the photo back. 'Oh, if there was only a way of contacting them, you know I . . . ' Then stopped.

Something on the edge of the photo. A satin pink. She had seen it before. It almost blended into the bush of giant mallow laden with pink flowers. But this pink, satin, shiny man-made stuff, out of focus in the background. She'd seen it before.

Hurriedly, she took the back off the photo frame and slid the photo out. On the edge of the photo was a jacket sleeve and she knew whose it was. *Linda old bag*, as Clive called her.

This was not a garden pond after all. This was taken at their own allotment. The boys were playing on Steve's plot. Right beside his pond. The stones were new. The pond must have been just dug. The same stones were now grey and encrusted in mud and colonised by tiny little alpines. The little boy was making a face in Linda's direction, probably encouraged by Clive, who – someone told her – used to let his boys run wild on the site. They stripped gooseberry bushes before the fruits ripened, especially Linda's, who grew the best fruit. She'd heard this was why Linda built her ridiculous fence all around her plot. To keep Clive's kids out.

'Why, this was a long time ago,' Padmini said.

Sylvia's eyes stayed wide and shiny, the photo now back on her lap. Then it struck Padmini. Steve's past comment about finding his garden gnome floating in his pond. Clive claiming to have seen Linda throw Bob's hand trowel into the pond after a disagreement over how her fence, now an overgrown hedge, took up two feet of his plot.

She began ringing Vijay, beside herself with excitement. Sylvia's eyes were shiny. Was it her own excitement she saw reflected in Sylvia's eyes, or were they somehow alive to the possibility of being on the verge of a great discovery.

Chapter Nineteen

Patel waited in a little room at the airport, his mind racing. Such quick work by the British authorities could only mean the system automatically red-flagged anyone associated with Zakir. He could not think how they got wise to his involvement in the Burj Dubai fracas. Did someone recognise him? He imagined little red lights blinking on the super-secret computers of the international police networks. Interpol, as it used to be called, somewhat quaintly. What was Zakir Bai up to? What was Majid's role in all this?

Patel wondered if he'd get any answers at the end of his hellish wait in a blank bare-walled room. No one told him anything but he guessed they were rustling up some interrogation expert to talk to him. They must be scratching their heads about his appearance in Dubai. Patel decided he'd tell the truth. This could very well lead to his dismissal from the force. No references would be forthcoming from Superintendent Skinner for his subsequent job applications.

Back aching from sitting on a plastic chair, he let his mind drift. Dismissed from the force. The shame. Thankfully, his father wasn't alive to witness this humiliation. He fantasised idly about becoming a Criminology lecturer at Leicester University. If they ran that programme still.

Walking around in jeans and Doc Martens, sporting stubble ... Maybe grow his hair into a ponytail, look cool ...

Students basically worshipping him, giggling as he walked past ... Googling his achievements ... What did Wikipedia say ... Height, weight, age, cricket stats ... Capturing two, not one, serial killers ... each case title linked to its own Wikipedia entry. Forced to leave the yard amidst an important investigation after a massive shootout with mafia dons from the Indian subcontinent. Students asking for details. Him keeping shtum on the classified stuff ... Dignified but mysterious silence ...

Such daydreaming screeched to a stop on the realisation that they wouldn't hire a lecturer with a criminal record. Two hours after he entered the room, a woman let herself in.

She came in with a bright smile and an apology for the delay, introduced herself as Marie D'Arcy. Just the name.

'And you are? You didn't say,' said Patel.

'That's right. I didn't,' she said. 'You can call me Marie.'

Anti-terror suspect interrogation expert, thought Patel.

Ms D'Arcy was a little, mild-mannered woman with dark hair heavily highlighted with blonde colouring, a startling red lipstick on her rather thin lips. She sat in front of him. Offered him a cup of tea, which he politely declined. She placed her bag on her lap. From it, she drew out a dozen glossy photographs and placed them on the desk.

'Is this you, Vee-jay?' she asked softly, her tone conspiratorial.

He studied the photo shot with a long lens camera. He was on a driveway, walking away from a building, its tallness and glassness distinct. In the blurry light, he couldn't make out the peach colouring of the shirt he sported – part of the waiter's uniform he'd nicked from the kitchen of the Burj Dubai Hotel. Close but facing away, Neha's distinctive head. The rest of her obscured by a palm frond. Patel was walking away but looking back. His facial features distinct as he stared straight into the hidden camera lens.

'Do you have anything to say about your presence here?'

'I'm sorry,' said Patel. 'I'm not sure where this was taken?'

He wanted to provoke a reaction from her for this blatant lie, but she wouldn't rise.

'In Dubai, ten hours ago,' she said, her voice completely neutral.

So she wasn't going to give him any information. Well, she would have to squeeze information out of him in turn. He'd been ready to confess all, but something about her manner made him wary of doing so.

'You still haven't told me what I'm here for?'

'We have some questions for you, DS Patel.'

'It's actually DI now. I was promoted three weeks ago.'

She gave him a look.

'Inspector,' she said, 'you were photographed walking away from a scene of bloody carnage. Two internationally wanted gangsters at a shoot-out. It's a miracle only one person was killed, and that it was an armed gunman, rather than an innocent bystander. But plenty of diners were shot, some injured seriously.'

He couldn't imagine why Simon hadn't intervened yet. Perhaps Neha couldn't get hold of him on the number he'd written on her arm before the meeting with Zakir. But Simon had been about to ship out to Pakistan. If it was black ops, he'd be uncontactable.

Patel wondered how to play it. 'Am I under arrest?'

'No.'

'I need a lawyer here to tell me if I should be answering these questions.'

'Have you heard of the Terrorism Act, Mr Patel?'

He sniffed British interest in this. This wasn't a case of terrorism in the Indian subcontinent. This was about terrorism on British soil. Hot damn!

'Is that what I am detained under? The Terrorism Act.'

'Loosely, yes.'

'Do I get my one phone call?'

'Technically, yes. But there are no phone lines running to this office.'

Office, he thought. *More like a broom cupboard.*

'You can give me my phone back?'

'Ha.' She made a 'sorry, not sorry' face.

He wondered why his mum had called so many times. It really was not like her. Something must have happened.

D'Arcy was speaking. 'Tell me what you were doing there, and don't say it's classified. I deal with classified stuff. I know whatever you were involved in wasn't official. You're on sick leave.'

'Have you heard of Simon Thacker?'

'No.'

'Well, that's coz he's very good at his job. He is MI6. If you get hold of him, he'll explain what I was doing there. I'm afraid I can't say much more. It really is classified stuff.'

'You're messing around with me, aren't you?'

'Never.' Patel made an expression he learned from his father who used it when he thought his son was on the verge of some naughtiness. 'This is too serious for jokes, don't you think? As you say, serious business, international gangster shoot-out. A life killed. I wouldn't mess with you, Ms ... D'Arcy.'

'Inspector,' she said. 'Special Branch.'

At last.

'The man you were meeting, Zakir Ashraf Bai, has been flagged up for involvement with Syrian criminals. We've been tracking his movements for some time now.'

Patel read between the lines that they had a heap of suspicions, but nothing solid on Zakir.

A slight hesitation in her manner betraying that she was

veering into unscripted stuff, she said, 'We've been looking for a young British girl, fifteen years old, dark hair, green eyes, last seen heading to Syria. It looks like the description matches your companion in your meeting with Zakir. Do you confirm?'

Hiding his shock, Patel said, 'Oh, you are mistaken about that.' What on earth was going on? What could connect such a girl with Zakir? But here at least he could be straight. 'The woman accompanying me is a twenty-eight-year-old Indian, young-looking, sure, and hair's dark, alright, and her eyes are more brown or hazel, like mine, rather than green.'

'She doesn't wear contact lenses?'

'Not that I noticed. And she's definitely older.'

'Ah. And you say your involvement with Zakir has been classified and authorised by MI6.'

'The highest echelons,' Patel said with conviction.

He held her stare till he could feel her relenting. Then he said, 'Let me call Simon Thacker.'

Pursing her lips, D'Arcy rang someone to check Simon's credentials, then, still not looking completely convinced, gave Patel her phone.

Hoping like hell, he pulled up the waiter's sleeve, and there it was, Simon's number where he'd scribbled it the previous afternoon.

He dialled. It rang and rang, then an automated voice came on. 'I am sorry, the number you have dialled is unavailable at the moment; please try again later.'

'Can I text on this phone?' he asked her.

'Sure, go ahead.' A hint of a smile on her face.

He wrote: Call back, urgent. Arrested. At East Midlands Airport. Vijay.

*

Clive had completely lost his appetite. He spent all morning sitting on the caravan step, staring at the horizon. He'd barely sipped any water. Guilt filled his belly, rattled his soul's cage.

He'd abandoned his wife, just as her sons had abandoned her. You couldn't say she'd done a single thing to deserve this treatment from any of them. *She* had been solid, dependable, loving. Not movie standard wife and mother, but enough. Put food on the table, did not complain about her lot. Got the kids ready for school, asked after the homework, did presents. Birthdays, Christmas. A&E trips.

While she didn't exactly fight their corner in the case of schoolyard bullying, or in a couple of fractious parent-teacher meetings, she'd made them a home, always did a Sunday roast. She listened to them, always willing to accept their version of events. With him, although the first flush of romance was a distant forgotten memory, she'd been loyal, dependable. Never argued with him in front of the kids. Always presented a solid front. Liked to get tipsy with a friend or two occasionally, never got drunk. And she was an attractive woman in her time. With a lovely laugh, and kind to everyone. No, she did not in any way deserve this abandonment.

Could he go back to see her? No, they'd arrest him. Throw him in the slammer. Guilty as hell. He was too old to become jailhouse meat. Ah, but life wanted to go on living. Even his pathetic little life.

He walked to the sea in the afternoon. Inured to the joys of families with little children on a bright holiday. A sad old man. He stood staring at the water. He thought of filling up his pockets with pebbles, come the night, and wading into the water. On and on, till he fell off the sand shelf, refused to kick his legs to swim.

In the end, he chose to sit in his car to die. He found an old rubber hose used to run water from the taps that used to be at the site. Gaffer-taped it to the exhaust. Stuck it into the back window. Gaffer-taped it up. Sealed the gap with a piece of board. And more gaffer tape. Sat in the car, gathered himself for a moment, switched on the ignition. The fumes made him cough. The cough burned his lungs. Too awful. He switched off the engine. Fell out of the car gasping for air, retching. Not a peaceful way to go. He tore the gaffer strips off.

Then he rattled around looking for rat poison in the caravan. He knew he'd bought some ages ago. He found mouldy detergent. The thought of imbibing detergent made him gag and retch once more. Probably not fatal anyway.

He found the box of rat poison under a pile of blankets. He could put it in strong coffee or a chocolate muffin. He squinted at the small print at the back. Seven years past its use by date. He wondered what happened to poison that was out of date. Did it become harmless? Go back to nature? He saw nibbles on the unopened packaging. Perhaps it even became food again for the rodents. A balanced source of fibre and protein.

He could just sit in his caravan and do nothing. Isn't that what some Native American elders did? Go out to the top of the mountain to die. *I may be some time.* Inuits went out into the snow, didn't they? The King died. The Queen died of grief. Could a man *will* himself to die? He took a walk, gazed at the mess in the other caravan.

He went home. The clapboard caravan home. He sat in the rickety chair and let himself be consumed by self-loathing. By the wish to cease to exist. But Sylvia. Who would give a damn about her? And his sons. What would happen to them, especially Peter? As a boy he'd always needed a push to do anything. Then he'd made the decision all on his own to follow his flaky, irresponsible older brother all the way to the land where water swirled the wrong way round, or so he'd read somewhere.

Perhaps some undertow would pull his sad dead body all the way to Australia. He'd wash up on the Great Barrier Reef and his sons would read about it in their local newspapers sitting in their wrong-swirling bathwater. So he did that. Filled his coat and trouser pockets with pebbles, stuffed them. Pushed into his shoes bits of grit and sand.

He waded into the cold sea. Gone midnight. Bit of moonlight now and then when the white lady peeped from her cloud covers. Bitterly cold so Clive shivered. He felt lit up from within by his fervour, his zeal to do the right thing, finally. His Pradas, a dead man's shoes, now taking him to his own death. To his watery grave. He imagined a kind of peace as he floated at the bottom of the ocean, eyes closed, hair waving like seaweed. He walked. The sandbank was shallow here, seemed to go on for half a mile. Did he choose the wrong bit of beach on purpose?

He hadn't thought it through. There was a sharp drop-off at another section of the beach, further up, with warning buoys. Why did he not go there? He had not planned it. Just made a beeline from his caravan to the water. Or perhaps his subconscious was trying to keep him alive, tricking him into choosing a shallow beach. Well, he would walk and walk, in water that came up to his midriff, till his knees gave out in exhaustion. Then he'd collapse and drown in four feet of water. In the three days he'd been here, he'd never seen the tide so far out. The water so low. Luck of the draw. The universe trying to keep him alive.

Just this afternoon, when the beach had been heaving with families, the sea had been far in. He could wait for high tide. He'd have water over his head in a jiffy, but it might happen in the daytime, when there were too many people about. Someone would pull him ashore, call the cops, the emergency services. They'd be on the lookout for him. Wanted criminal on suspicion of homicide. Him, Clive. Homicidal maniac. Sad old thief.

He sobbed as he stood there in the freezing water. He felt the warmth of life ebbing away. He walked further. He should have gone and brought Peter back last autumn. Sylvia had pleaded with him. Peter had asked for money. Clive had shouted at him on the phone, called him a pussy. Steven called a few days later to say Peter was ill, needed to come home, but was refusing to go, refusing to speak to anyone. Sylvia had pleaded, 'Take money out of the pension pot, go and get him.' Clive had refused.

He knew now that Sylvia, after he point-blank refused to discuss the matter, had been stewing and worrying, and that's what had caused the stroke. His fault. He sobbed.

He could go back and face the music. At least he'd see her settled into a care home, much as she hated strangers looking after her. That would be worth becoming jail meat for. Perhaps he'd even get away with it. After all, the British police did mess up evidence often in cases, sometimes leading to criminals getting away scot-free. He'd read in the *Mail* that rapists and murderers were let off due to filing errors.

If that miracle happened, he could really track down Peter, offer him help.

Yes, he would, he promised Sylvia in his head. Whatever little they had, he'd offer it to Peter. That would make her happy. To do that, he'd go back and face the music.

He turned back. The shore was far away. So far that he couldn't see it. He could barely move his legs, now numb and stiff and cold. The tide still pulled him deeper in. He had no energy to trudge back to shore against the tide. Like the plonker that he was, he would die in a puddle, after all.

Chapter Twenty

All along the M5 the rain clouds chased Lawrence. When he reached the Anglesey service station where Clive had filled his car with petrol all those years ago and opted to save the receipt for tax purposes, the rain caught up. Chucking his half-eaten jackfruit wrap and empty Coke cup, Lawrence hoicked up the collar of his Polo T-shirt and dashed to the car. Inside, he used a couple of paper tissues to wipe the raindrops from his beard and topknot.

He wished he had brought his waterproofs. Had the foresight. But at least he had the cleverness to download Google Maps. He opened the app, carefully spelled out the name of the Welsh town that had issued the flood-risk letter. The campsite itself did not seem to exist any more. And he wasn't sure how close it was to the sea. Was it located on the floodplain beside the sea or a river? Plus, there were two rivers and a big stream in the vicinity; did the rivers have floodplains too?

He missed his little munchkin. Lawrence normally put her to bed four times a week, when Magdalena had night shifts. Magdalena's mum had come to babysit. Muffin had been excited to see Granny, but by tomorrow morning, she'd be missing her daddy. He wondered how long it would take to find Clive. When he'd get back. He needed to be able to tell her what he did for a living when she got older. He knew that other parents, doctors, engineers, did career days. What could he say? An odd-jobs man? No. That was like garden clearing or maintenance work. Someone who hung pictures, repointed bricks. He could present himself as someone who got things done. An enforcer – like something out of *The Matrix*, he could pretend, except preschoolers wouldn't know *Matrix* from Lego.

He found three potential sites on Google Maps, and drove to each of them, but all were functioning, full of families, kids. Unlikely places for a lonely old man. The flood-risk warning could mean the campsite closed a few years ago. He chatted to a couple of the ladies who ran the places, people running a business were always keen to chat. Every visitor a potential customer, he supposed. *Yes, it was possible. Did ring a bell, yes. A campsite on the bay that closed due to flood risk. Couldn't remember the site name.* But he wasn't convinced they weren't just humouring him.

Lawrence wanted to give up and head back. He'd be too late to put the little poppet to bed. But, if he left now, he'd be home before midnight. Could fix himself a drink, put his feet up, watch a film, wait for Magdalena to come back, make her a cup of tea before she went to bed. She was weird like that. But then his job description wouldn't fit him. He wouldn't be the guy you went to when you wanted something done. He'd be the guy who might get things done for you, if he could, weather permitting.

Ah, fucking weather. It had been such a beautiful day. Where did the rain come from? Why on earth did he put on a Polo T-shirt? Not his style. Something he'd picked from a charity shop, to humour the kid at the till who'd seemed unnerved by his presence. He suddenly felt so unhappy he wanted to tear the T-shirt off and throw it away.

That's it, he decided. He would do this one last job, do it well, take the twenty grand, and use it to start leading the life he wanted to. They'd be poor for a while, heck, even for a long time, but hey, it was worth it. He'd look after his daughter, work his socks off to make his new café a success. He would serve scones with a separate jug of cream.

The rain came on heavier as he stood in the middle of yet another field, where there used to be a campsite. He opened Google Maps on his phone to check if he was on the right field, held his hand over it to keep the rain off the screen. A sheep bleated suddenly, very close by, startling him, and he dropped his phone in the mud. Just a short fall, but the dang thing fell vertically, hit a jagged stone sticking out of the wet grass. He shooed the sheep off. The screen was cracked. Frozen on the Google Earth image. He could not get it to switch off. He swore. Now what?

He held the button down for several seconds, until finally, the phone screen went dark. Then he got in the car, wet clothes squeaking against the leather interiors, and drove to the nearest beach.

He sat looking at the sea, then brought out a slightly crumpled photo from his door sleeve. Two boys laughing, kicking a ball by a caravan. He studied the landscape in the background. A sandy beach, turning pebbly to the left-hand corner. He smoothed it best as he could. It had got crumpled when he'd hurriedly pulled it out of its frame and stuffed it into his back pocket. He'd remembered a photo album in the TV cabinet, found one of matching dimensions and content, the younger boy next to a lake or a pond, and had popped that into the frame. Even positioned the frames exactly as they were.

Alyyuth Campsite is a modest campsite, no toilets, nothing, on the edge of a clutch of lodges for people who needed more facilities, a good bed, central heating and baths. He knocked on the little office door. No answer. He walked around. It did not look like a family sort of place. Nothing for kids. No playground equipment, no pool. No petting animals in an enclosure. Just a view to die for, of yonder hills and a castle in the distance, just air so fresh it seemed to kickstart new cells in your lungs. He took a walk around the campsite. A couple of apple trees with the flowers dropping, little nub apples forming. Lichen grew on its branches. He knew that lichens did not grow in polluted air, like in Leicester for example.

He tried the door again, and a woman opened it. He told her he was a private investigator and asked if he could meet her about a man he was tracking, wanted back in Leicester for a crime he couldn't disclose details of, and known to have a caravan on this site.

'There's no one from Leicester here,' she said.

'He wouldn't have told you he was from Leicester,' Lawrence said.

'Oh, they don't have to,' she said. 'We take card payments. The address pops up.'

'Recognise this? Your site?'

She narrowed her eyes over the flood-risk notice. 'Name's the same,' she said. 'But as you can see, we are high up on the hill. No flood risk. Not near a river or sea either. Nearest significant water body is the sea, Conwy Bay, twenty miles thataway.'

'How long has this campsite existed?'

'Oh, near ten years.'

'Ah. This letter's dated twelve years ago.'

'Perhaps they closed it down due to insurance issues and all. I remember there was some big flooding around then. Some people's homes had water in, had to be evacuated.'

'You think this campsite's name was taken from the previous campsite? Could it have been near here?'

'I'll ring my dad. He named it. He's good with memories from years ago. Clear as day to him. But what happened yesterday, not so good.'

Lawrence had to bear witness to her long, ponderous, round and round the garden conversation, until he caught her eye and pointedly looked at his watch, inspiring her to finally come to the point. She quietened to listen to what her dad had to say on the matter, just occasionally grunting to show she still listened.

Lawrence restlessly tapped his feet, fingered his topknot, brushed his beard.

Finally, she said goodbye, after repeated promises to visit.

'So that was interesting,' she said.

'Was it?'

'Yeah, he said there was a campsite with the same name years ago. He'd heard people remarking in the early days. Named after a clutch of pretty woods Dad played around in, and possibly near to where this bay was. He reckons it must be near Crickly Bay.'

'How do I get there?'

'It's just a small bay, narrow roads. Go straight on this one to Conwy, then go north, and a mile or two along and you'll find it. Just put it in the satnav.'

'I was using my phone. It's broken,' he said. 'You have a roadmap I could borrow? I could post it back to you.'

'Gosh, who uses those any more? No, sorry.'

Lawrence walked back to the Subaru, wishing he'd given in to Magdalena's wishes and bought a new car with an inbuilt satnav. Then a spark lit up in his brain. Hang on, wait a minute. He opened the boot and found the false panel in the floor, clicked it open, and voilà, his trusty old road map for Britain, lying there undisturbed for ten years or more.

'Ha ha. Take that, technology rubbish,' he chortled.

He leaned over the open boot, his head inclined to keep it

out of the rain. Icy little spears of water drenched his back as he bent over the map and traced a finger around the drawings of little roads around Conwy and Straclyth Bays. It occurred to him if the campsite still had a few abandoned caravans it made an ideal hiding place for Clive. Unless it was all underwater, then Clive could be in Scotland for all he knew.

Chapter Twenty-One

This is purgatory, thought Clive. He hadn't paid much attention to heaven and hell, the afterlife and all that in Sunday school. But the idea of purgatory had struck him, long ago, as something interesting, a sort of a waiting room, where you were in limbo. Where there was no air, no feeling, no sound, and you sat or stood, mired in suspense, awaiting your sentence.

In his particular purgatory, Clive found himself mired in the cold ocean, weighed by his age, his physical frailty, the enormity of his guilt, his fatigue from going on living. Outside of his torment, the sky was a metal black. The teasing moon had finally vanished, leaving the sky covered in clouds. The air so still he could have been in a vacuum. No breeze to indicate he was still on earth. *Perhaps he'd died already*, he thought, but that was nonsensical thinking.

It took ages. It took a lifetime. Inch by inch, looking at a far light on the shore, he willed his limbs to move. He fixed upon that lamp as a beacon; God, perhaps, calling him. He didn't really believe in God, had no reason to. He hadn't done anything for a god, and didn't think God or the gods gave a monkey's about someone like him. Fair enough. But now, it comforted him to think of the light on the shore as a beacon guiding him with a kind of benevolence ... a divine benevolence. Why not? *Hey, pal*, a part of his own exhausted mind said to him in an American-cowboy accent, *whatever gets you back on that shore, yeah?*

He was still far away from the shore when the daylight died. A great almighty rain shower came down to test his newfound faith in his repentance and will to live.

Lawrence waited for two minutes on the crossroads, unable to decide whether to take the left or the right. The left took him back to Leicester for just after two a.m., the right took him further up the coast in the failing light. He'd give it another hour, he decided.

Two hours later, the sun had well and truly set. Pitch-black now. He felt wet, cold and hungry. He flicked on his full beams. Little country lane bordered with overgrown hedges. He wished he'd stopped at the Spar he'd seen twenty miles earlier and bought a sausage roll and a packet of crisps, as his first instinct had been. But his better nature prevailing, he'd decided to wait for an M&S or something. He didn't want to get indigestion. Foolishly he'd wished for a quinoa salad. Stupid. Of course they wouldn't have an M&S in the sticks here. Spar or nothing. Should've gone in. Now he was stuck here, starving, no inkling where the homicidal grandpa lurked.

He checked the petrol gauge. Running pretty low. He reckoned he'd have to turn around soon, head to a B&B or petrol station.

He looked for somewhere to turn around. The hills dipped steeply. The wheels spun in the mud for a second, Lawrence held his breath, till, to his relief, the car obliged and turned. He stopped the car, just breathed for a few moments. Visibility was piss-poor. He could just about make out he'd stopped on a verge, the valley blanketed down in front of him.

And then, just like that, as if there was a showman who'd decided to whip away the curtain and reveal the entertainment, the rain ceased, the moon came out, and there, right in front of him, in a low field of puddles, stood a clapped-out caravan, and beside it, Clive's wheelchair-adapted van.

The weight of a drowned man under his clothes, Clive dragged himself out of the ocean. He lay gasping on the beach for an eternity till he caught up with his breathing. Then began the freezing trudge through the sand. When he got to the caravan, his teeth chattered, and hands felt half frozen. He could barely wriggle his fingers. It rained hard as nails. He stumbled into the caravan and found the kerosene stove. Found a matchbox. Fumbled the matches with his violently shaking hands and the matchbox flew and matches fell on the floor, where he'd dripped a puddle. He rooted in the kitchen drawer and found a lighter, and with his trembling fingers tried to light it. No strength in his thumb.

He began to weep, out of his mind with fatigue and cold. Then he fished his car key out of his sodden pocket, dropped it twice, stumbled out and lurched in the blinding black rain into his car. He turned the key. To his relief, the engine started instantly. He turned the heat on full blast, noted the petrol warning light come on. He couldn't remember if it had come on yesterday or today.

He closed his eyes and slumped on the wheel, head in his arms, too exhausted to think. To decide if he could afford for the petrol to run out, the petrol station miles away. Was he suffering hypothermia, would he survive the night, would he ever see Sylvia or Peter or Steven again, and finally, did he deserve to be still alive, after all the terrible things he'd done in his life?

*

Lawrence wondered where Clive had gone. The caravan was a mess. It looked like the one in the picture, though much dilapidated. Inside, a big puddle on the floor.

'Oh heck,' he said, as he surveyed the carnage. Matches floating in the puddle of water on the floor, a kerosene stove on its side, a couple of wet towels on the chair. There was his wallet. Right on the little kitchen counter. It felt dry. Inside, a bundle of cash, about four hundred pounds in twenty-pound notes, driving license and a couple of debit cards, a Tesco loyalty card. Where had he gone without his wallet?

Lawrence came out of the caravan, looked around for torchlight. Perhaps he'd gone for a walk and would return soon. The car was still here. He couldn't have gone too far. He wished he still smoked. He badly needed a fag now. He noticed the car. Perhaps there was some information in there. He approached the car. He'd have to find the car key to open it. He half turned to the caravan. But maybe—

Experimentally, he tried the door, and it opened. He stumbled back in shock. A human form in the driver's seat, slumped over the wheel.

Chapter Twenty-Two

After two hours of twiddling his thumbs, biting his nails, relenting, he accepted a cup of tea, then two, then some biscuits, then even a Boots sandwich. By now D'Arcy seemed to be convinced that Patel was no bad guy. Hell, he was a celebrity good guy. She spoke of following protocol, having to abide by the rules, even if he were the prime minister.

Yeah, right, Patel thought. Like hell she'd have arrested the PM and sat him in this room for hours, following protocol. And she denied him a lawyer and a phone call.

Simon called at last. 'I've spoken to them, they'll let you go now.' He sounded tired.

'Thanks, pal,' he said to Simon.

'No trouble.' There was a strange quietness in the background from which his voice emerged.

'Where are you?'

'On a jet plane,' he said. 'Calling from a very expensive satellite phone.'

Patel thought of Dr Evil in his undersea lair, with a big, rectangular grey satellite phone with the long antennae, and wondered if Simon's phone was similar to that contraption. 'I suppose you can't tell me what precisely you are doing on that plane?'

'You suppose right.'

'This got anything to do with Zakir and co?'

'Can't tell you, dude.'

'Dude.' They liked their mock-American parody.

'Where's Neha? She alright?'

'She wasn't nicked. Just me. They got a picture. Paparazzi, I expect. I sent her to see my mum.'

'Oh good. Safe as houses. You don't need me to send someone to keep an eye?'

'Nah, she can look after herself. She's a grown woman.'

Simon sighed.

'So what's happening in Pakistan? I need to know if it's to do with Majid's death.'

'Not at all. Not sure Zakir's involved either, but I wouldn't bet on it. Intel scarce at the moment. Our mole who led us here turned up gagged and bound, in a bag in a Karachi sewer.'

'Alive?'

'Doornail.'

'Are you flying back to the UK now?'

'Yes, landing in thirty minutes. There is some serious breach in one of the big MOD armament holding centres in Pakistan. We are looking into what's gone missing. A whole bunch of stuff. A whole lotta mess.'

'It's not classified?'

'Aw shit, half of Pakistan knows. They're celebrating. It is going to be in the *Daily Mail* tomorrow. You can even tell your girlfriend.'

He could imagine the grief Simon would be getting from his superiors.

'Who's got to carry the can?'

'Yours truly, who else? I'm in charge of this mess.'

'Well. Good luck sorting it out. Perhaps you can drop by if you're in the area.'

'Unlikely. But I'll try, if I'm indeed in the area. You take care, bro.'

'You too, mate. Thanks for the help.'

'Any time.'

Patel hung up, missed Simon intensely for a second. They used to practically live in each other's clothes. Oh well, he probably wouldn't see or hear from Simon for another ten years, he thought.

The release of Patel from Her Majesty's custody was easier said than done. D'Arcy had long left, to interrogate other crims or suspected crims in Heathrow or Gatwick or wherever. A jolly Berkshire fella called Timothy then took over, and got Patel to read and sign an account of his interrogation, a mind-numbing document that he had to first slowly write up. Timothy, cheerful, unhurried, set to work.

'Sorry,' he said, 'usually these things take a while. Never had anyone released so quick.'

Patel refrained from gnashing his teeth. He'd been here four hours now.

'Look,' he told Timothy, 'can I at least have my phone back? My mum's been trying to reach me. I'm sure it's an emergency.'

'Sorry, sir, we cannot get back to you your personal effects until I present the release papers to the holding officer, and I cannot get the release papers before getting a signed and witnessed statement off you.'

Patel sighed. There was nothing he could do. He knew they were sticklers because he was one of them. Paperwork was the bane of a cop's existence, but if they did not dot every i and cross every t, they'd be stuffed when someone sued them for wrongful arrest.

'You can borrow my phone, sir, and call your mum?'

He had no idea what his mum's landline number or her mobile number was, or even his own. All the information was stored in his phone and laptop, to which he had no access.

'Never mind,' he said. 'It'll have to wait, I guess.'

Finally, after another hour, he was allowed to go. By the time he retrieved his phone from it's security wrapping, the battery had given up the ghost.

Of course, he said to himself. *Oh well, I'll be home in two hours.* He wondered if his mother had heard about the shoot-out in Burj Dubai on the news, and had put two and two together. Of course she would have. She liked to follow all the Bollywood gossip. She was probably an expert in all the various ways the Bollywood actors and the mafia were entwined, and in turn connected to the Middle East, Sharjah, cricket, etc. In fact, he ought to ask her about this cricket betting business. What was all this about Indians betting on English county cricket? That was beyond bizarre. A truly globalised world.

He had to wait for a taxi. They'd never been so busy, said the harried woman at the taxi booking desk.

Patel decided to be zen about the whole thing. Still, a niggle of worry about his mother. He left the queue to find a charging point for his phone. No joy. Every single charging point was taken. Inclement weather, a dust storm over the Arabian peninsula had caused lots of cancellations, and an influx of people waited, connected to their phones with the charger cables like babies to their umbilical cords.

He gave up and decided to just get home. When he rejoined the taxi queue, it was even longer. *Oh heck*, he thought. If it was a real emergency, his mum would have called an ambulance or the police. The fact that she'd called him several times meant she was fine. It was probably just something she wanted to talk to him about urgently. Maybe Clive had turned up and was in trouble again. Perhaps Clive's tormentors had ... no ... he wouldn't think the worst. He would stay positive. Hemmed in by the queue, he fidgeted, tutted, making the rose-hued beauty in front of him turn slightly, with a frown of disapproval directed at Patel.

Reassuring Sylvia until her trembling subsided, promising that she'd be back straightaway as soon as they found something, anything, or even nothing, Padmini settled her in front of the telly. Luckily, there was a World War II film on and Sylvia seemed to immediately engross herself in it. Padmini gave Sylvia's cheek a pat, and thought she could see a hint of a smile on her face. She left the house in high spirits, feeling sure she would find the bag. *A bloodhound on the scent, that's me*, she thought.

She looked left and right, crossed the road, and walked towards the allotment gates. She stopped suddenly, heard a corresponding sound, as though someone else had stopped behind her. She turned but saw no one. The street was dead empty. She checked the time. Two in the afternoon. Some of the green bins were still out on the pavements, haphazardly, the bin men long gone.

She'd assess the pond first, she thought. Neha might have some idea. She was a bright young girl. Woman, she corrected herself.

She unlocked the gates, slipped in, and pushed them back together, pulled the latch in place and hung the lock so it looked secure on casual glance. Padmini couldn't fathom how so many people had lately been going in and out through the locked gates. Something to do with the metal latch. She'd have to write to the council about it.

She heard music blaring from one of the terraces. The eccentric man who grew plastic flowers in his front garden. Once his face had popped up above his twelve-foot fence, startling the life out of her. He'd just stared, glumly, not even surprised at the foul language that erupted out of her at the sudden sight of him. She'd apologised, and he'd not spoken a word. Really, he should've apologised for startling her so. What was he doing, popping up like that?

Startle she did, when she nearly tripped over a furry creature in the overgrown grass. She cursed, managed to right herself, and the little mutt started yelping and scooted away in fright. Then stood there by its gate with the big 'Beware of the Dog' sign, wagging its tail. She tutted at the mess it had left behind, scanned the house. She caught sight of a face in one of the upper windows, waved and gestured at it. Unsurprisingly, the form backed away and she couldn't see it any more. She knew it was the man who owned the dog, and that he'd continue to let his dog out into the allotment to do its business, but at least she'd made her point, for whatever good it did.

Past the unofficial tip where Majid's body was found, on to Steve's plot. She gazed at the pond, wondering if she ought to ask someone to help. Usually there was someone around, but not today. She heard a twig snap, turned eagerly, but didn't see anyone.

She scanned around, warily, but she didn't hear anything else. The pond dully reflected the cloudy sky, the air heavy with the thunderstorm that was forecast. No guarantee, in a place like Leicester, which was blessed with a dry-ish microclimate.

She'd rung DS Codman, who'd given her his mobile phone to get in touch in case Clive rang her. He'd said, 'What bag?' Then made it clear it was Clive he wanted, not some notional leather bag.

Padmini wasn't so keen on doing this sort of thing herself. But she couldn't sit at home waiting for Vijay to turn up. What if those rough men had the same idea? She'd spent twenty minutes trying to get hold of Vijay. Then she had a voicemail from Neha, saying, rather obscurely, that Patel had been delayed but she was on the way to see her from the airport.

Although why one of them should be delayed and the other not when they were travelling together, she could not fathom. Something to do with his job, she supposed. Then she'd looked through her allotment contacts, found Steve, plot sixteen. His phone went to voicemail. She said, 'Steve. I'm sorry to not give you much notice. But I'm going to dredge your pond. You know how your wife's garden gnomes have mysteriously disappeared over the years, I have an idea where they might be. Along with a few other objects. I'll place any gnomes I recover by your shed. Cheerio.'

She hoped Steve wouldn't take umbrage at the lack of notice. If he did, she'd tell him to take it up with the committee, which was basically herself. Not quite cricket, but needs must.

She decided to consult Neha when she got here, about how to tackle the pond. She checked her watch; her train should be arriving now. She brushed the dirt off Steve's plastic chair and sat down on it to study the pond, whose calm surface hid untold treasures thrown in over the years by Linda, fuelled by pure spite. She hoped like hell Majid's bag was in there.

Lawrence fought his distaste as he pulled the soggy, whimpering heap from the car. Sprawling on the wet mud, the figure heaved and sobbed some more. Looking at the pathetic, snivelling mess drip into the mud, it was all he could do to refrain from aiming a kick to the old man's head. There had always been an incipient bully in Lawrence which he tried his darndest to keep in check. He mostly succeeded. So far.

He swore at Clive, who seemed oblivious to his presence. Indeed, he seemed delirious. Shaking and shivering. Lawrence wondered if he'd lost his marbles. Leaving Clive cowering on the ground for a minute, he went into the caravan. It was too small for his big frame. If he turned abruptly, the whole thing listed, creaked. Thank goodness there was still a bit of light from the moon. He found a lighter in amongst the mess on the floor and lit the kerosene lamp, set it to blazing. Almost an antique, the darn thing worked like magic.

He shoved all the small mess out of sight; the big mess, wet towels, etc., straight out on the muddy grass outside. He fetched a plastic broom and swept as much of the puddle and mud out. He found a couple of dry blankets, a couple of kitchen towels. 'That'll do,' he muttered, laying them ready on a chair.

He strode out, nearly stumbling down the step of the creaking, listing caravan, cursed at himself to be more careful. He needed a twisted ankle like a hole in the head.

Clive lay on the ground, flailing around and weeping. Lawrence felt a red mist descend in front of his eyes. He closed them and breathed till he could see no more red. With one fist he grabbed Clive's collar and hefted him up on his feet. For a moment it looked as though his knees wouldn't hold him upright, they wobbled and gave way. Propping him up against the open car door, Lawrence began stripping his clothes off him. He noticed with distaste that the man still wore the Prada shoes, now squelching wet. He pulled off the shoes. Felt something heavy in both pockets. He turned the wet pockets inside out with difficulty, and little heaps of sand and pebbles fell out. Had he gone beach-combing in this weather, or was it a sign of him suddenly gone bonkers?

He pulled Clive's coat off, and before throwing it to the ground, checked his pockets, found more stones and sand in them. What the hell? And half a brick. Why on earth did he pick up that? Who collected broken masonry? A half-wit, that's who.

Lawrence, overcoming his revulsion at the sight of the old man's body, stripped Clive to his undies. He flinched to touch him, but nevertheless had to. He pulled Clive into the now warm caravan. He shut the door, ensconced Clive into blankets on the rickety chair and pushed it near the fire.

'What the hell you playing at, old man?' he asked, hating the way the old accent crept up on him, and that tone of uncouth rudeness he'd picked up from the men and women in his family. Proud ruffian clan that they were.

Clive muttered something. The colour seemed to be coming back to his cheeks. The trembling in his limbs had subsided.

Lawrence waited, watching, thinking. Clive had stopped muttering, now sat staring at the kerosene fire. What was going on with him? Why had he been walking around in the rain? Granted it had rained. But did that make a person THAT sodden?

'What's going on with you?'

Clive raised weary eyes to Lawrence. None of the old fear in them. It was as though the spark had gone out in his eyes.

'What are you doing here? Did you kill that old bird?'

'Yes. No. I didn't mean to.'

'Did you confuse her to death?'

'No. I don't know. I was angry.'

'If anger could kill, we'd all be dead long ago.'

'How did you find me?' Clive asked.

'I looked around in your house. Saw a photo of this caravan. A letter about flooding, not in Leicester, kinda Scandinavian sounding, I thought. Some Welsh name it turned out to be. Just to be sure, I asked your wife.'

'She spoke?' Clive looked flabbergasted.

'Her eyes told me the answer,' said Lawrence. 'There is real communication beyond language, hey? Her eyes. They spoke. Fear in them. Truth in them.'

'How is Sylvia?'

'The same. That Patel bird's looking after her. And the carers. They still coming.'

'Thank God,' said Clive. Looked relieved. 'Thank you,' he said, the pathetic buffoon.

'What were you doing, so sodden, like a drowned rat? Pockets full of sand and stones, digging in the ...'

Lawrence stopped speaking. He stared at Clive's face. He had a peculiar look, relief and guilt both on it. He seemed almost glad that Lawrence had come. His nemesis. Guy who roughed up this pensioner so bad. Made his life hell. Kidnapped his wife. Why was he relieved that Lawrence was here? Sand and stones in pockets. Where had he heard that before? Then he understood.

'Ah, you git.'

Clive didn't speak. His eyelids moved, twitched, still gazing at the fire. Drowning in the sea. That was the plan. He had been off to top himself. The bloody silly git.

'So you saw Sylvia,' said Clive, in a barely audible whisper. 'Being looked after.' He nodded to himself, as if satisfied.

Lawrence was left to feel like a heel for nearly kicking Clive's head in when he'd been sobbing and trembling in the mud.

'What's going on with you, man?'

Clive glanced up, just fleetingly.

'So what are you here for? Counselling? You my counsellor? The council send you?' He laughed feebly at his own joke.

Deathbed humour, thought Lawrence. *His own deathbed. The idiot.*

And to think, Lawrence had a hand in forcing him to his

death. Pushing aside that thought, he said, 'Why have you got a cop involved, man? You an idiot?'

'I didn't,' Clive said, clearly lying. 'He ... he just involved himself, being the allotment secretary's son.'

'What d'you want to hang with a copper for, man? Now look at you. On the run. Murder, theft, even suicide used to be a criminal offence not long ago, you know that? How could you do this to your wife, man?'

'I didn't know what to do ...'

This was not where Lawrence wanted to be in life, hounding some pathetic fool. He wanted to be home in bed, next to his wife, looking forward to an early start, up with the lark, to opening the shutters of his café, letting the coffee smells waft over onto the pavement to lure the punters in. *Good morning. What can I get you?* The sight of him associated with croissant buns and a half cappuccino, a whiff of the pastries and a sniff of the beverage siphoning life into a sleep-numbed person heading to a dull office day. To create for them their only bright spark in the whole sodding day. That was what he dreamed of doing.

He looked at Clive, sobbing afresh. And then it struck him. Here was a man at the absolute plunge-end of despair. A man at the home-stretch of his life's race, stuck fast in mire. Of his making, no doubt, unable to get out. Here was Lawrence, and he wore metal-edged boots with which he could kick him down and under the mire so he could emerge no more, or he could pull him out, and stick him back on the road.

Lawrence took a deep breath. He didn't see why he should do the bugger a favour. Then he thought of the pathetic bits of brick and stone and sand in Clive's pockets.

'What were you doing, filling up your pockets with stones?'

'I ...' Clive faltered. Shame in his eyes. 'I just wanted it to end.'

'Your wife is still waiting for you to go back, you twerp.'

Clive nodded. 'That's what pulled me back.'

'Did you go far in? You were soaking.'

'Maybe half a mile? Low tide. Flat as a pancake. Or I wouldn't be here.'

'Not so easy, topping yourself, is it?'

Clive nodded, agreeing. 'Didn't have the stomach for any-thing dramatic.'

'So why were you sitting in the car then?'

'Didn't have the strength to light the fire in here.'

'Ah, so started the car to warm up?'

'Yes.' He made a feeble attempt at a chuckle. 'Ran out of petrol.'

'Lady luck not on your side, eh?'

Clive nodded, dejectedly.

In a way, he supposed he saved Clive's life. Could've just died sitting in the car out there.

'On the other hand, lucky I came along to light the fire for you.'

Clive nodded, expression unchanged.

'Well,' said Lawrence, sensing the time had come now to broach the business of his being here.

He could not muster the words of threat. He could not muster the menace from within. He felt soft and still. He'd saved this man's life. But he'd also been the one to push Clive to the end of his tether.

He could have caused this man to die, which would have been tantamount to murder. Hounding a man to death would be a valid reason for prosecution. If the evidence could be found, they could have a legal case against him.

He'd done a lot in his life, but Lawrence had never killed a man. He'd put two in hospital, one in a neck brace, one with internal bleeding. Both came out fine, no grudge held, no hard feelings, paid the money with interest. But this was more. On the verge of turning his back on the career, he'd hit pinnacle, or rock bottom. He did not have the stomach or heart for it any more.

Lawrence sighed. A big, long, noisy sigh, and all kinds of pent-up tension released from him.

'Listen, man. This is what you will do. Gather yourself, get dressed, go back to your missus. No one will bother you any more. You won't see me again, except now and then on Queens Road, or in my new café on Allandale Road.'

Clive started, as if he thought he'd been dreaming and was trying to wake.

Lawrence leaned forward, spelled it out clearly. 'Go back to your life, pal.'

Chapter Twenty-Three

Leaving the lottie gates open for Neha, Padmini walked to Steve's pond. A flash of rain had drenched everything but now the sun shone. She wondered if there was something between Vijay and Neha.

She paused, by Mason's plot, cast a critical eye over his geraniums and delphiniums, all abuzz with bees. She wished she'd rung Mason. She couldn't bring herself to. There was a slight flirtation in their interactions, making her much too self-conscious about ringing him out of the blue. And what would Mason think of her if they failed to find anything? She could be wrong about her hunch, after all, and wrong about starting to read Sylvia's expressions.

She waited by the pond for Neha, who arrived, a bundle of nerves. She seemed lost without Vijay by her side.

'Why didn't Vijay pick up his phone?' she asked Neha.

'I think there wasn't any signal in the middle of the airport,' said Neha. 'They just whisked him away.'

How important Vijay had become, Padmini thought, that they barely let his plane land before collaring him for reasons classified. Still, it wouldn't have hurt to take her call, she thought, not buying the 'no signal' spiel. But that is what you got from your children. They ignored you till they really needed you.

Together, they ascertained the pond's depth. Padmini used a

bamboo pole normally kept for runner beans. The pond's depth was about a metre and a half to where she could reach, about a third of the way in.

'You're young and fit,' Padmini told Neha. 'You go in. I'll stay on the shore and hold out this sturdy branch. You can grab on to it for your balance.'

Neha stared dubiously at the murky water. She walked around the pond with the bamboo pole testing the depth at various places. 'I can feel objects. Let's try lifting things out with a stick.'

They dredged with some watershoots from her badly pruned Golden Delicious. Pulled out weedy clumps. Something with a bright red-painted cone came up and plopped back down.

Padmini studied the pond. Thick mat of pondweed. Flies abuzz in the sun. Nature hostile. Unwelcoming. The sticks were too feeble. Someone had to go in. Neha refused. Even after Padmini offered the use of her shower after.

'Go on then, you are the investigative journalist. Wouldn't you do anything to get at the truth?'

'There are creatures in there.' She mock-shuddered.

'You grapple with gangsters, break the law. What's a bit of wading into a pond, eh?'

'No chance. Anything could be down there. A metal trap.'

'Well, this isn't exactly Sleepy Hollow. Just a garden pond.'

'It's huge. It's two metres deep just this end.'

'That's the lily end. It needs to be deep. The rest of the pond will be quite shallow.'

'I have nightmares about giant octopus tentacles grabbing my ankles in a pond just like this one. Recurring nightmare.'

'I don't believe you,' said Padmini. *The girl's making this up,* she thought.

But then, Padmini herself had no desire to plunge into the

dirty grey water. She had no problems with swimming pools or the ocean. She'd never been keen on river and pond swimming, where you often had weeds and reeds brushing against your legs. She was allowed to be reluctant; an older woman's prerogative. Neha needed to step up. She felt disappointed in the girl, even as she reminded herself Neha wasn't a girl, but a grown woman.

Then it struck her. The perfect solution. Her cousin in Oadby had gone fishing once. And he had bought all the gear, including chest-high waders. Used them just once. He absolutely hated fishing. All the stuff he left in the garage, untouched for nearly three years now. She rang him, and he said she was welcome to borrow them, keep them for herself if she wished. He seemed extremely uninterested in why she might want them. She rang off and told Neha the good news.

'See now, you don't have to fear the cold, grey water. You will be completely waterproof.'

'Nightmares aren't logical,' said Neha, with a stubborn tilt to her chin. 'Even if I were in a shark cage, still I wouldn't get into that pond. I'll have panic attacks. I might faint.'

Padmini sighed. 'Right. I'll go and get the waders. You stay right here by the pond. Keep an eye in case anyone else has the same idea.'

'Yes, aunty,' said Neha.

Padmini couldn't fathom what she'd done to deserve the 'aunty' appellation.

Again, as she left the allotment, this time locking the gates firmly behind her, she heard a rustle behind her. It could be that daytime fox, she thought. Someone in one of the houses backing onto the allotment fed the foxes regularly, and the creatures now turned up at high noon to beg for food. Bold as you like.

She looked around as she went home, just to make sure, and after getting her car keys, studied the street from her window for a good while, but didn't see any two men that fit Clive's description. Only a Muslim man went past her house twice.

When she returned with the waders, she found Neha fast asleep, curled up on the grass right by the pond. *Hardly keeping an eye, is it?* she thought. But she supposed the girl was travel-fatigued. She'd give her the benefit of the doubt.

After the comedy of getting into the waders, she woke Neha.

She gave her a sturdy stick. 'Hold this for me,' she said. 'I'll take it after I get into the pond.'

'OK,' Neha said, yawning and rubbing the sleep from her eyes. 'I must have fallen asleep,' she said.

No shit, she thought. For such a bright thing, she seemed rather daft at times.

Padmini carefully sat on the edge of the pond, lowered her legs into the water. After a few seconds she could feel the cold seeping through to her legs. Feeling unsteady under her boots, she gripped the stick held out by Neha. She was somewhere around one third of the way into the pond; the water was up to her chest already. She wondered if Steve had got a digger to build it. Before her time, of course.

The pond teemed with life. Newts, tadpoles, all manner of snails, even little stickleback fish.

Padmini waded here and there, swishing the stick under-water, sorry to be disturbing the creatures. All for a good cause, she told them. Nettles six foot tall had bowed down over the pond edge and stung her waving arms. Contrary to her expectation, the bottom of the pond wasn't smooth. It was like standing on a mound of moving objects, all invisible. She needed goggles to look underneath, but too late now. In any case the pond water was churned up and muddy. She had Neha bring her a fork from her own shed. She dug into objects on the pond floor and brought them up randomly, hoping she didn't pierce the pond liner in the process.

Slippery, heavy things were garden gnomes. Often she felt one of them slide and had to put her bare arm, right up to her shoulder, underneath to grab one as it slid off the prongs of the fork.

Neha patiently waited, transfixed by Padmini's shambolic hunt for the leather bag. Padmini perceived Neha's amusement, and her attempt not to laugh at Padmini's ungainly staggering around in waders.

'Heck,' she said, as a garden gnome slipped from her hand and plopped back into the pond, splashing her cheek.

'Bugger,' she cried as she bent too far to grapple with a rusted old watering can caught on the prongs of the fork and the murky cold water slipped over the top of the waders, drenching her chest.

Neha looked at the sky, looked away, hard pressed, in Padmini's eyes, not to giggle.

And then finally, the fork prodded something, not soft as mud, and not hard as ceramic or metal, but something in between. Leather.

Lawrence left Clive in the early hours. He pulled over into a service station for a kip. Momentous decision-making had knocked the stuffing out of him. But he had business to conclude before he could rest. He called Mr T.

'Yo, man,' he drawled. It was best to affect a casual air when giving important news. 'Mixed results. Clive won't be a problem any more, you don't have to worry about him, but there ain't no bag.'

He listened to Mr T, said, 'Oh yeah? Well, glad someone

else was on the case, eh? Yeah, I know, sayonara to my twenty thousand. Yeah. I still quit, man. Getting too old for thrills and spills, ya know?'

Mr T said something like, 'What can I say? It's your life, brother.'

That was good enough for Lawrence.

He slept solidly for hours, stretched out with legs folded on the back seat. When he woke stiff and cramped, he realised he could still make it in time to pick the little critter up.

He got home with time for a bath before picking her up, all the better for cuddles. He longed to wash off the smells of sea salt, mud and an old man's tears.

Just as the bath got nice and hot and he was about to step in, the doorbell went. He ignored it. Parcel for next door, usually. The doorbell rang for a long time, but Lawrence resisted. He wanted to cling on to his secret, his release, for a bit longer before he had to face other people. Finally whoever it was gave up, and left him in peace.

Padmini unlocked the front door of her house, told Neha to fetch a black bin bag from the laundry room. Neha held the bag open and Padmini carefully placed the dripping wet bag inside it. Gagging from the pond stink and freezing cold, she peeled off the waders and boots outside her front door, took herself straight to the shower. Five minutes under the hot shower revived her. Quickly she dried and dressed, knowing Neha was impatiently twiddling her thumbs.

She rang Codman. He'd given her his personal mobile number in case Clive contacted her. He answered on the first ring.

'Yeah?'

'We found it. The bag.'

'What bag? Who's this?'

Padmini explained. Codman remained uninterested, and unimpressed.

'Have you checked what's inside?'

'No,' Padmini said. 'I didn't think I should. You think I should have?'

'Yeah, in case there was a bomb or something.'

Padmini had the distinct feeling he was being sarcastic.

'Right,' he said. 'I'll send a constable over. You can hand it over to her.'

'What time?'

'What time? Soon as I can. Sometime today.'

Padmini hung up, feeling like someone had punched her in the stomach. All that effort, for this response. Two dangerous men threatening life and limb in search of this bag, and the investigating officer, if he was still that, so unimpressed at its discovery.

She looked at the bag. *Sod it*, she decided. She'll take a peep while waiting for this constable Codman was sending her way.

They covered the breakfast table with old newspapers, and carefully upended the bin bag. The valise thumped out. Dark pond water and gunk oozed all over the newspapers and dripped down the table leg. With a pair of Marigolds on, Padmini opened the flap and brought out a bundle tightly wrapped in a shopping bag and secured with rubber bands.

The money was soaking wet. Days in the pond meant the water had seeped in through leather and plastic. They sat at the dining table, the two of them, and began counting the money. The notes were too wet to be separated, but luckily, they were in bundles of twenties and fifties with a cashier's band printed in waterproof ink. Bundles of ten thousand. Twenty in all. Two hundred thousand pounds.

'The value of a life,' she told Neha, who nodded glumly.

Padmini spied tears in Neha's eyes. Perhaps this was a bit of an anti-climax for her. The presence of money suggested the whole affair to be cheap and shoddy, rather than something complicated and exciting. Not involving high morals or passions. Nothing poetic about a sordid death over bundles of cash. Or perhaps Neha felt let down because this wasn't front-page stuff; barely worth a byline.

'Why was he carrying this cash?' said Neha.

'Who knows? Perhaps to buy a sports car. People do that in Leicester. Pink Lamborghinis. Modified. Spray painted. What do they call it? Customised. I've even seen a gold Bentley.'

'He wasn't interested in cars. Anyway, how would he get it to India?'

Padmini said, 'I'll leave you and Vijay to figure it out. Where is he, anyway?'

Neha just shrugged. She gingerly picked up the edge of the front flap of the bag. It lay on the table, close to her. 'Smells disgusting,' she said.

'I'd better wash it.' Padmini stood up, fighting a bit of dizziness. The old low blood pressure. She'd have a lie-down in five minutes.

'How do we dry the money?'

Padmini thought for a moment. 'Best to leave them in bundles. Spread them out in the airing cupboard. That one, there's a slatted shelf above the boiler. There.' She directed Neha, while holding the bag under the kitchen tap, rinsing it out. First, she'd rinse, then use Ecover washing-up liquid. Shouldn't damage the leather.

'What's this?' she exclaimed. She'd unzipped the front section to rinse it thoroughly and found a sodden piece of card in there.

Padmini turned off the tap, carefully extracted the card and lay it on the counter. A business card. The letters almost faded. She couldn't read the ones that were still visible without her glasses. Her glasses were upstairs, by her bed. The card was falling to pieces. Carefully she turned it, some letters and numbers handwritten, also half-faded. As she lay it back down, it tore further, the corner she held dissolving into mulch.

'Oh dear,' she said. 'Best lay it here till it dries.'

Neha nodded to Padmini as she finished laying out the notes.

Padmini lay the card on the counter. 'I'll get my glasses,' she said, but before she could reach the stairs, she heard a tinkle of breaking glass.

Padmini and Neha froze, looking at each other.

'Does Patel usually come that way?' said Neha.

'No,' said Padmini.

'It's from the back.'

'What shall we do?'

'I'll check. You put the bag away.'

Padmini nodded, suddenly frightened.

Neha tiptoed out of the kitchen. Padmini quickly shut the airing-cupboard door and looked about. A plastic bag with overgrown courgettes the size of marrows lay on the counter. Vijay hated courgettes. She grabbed the bag, twirled the handle around tight and popped a couple of rubber bands around it. Just as she was about to stuff it into the bag, a hideous hooded figure, face hidden by something black appeared.

The man, for it was definitely a man, said, 'Pop it right in, luvvy, and hand it over.'

Padmini meekly stuffed the courgette bag into the leather bag. 'Where's Neha?' she said.

As she held it out, she thought perhaps she should put up a token protest, or he'd be suspicious, so she withdrew her arm, as if reluctant, and the man stepped forward to grab it.

At the same time, Neha launched herself on him with a piercing shriek.

Like something out of nature, a fury, Neha attacked him with claws and teeth and nails, shouting, 'Tell me, you bastard, what happened to Majid. Did you kill him?'

Padmini stood there frozen, still holding the bag. What should she do? Call the police, she thought. But she couldn't. Or there'd be trouble about tampering with evidence, no? Vijay would be in trouble. They'd put it in the *Leicester Mercury*.

Neha, astride the man who was shouting incoherently through his twisted balaclava – the word came to her, yes, that's what it was called, not baklava the sweet – saying, 'Get off, you bitch,' or words to that effect.

Still scratching and gouging the man, Neha screamed at Padmini, 'Run, aunty, get away. Go find Vijay. Call the cops.'

Padmini was obliged now, to run. She couldn't very well admit to only holding courgettes. As she squeezed past the struggling duo, the man pushed himself up with a grunt, throwing Neha off him. Padmini began to run.

She felt an almighty thud in the small of her back and went flying into her own conservatory. In her haste, she'd run to the back of the house, rather than the front. Her feet flew from under her, and the bag went flying, and she landed on the floor. She heard, rather than felt, the sickening crunch in her arm. Her head caught the corner of the mangowood table and she saw spots.

Among the spots she saw Neha flying low over the floor, almost at knee level, launching, arms first like Superman, into the man's legs. He fell forward with a grunt and an oath; bang went his elbow on the ground.

Padmini felt his pain as he yelled out, and then swore at him as he kicked at Neha, winded from her attack. Like a slippery eel he struggled out of her grasp, grabbed the bag.

Good, thought Padmini. She shouted, 'Go now. Take the bag.'

But Neha wrenched around, struggling to stop him. Padmini couldn't tell Neha to let him go, that they were only courgettes in the bag. Then to her horror, she saw the man grasping Neha by the neck, squeezing.

Before she knew what she was doing, Padmini launched herself at the man, whose other hand had freed itself from Neha's grasp and was diving into a pocket. As she landed on him, she heard the flick of a blade.

It sounded like ... but her thought was interrupted by a searing pain.

Then suddenly, the man leapt up, dragged Neha into the house.

Before Padmini could protest, *Hey, where are you going with the girl? It's the bag you want* ... a wave of dizziness overcame her.

She startled awake when the man crashed through the glass. Out in the garden, he loped across the lawn and jumped over the compost bin and the fence, disappeared into the access road beyond.

Padmini tried to get up to see where Neha was. A cup of tea to get over the shock, isn't that what they gave her after each of her children's births? But why was it shocking, the birth of your own child? She frowned, trying to make sense of this puzzle, but gave it up and went to sleep.

Chapter Twenty-Four

Clive spent half an hour on his knees in front of Sylvia, begging her forgiveness. She was silent, eyes wide and transfixed as though in wonder at her husband's behaviour. Then Clive showered long in scalding water. When he got out, cleansed and feeling a lot better already, the carer had left, after settling Sylvia in front of the telly.

Clive felt slightly embarrassed about the impression the carer was leaving with. He'd just let himself in through the door, stinking to high heaven, shabby and skin still salt-encrusted, his knees giving way with relief at the sight of Sylvia alive and well and being looked after. He'd just gone straight to Sylvia, still in the stairchair at the bottom of the stairway, and just crumpled in front of her, clutching her knees. The carer hadn't said a word or interrupted in any way. He was thankful for that. The woman probably overstayed her allotted time in order to let him finish crying.

Now, brighter inside and out, he told Sylvia, whose eyes were fixed on an afternoon World War II film, 'I better go and thank Mrs Patel. And then, I suppose I've to face the music, eh?'

He waited, eyes on her face, for a response from her, something reassuring, but she didn't move her mouth or take her eyes off the television set. He felt the stone inside his chest swelling and hardening once more. Silently, he left the house and walked the long way around to Mrs Patel's house. The buzzer went three or four times before he realised the distant banging he was hearing wasn't building work in a neighbour's house, but coming from inside Mrs Patel's house.

The front door was locked. He couldn't open it. Somehow he managed to heft himself up on a broken chair abandoned on the pavement and unlock the side gate. He rushed into the passageway and to the back where he immediately saw the broken glass strewn over the patio.

The conservatory door was unlocked. He opened it, and heard the loud banging coming from the living room. He went through, calling out, 'Hello, where are you?'

He heard Neha's voice. 'In the front room, quick, let me out of here.'

Clive got the gist of what happened from her as he struggled to get the door open. But he had no idea where the key was. He was an old man, and the door was solid.

'Find Mrs Patel,' shouted Neha.

'Where is she?'

'In the conservatory.'

'I didn't see her. Hang on, let me check again.'

Clive shuffled back to the conservatory and his breath strangled in his throat at the sight that he'd completely missed in his hurry to get inside the house.

Right by the conservatory door, half hidden by an armchair, lay Padmini. She looked unconscious. As he knelt to feel a pulse, his trousers soaked up like a sponge, her sticky, still warm blood.

Lawrence had a hot bath, soaped and scrubbed the filth and tiredness out of his skin and hair. Towelled dry, he felt like a new man, in every sense. He dropped his phone off at the repair shop on the way to preschool. He would bring Muffin home and construct a mega marble run with her. Play till dinnertime. He'd make her fish fingers and chips for tea. She'd love that. He'd say kindly, 'Easy on the ketchup, hun.'

Traffic snarl crossing London Road. Tomorrow, Lawrence thought, he'd go to the bank. Ask for a loan application. He had five grand in savings. He'd write a business plan. Perhaps find someone to do it cheaply on Fiverr.com. Lawrence, full of plans, ran his fingers through his beard, reached the preschool and got out of the car.

The preschool gates were still closed. Lawrence waited with a small clutch of parents in the outside porch area. Instinctively the parents who arrived avoided the side where Lawrence stood, leaning against a pillar, occupying not just the space he was physically occupying but via his aura, an extra metre around him. The newcomers jostled subtly for space on the other side of the porch.

'Hey, man,' chirped up a voice that made Lawrence's hackles rise. Ringo. He sauntered up and leaned against the wall right beside Lawrence, as if he were an old pal or a nephew.

'Hey, Ringo.'

'Wassup, man, what happened to your phone?'

'It broke. Long story. What are you doing here?'

'I was sent to find you, man. Mr T couldn't reach you. I even rang Maggie, but I guess she doesn't carry her phone in the operating theatre.'

Maggie? Lawrence began to get hot under the collar about Ringo phoning Magdalena, before he realised she'd probably given him her number after leaving Muffin with him the other morning. In case Lawrence didn't wake up in time or something.

'Yeah,' he said, simmering down. 'She won't pick up when she's on shift.'

'That's what I thought,' said Ringo.

Lawrence looked at the preschool door. Still closed.

Ringo leaned further, making himself more comfortable on the wall, said in a low voice, 'Any luck?'

'No. No sign of the old man.'

'Tough. Mr T won't be happy to hear that.'

'I quit,' Lawrence said.

'What do you mean, quit?'

'I mean I quit. The business. Turning over a new leaf. All that jazz.'

'Seriously? What are you going to do then, become a yoga instructor?'

Lawrence forced a laugh. 'Well, why not? That's not so bad. No, I'm opening my own café.' He felt a hint of pride as he said the words out loud for the first time ever.

'Jeewizz, yo,' Ringo said. Lawrence winced at his expression, like something out of a crappy American sitcom. Then Ringo began laughing.

Some of the parents glanced over at them. Lawrence waited patiently for Ringo to get over his chuckles.

'Have you got a pussy down there as well, man?' Ringo said.

Lawrence grabbed Ringo's collar and squeezed till the little shit began choking. 'Laugh at me, then,' Lawrence said. 'One more time, go on.'

Ringo put his hands up and squeaked like a mouse. Lawrence relaxed his grip a tad.

'Yo,' Ringo spluttered. 'Just kidding, man. Just messing with you. Didn't mean no disrespect, man.'

Lawrence noticed a nice Asian dad watching, his mouth open. One or two other parents were pointedly looking away. Lawrence let go of Ringo's collar, smiled, dusted him off with a few thumps, put an arm around his shoulders. 'Best not to make a nuisance of ourselves at the preschool, eh? Don't want to scare the little kiddies, now, do we?'

'Good luck with your café, bruv,' Ringo said.

'Thank you,' Lawrence said.

He waited for Ringo to leave. Instead, Ringo said, 'They're running a bit late, aren't they?'

'Hey?'

'It says pick-up time three-fifteen. It's gone twenty past, innit?'

'Yeah,' Lawrence said, wearily. 'They run late most days.'

Still Ringo waited. Lawrence wondered if Ringo was genuinely fond of kids. Perhaps he found them compatible with his IQ, Lawrence thought.

Ringo watched the door with a bovine look on his face, and Lawrence didn't want to tell him to scram in front of the Asian dad, who hovered close by like a fascinated fly.

The doors opened, and Munchkin was the first one out.

'Daddy,' she shouted, then her eyes fastened on Ringo. 'Hey,' she cried, and ran to him, and began bouncing up and down, telling him all about the reptiles that'd been brought to be shown to the kids that morning. Then she demanded, 'Uncle Abdul, are you coming to pick me up every day?'

Lawrence frowned, wondering if he'd heard right. Ringo, holding Chloe's little hands, smiling, with his eyes darting to Lawrence, said, 'That was just a joke, sweetheart. It's Ringo, remember?'

Chloe sighed dramatically. 'OK then,' she said, with a great show of tolerance for an adult's unpredictable ways, 'Uncle Ringo, will you come to pick me up every day?'

One of the staff, Mrs Bingham, smiled at this exchange. To Lawrence's annoyance, Ringo told his daughter: 'If you want me to, sweetheart.'

Chapter Twenty-Five

Patel sat in the over-bright waiting room with his head in his hands. How could the whole world come crashing down in an instant? Beyond the double set of glass doors at the end of the room lay his mother, surrounded by faint beeps of the machines punctuating her fight for life.

He felt the movement of someone gently seating themselves beside him, looked up to see Neha, her head bearing a huge bandage, her arm in a sling.

'OK?' he managed to ask.

She nodded, winced. 'It will all mend,' she said, wearily. Tears stood in her eyes, threatening to fall. She looked so pale and exhausted, he wanted to put his arms around her, for his own comfort as well as hers.

'I hate hospitals,' she said.

'You ought to go to my house, get some sleep,' he said. She shook her head no.

'The police want to interview me again. They are coming here. I imagine they'll want to talk to you as well,' she said. He nodded.

It was midnight by the time Patel and Neha got home. Patel's sister had arrived from Nottingham, after finding childcare, and she'd ordered him to go home to rest, and take Neha with him.

He had no intention of protesting against her decree, just as he didn't while growing up.

He was touched to find Clive fast asleep in an armchair. He made a cup of tea and gently woke him. 'She out of the woods yet?' Clive asked, hopefully.

Patel shook his head. Clive nodded sadly and took his cup.

'You've left Sylvia on her own?' Patel asked.

'No, I finally plucked up the courage to call one of her friends, and she agreed to stay the night. I had to be here, to ...' Clive's voice trailed off.

Patel nodded, understanding. Clive had found his mother in the nick of time. Even ten minutes later, she might have been dead. The intruder had dragged Neha into the downstairs study and locked her in, before disappearing. Patel assumed he'd run away in a panic, or he wouldn't have left Neha alive to provide clues about him to the police. Either that, or he was ruthlessly efficient, and knew Neha couldn't identify him in a million years.

Patel felt himself drawn to the conservatory. It caused him physical pain to see the police tapes, the grey fingerprinting dust over everything. He shut the inner door, remembered to breathe again.

That fucking bag again, causing so much misery. The police had taken Clive in for questioning, both over the attack on Padmini and the circumstances of Linda's death.

He found Neha in the kitchen, filling a glass with water. Deep circles under her eyes. She shivered.

'Let me turn the heating up,' he said, reached around her to open the boiler door. He was stunned to find hundreds of twenty-pound notes drying in the airing cupboard, instead of the usual dandelion roots or thyme his mother put in there.

'So there's that small triumph,' he said dully, once they'd

counted the money and found all two hundred thousand pounds intact. 'We got two hundred thousand pounds for my mother's life.'

'Don't say that,' said Neha. 'She is still fighting. Don't give up.'

Patel felt tears on his face. Now he did reach for her, and gently, taking care with her wounded arm, she gave him a hug.

'You know,' she said, pulling herself away, 'we did find a card in there too, but it's all mulched and soggy. We put it to dry by the sink.'

Patel said, 'I'll take a look. You get yourself off to bed now.'

Neha nodded, swallowed the pain medication the hospital had given her, refilled her glass and took it upstairs.

Patel stared at the scrap of card that had been underwater for days, now in tatters, dried out on his mother's kitchen counter. The ink, not being waterproof, had entirely faded away, leaving just a ghost of the letters that had been there. He held the magnifying glass and concentrated, the babble of voices – his tired mother's, sprightly Neha's and the recently returned weepy Clive's – swarming about him.

He turned the card over, and was astonished, because he hadn't expected to find anything. But something scribbled with a ballpoint pen had withstood the soaking. Part of a series of letters and numbers and symbols.

By morning, he still hadn't figured out what it could all mean.

When Neha appeared downstairs, he showed her. 'Perhaps it is code,' she said, excitedly. 'I can ... I mean, I'm interested in code-breaking, a bit ...'

'What could the code be for?' Patel said.

'A numbered Swiss bank account?'

'There are numbers and letters mixed up,' said Patel.

'Harder to crack,' said Neha.

The last few symbols, three or four, were mulched into the paper, beyond hope.

Neha copied out the letters on the card and passed it to Patel. They pored over it together.

'It's usually Mr or Miss or Ms or Dr, isn't it?' said Neha.

'Or—' said Patel.

'Could it be—?' said Neha.

'Yes,' shouted Patel.

He could've kicked himself. If he'd woken Neha in the night, he needn't have spent the hours agonising.

He looked at the letters he'd written down. If he changed the o to a and filled in the missing stems and curlicues, the name that emerged was a very familiar one indeed.

Chapter Twenty-Six

Forty-five minutes later, Patel pulled into the drive of a large country house. Neha was fast asleep beside him. She began to stir when he parked the car and turned the engine off.

Perhaps it was part of her journalistic qualities, he thought, this ability to kip when she could, so she could be alert in the late hours of the evening when things began to happen.

He faced a sprawling late-Victorian mansion. Rustic pots bearing a riot of flowers were clumped around the touched-up façade. Patel looked for a knocker or a doorbell and found, to his surprise, a sophisticated intercom and alarm system beside the front door, artfully tucked away behind a hanging basket. Neha took pictures of the security system. Patel pressed the call button. Immediately, Sir Roger's friendly voice boomed through. 'Patel, come on in. Door's open. I'll be down there in a minute.'

Patel and Neha pushed the heavy door open and entered the hallway. Through the connecting doorway they could see the vast living room, which was empty, the walls adorned with modern scribbles in tastefully simple frames. The hallway itself was as big as his London living room, functioning as a kind of waiting room, with a couple of French antique settees. The dark walls were covered in framed photos. You had to look carefully to perceive the great and the good on various significant occasions, some professionally shot, some informally. His erstwhile mentor, Sir Roger, was in all the photographs, ranging from his humble county days to now, when on any given day it seemed, from the photos, Sir Roger posed, laughed, talked, with personages as varied as the Queen, Alex Ferguson, Sachin Tendulkar, Alex Scott, Narendra Modi, Theresa May, the Dalai Lama and Isa Guha. Neha reeled off the names like a delighted teenager.

'Hidden away in the dark corner of the hallway,' she said. 'Very modest of him.'

'Except when you're buzzed in,' said Patel, 'you have plenty of time to enjoy the coverage while you wait for the big man.'

Neha smirked.

'We English know how to do subtlety,' he said.

'Humble-brag?' she said.

'That will be when he shrugs off the importance of these connections which he brings up casually in conversation.'

'Wow,' said Neha.

They waited five minutes before Sir Roger appeared. Neha had studied every single photo. Patel wondered why Sir Roger took so long to climb down the stairs. He'd called half an hour ago from the car, so it wasn't as though their visit was unexpected.

Sir Roger looked preoccupied even as he smiled and ushered them into the open-plan kitchen and living room. When Patel told Sir Roger they'd found his card in Majid's valise, Sir Roger expressed surprise, but immediately admitted he'd probably given it to Majid.

Patel showed him the leather bag, still damp from its residence in the pond and subsequent rinsing.

'Do you remember this bag? Did you see Majid or anyone else carrying it recently? Do you have any idea who could have given it to him?'

'Sadly, no,' said Sir Roger. He barely looked at the bag. Patel waited for him to ask what had been in it. But, to his surprise, Sir Roger said, 'May I see the card? My card that you found?'

Patel drew from his pocket the Ziplock bag in which he'd placed the fragments of the card. 'Got a little bit soggy,' he said.

Sir Roger frowned, took the card in its Ziplock bag, and carefully turned it this way and that. He paused ever so slightly on the characters part-obliterated on the back of the card. He seemed to be on the verge of asking about them, or making a comment, but changed his mind, and handed it back.

He said, 'Must have taken you a while to piece together that it was my card.' His eyes jumped from Patel's to Neha's, as though wondering who to give the credit to.

'Oh yes,' said Neha. 'We had to work it out like some kind of Da Vinci code.'

Sir Roger laughed, but it was forced. Patel noticed a slight tremble on his left hand. Either he was nervous or unwell.

'Sorry, I hand my card out left and right. No idea who the bag could belong to. But Majid knew so many people. It may be worthwhile to ask around in the dressing room. Perhaps you could go along tomorrow. I can phone the security to hand you an all-access pass.'

Sir Roger, Patel knew, meant the first one-day match at Lord's. 'Will you not be there yourself?'

'Ah, no. Sadly not. I have another, important engagement.' Again, Patel detected the slightest hint of nervous tension behind the relaxed, smiling demeanour. Sir Roger obligingly gave the names of cricketers, from England as well as India, who he'd seen talking to Majid. He also gave the names of auxiliary staff.

Patel excused himself to use the loo, with a look at Neha. He hoped she read the look, which conveyed the request to keep

Sir Roger occupied with conversation. Sir Roger directed him to the downstairs cloakroom. 'Past the hall, on the left, behind the staircase but before the garden room.'

Patel paused by the stairs. They could just see him. Neha walked over to a painting, asked Sir Roger something in a low voice, forcing him to turn his head towards her.

Slipping off his shoes, he noiselessly padded up. Four bedrooms, the family bathroom. Another flight of stairs. Second-floor office. More modern scribbles. No photos on the desk, which surprised him. He'd googled images of Sir Roger before leaving Leicester, and had found a photo of him at this very same desk with a clutch of frames on it.

Under the empty desk, drawers. They were full of papers, paperclips and other stationery. Nothing useful on the papers. Just day-to-day stuff. He went to the corner filing cabinet. Fourth cabinet locked. No keys. No keys in the desk drawers.

Patel patted his pockets. Ah ha. He had Neha's little set of skeleton keys, that he had asked to borrow earlier. He used all his powers of concentration to manipulate the little keys without fumbling. The third key fit. As silently as possible, he pulled the drawer open.

A slip of paper with bank details, codes, passwords, etc. Nothing that looked like the code on the back of his business card. He lifted up the paper. A brown envelope underneath. He opened it. A folded photograph on plain paper, from a home printer. The ink saturated the paper, obscuring the details.

Patel squinted, focused on the image. A blurry or tear-stained face of a woman, her mouth pursed or in the act of speaking. She wore a head covering. Patel looked closely at her features. Possibly a white woman. You couldn't see the colour of her hair, which was tucked under the hood.

He examined the edges. It looked like a screenshot from a

Skype meeting, quite pixelated and of poor quality. He put the photo back in the envelope, slipped it under the paper, locked the drawer. He left the study, padded down to the ground floor to flush the toilet.

When Patel rejoined Sir Roger and Neha, he'd only left the room for a few minutes. But there was a distinct unease in the air. Neha and Sir Roger had moved to the other end of the open-plan kitchen, and stood studying a scribble that either represented a banana or a water jug. Neha's fluster made Patel wonder what had happened.

'Sorry about that,' said Patel.

Sir Roger said to Patel, 'I was just asking Neha if she's decided on a career path yet. Journalism course, is it? Which universities are you applying to?'

Patel laughed, intending to correct Sir Roger's mistaken impression, when he saw the look on Neha's face.

'Tell him, Neha,' he said, and watched her face keenly as she told him she was already a professional journalist.

Sir Roger seemed at a loss to respond to this, and seemed embarrassed. Neha looked even more flustered.

Patel wondered again what had gone on in his absence. Why didn't Neha say anything if Sir Roger had behaved inappropri-ately? She was the type of girl to kick him in the balls first and complain later. Sir Roger only seemed preoccupied, struggling to make small talk, and not unduly interested in Neha. He looked at his watch now, trying to keep his hands still.

'Sorry,' he said, 'just expecting guests.'

'Family?' Patel asked.

'Yes ...' said Sir Roger, his face blanching. 'Family.'

They took their leave. It seemed Sir Roger tried not to look relieved.

*

'Well, that was fruitless,' declared Neha. The chirpiness in her voice had a brittle quality.

'Do you think so, really?' Patel said. He'd been about to mention the girl in the photo, but something made him hold back. 'Did anything about Sir Roger strike you as odd?'

'Not at all.'

'Sir Roger is usually prone to small talk.'

'I thought he was pretty chatty.'

'So what did he say to put the wind up you?'

'Wind up me?'

'You looked strange, when I came back into the room. He said something about university?'

Her laugh sounded forced. 'He thought I was applying to do a journalism degree.'

Before they set off back home, Patel made a call to Simon.

'Simon, could you get some of your intelligence chaps to find out something for me?'

'Sure, if I can spare a moment from my fight to save the world from jihadist terror, yes.'

'Some background, I mean the real dirt, on Sir Roger Wallace.'

'Seriously? A knight of the realm?'

'Also, the contents of his Skype conversations. Video feed.'

'We need all sorts of permission. Invoke the Terrorism Act ...'

'Invoke it.'

Patel and Neha barely spoke on the ride home. He studied her when he could safely take his eyes off the road. She seemed deep in thought. He wondered who this young woman was, sitting beside him. He also wondered about Sir Roger, who had so many irons in the fire. What had gone wrong with him and where? He worked at the puzzle, the jigsaw pieces constantly eluding his grasp.

Neha also seemed preoccupied.

'I just don't see it,' she said eventually, as they turned onto London Road. 'He's such a nice old man.'

'Not that old,' he said. 'Sir Roger's only fifty.'

She shrugged, as if it didn't make much of a difference to her.

Patel's eyes widened, as he grasped the first linking piece.

They were passing the petrol station in Oadby. Patel made a sudden decision and screeched into a filling bay. The driver behind them honked in anger.

'Sorry,' he said to Neha.

She shrugged. 'Nothing to Indian driving,' she said.

'Just remembered I need to get petrol,' he said.

Neha glanced at the petrol gauge, but if she saw where the gauge stood, she didn't say anything.

'Get me some chocolate,' she said. 'I'm starving.'

'Yes, oh queen,' he said, forcing a jocular smile.

Patel grew serious as he filled up with petrol. In the queue to pay, he stood to one side, letting everyone else go past in front of him as he googled the contact details for Neha Sinha. He found a number and dialled. His eyes widened when the voice-mail message played. Stumbling to find the right words, he left a message, asked to be called back as a matter of urgency. Then he sent another text to Simon. Neha Sinha, journalist?

Patel came out of the kiosk, a bar of Dairy Milk and a bar of Snickers in hand. He handed the Dairy Milk to Neha and said, 'Sorry, took a while to find my favourite,' waving the Snickers at her.

Patel parked his mother's Audi outside her house. Neha put her hand on the door handle. His phone rang.

'Wait,' Patel said.

'Hi, Neha,' he said on the phone. Listened for a while. Then said, eyes on Neha's face, 'Oh, I see. It must've been someone pretending to be you. I thought I'd check.'

He listened.

'Oh, I did consider that the death by drug overdose of a famous actor is your line of work. Yes, UK is a bit far, yes. You could just ring people up, that's what I thought. I'm glad I checked. Thank you.' He listened. 'I appreciate your compliments. To India? Oh, not any time soon. If I did, I'll be sure to look you up. If ever I'm in Delhi. To be sure. Thanks. Bye.'

Neha smiled, but under the nonchalance he could see the serious worry. 'Is this time for a joke? Who was that?'

Before he could answer, Patel's phone rang again. Simon.

'Hey, Simon.'

'What the hell kind of complication is this? Who is this woman?'

'I think I have a good idea.'

'Be careful,' said Simon. 'Keep her away from her phone. It could be a remote trigger. I've sent a team on its way to you.'

'Call them back. She's not— It isn't necessary.'

'Hey, don't go soft on her, man. She might kill you.'

'Just call them off. I'll ring you back. I'm not in any danger.'

'I'll have them on standby. If I don't hear from you in five minutes . . . '

'Make it ten.'

Patel put his phone back into his pocket and turned around. Neha looked puzzled at the cryptic one-sided conversation she'd heard.

'What on earth?' she began.

'Who are you?' Patel kept his voice dead level.

'Who am I?'

'Yes.'

'Neha Sinha, journalist.'

'You are not.'

She laughed. 'What the fuck, Patel? Google me if you like.'

'I have. And yes, there is a Neha Sinha. Well-known gossip columnist. But she is in Mumbai at the moment, completely unaware of your existence, and only interested in Salman's poodle and Kajol's weight-loss.'

'I'm insulted.'

'You've committed ID fraud, stealing a real person's identity to conduct illegal activities.'

Neha laughed, pretending disbelief.

'You've used a counterfeit or stolen passport, obtained a visa under false pretences.'

'The passport came with the visa. All inclusive.'

Patel took a deep breath. 'The worst of all your lies,' he said, 'is the fact that you're a teenager, a runaway from home.'

'I'm not a teenager!' Neha cried. 'How dare you?'

'I did figure you're like a sulky child sometimes. Now I know you are one! How old are you?'

'None of your business!'

Patel winced. 'Simon thinks you're a suicide bomber.'

'He's anti-terror police,' Neha said, hotly. 'He'll say that about everyone.'

'Tell me the truth. Now. If I don't call Simon in five minutes there'll be an armed assault force on our heads.'

He'd already pieced together the rough outline of the story, and she confirmed it. She'd run away from home to find out the truth about her father's death. Her mother thought she'd gone to stay with a friend. The home situation had never been great. Patel built a picture of a smart-alec, headstrong brat with too much freedom due to her parents' broken marriage.

'And what's with your laptop, and getting hold of police documents, and skeleton keys?'

She looked cagey. 'I'm good with coding, you know,' she said.

'You're a hacker,' he said, amazed. Now it all made sense. 'But how did you get hold of so much intel, and the ID?'

She told him she also had other whizz-kid friends who liked to create havoc with their computers. One of them had been in trouble with the authorities and had to get himself a new ID. He procured a fake passport for her in the name of Neha Sinha.

'Seriously? A fake passport in a real person's name?'

'To be honest, it's a real passport, made on the real machines. The Indian government doesn't pay good wages. The chaps who work there just print a few extra on the side, completely fake, but completely real, and report the booklets as damaged and destroyed. Not cheap.'

'So it's your photo with Neha's details.'

She nodded.

'But you didn't create a fake profile in case I looked you up?'

She nodded again.

'Is this a large-scale operation?' He wondered how many foreign terrorists were getting into India using this scheme.

'Very small. Just one or two a year. Which is why it's successful, and the chaps don't get caught. Indian passports aren't in great demand. Indians need a visa to go practically anywhere. Which is why a real visa stamp on a fake passport costs a bomb.'

'And where does a young person such as yourself get hold of so much money?'

'I just transfer the money from one account to another, then another, till all trace of it disappears. I pay from bank accounts that never get checked by people too rich to care. The kind of people who wouldn't miss a few thousand here or there.'

'What sort of people?'

'Some of them very well known. Some of the wealthiest people on earth.'

'Like Sitaram. That's why the interest in his security system in Mumbai?'

'I owe my friend a favour. I gave him the intel about Sitaram's security systems. No idea why he wanted it.'

'Wow.'

'Yeah. Well, don't tell anyone this. Or my friends will get into trouble.'

'You do realise I'm a police officer sworn to uphold the law?'

She shrugged. 'As you like to say, not your jurisdiction, is it?'

'Touché.' He grew serious. 'How old are you?'

She looked sheepish. 'Nineteen.'

He groaned. His mother had been arranging their marriage in her head, he was sure of it.

'Truth, please.'

'Honest,' she said. 'Birthday two months ago.'

He clutched his head, groaned again.

'I'd better call Simon. Then ...'

'Then?'

'You can tell me why you decided to find your father's killers yourself instead of going to the Indian police.'

Chapter Twenty-Seven

By ten in the morning Lawrence's day turned from the best day of his life to the worst. The very worst. He'd woken up and smiled. He let Muffin have Cheerios even though it was Wednesday, and Wednesday was usually Weetabix day. He took her to preschool, then popped to the bank to see the manager about a loan.

The manager, a neat diminutive chap who wasn't fazed by Lawrence's size, barely heard a word Lawrence said, pitching his idea, before he began listing all the requirements before they even considered his application. Lawrence's head spun. Business statement, bona fide surety, etc. Plus they'd check his credit and criminal record.

Lawrence tried not to get irked. He knew as much as the second guy that all bankers were criminals. Just that they had law-making politicians in their pockets so they didn't have to go to jail. He didn't see why a petty crime conviction should count against an otherwise honest punter from opening his own business. It wasn't fair.

Of course, none of it mattered if he had a lump of cash. He could open a business in his wife's name. Magdalena would like that.

He went to Francis Street to get himself a cup of coffee and work out notes for a business plan. Daydreaming of the day when he would open his own, taking notes on the competition while he was at the café, what they did right, and what he could do better.

He walked up to the phone shop, where they charged him an extortionate amount of money to have fixed his phone. He paid it glumly. Just when he had to tighten his belt, he was forced to shell out. Still, cheaper than a new phone. He turned the corner towards his house, checking his phone for missed calls, when he noticed the police cars surrounding it.

He stopped, turned his phone on. Voicemail messages, one of them from the preschool, then several from his Magdalena. Hiding behind a fence, out of view of the cop cars, he dialled voicemail, and the preschool manager came on.

'Lawrence, this is Greenfields Nursery calling. Your brother has come to collect Chloe saying that Chloe's mum and yourself have rushed to hospital where your mother is dying, and that it is her dying wish to see Chloe. I tried ringing you as well as Chloe's mum, but we cannot get hold of you. Perhaps there is no network in the hospital ward. You have not put down a third party authorised to collect Chloe on the form.' A pause, some shuffled papers.

'I'm sorry, but I cannot send Chloe with your brother. Please call us back when you get this message.'

Lawrence heaved a sigh of relief and quickly pressed buttons to hear Magdalena's messages.

His heart turned to ice as he heard her hysterical, frantic voice, sobbing, shouting, that Chloe was gone.

As he was about to dash towards his house, a hand fell on his shoulder. 'Hey, man, how's it going?'

Lawrence dropped his phone and grabbed Ringo's throat. 'Where's Chloe?' Lawrence spoke through clenched teeth.

Ringo put his hands up, choking and gasping, indicating he wanted to tell him.

Lawrence reluctantly loosened his grip. 'Speak,' he spat.

'Chloe's safe. Let's get into the car and talk about it, eh?'

Further out of sight from the cop cars, behind a closed-down shop, they squeezed into Ringo's car. Making a supreme effort to control himself, Lawrence asked Ringo, 'Where is she?'

'She's safe. Don't worry about her.'

'How did you ...?'

'Turned out to be as easy as nicking candy. Tried the pre-school first. They said safeguarding blah di blah. They couldn't get hold of you or Maggie. They don't know about your broken phone and about Maggie working in the operating theatre. I told them there's no phone signal at poor Mama's hospice bedside. They know me now, don't they, as Uncle Ringo?'

Lawrence couldn't believe the kind of lowlife Ringo turned out to be.

'Then you went to my house? My house?'

'She was in the front garden. It's collateral, innit?'

'What the fuck, Ringo?'

'It's not Ringo, is it? It's Abdul Karim.'

Lawrence only then noticed the skullcap on Ringo's head, and the fact that he was wearing a white sherwani.

'Is this a joke, man?'

Ringo grinned, nodded to himself several times. Then the anger Lawrence had noticed once before came roaring back. 'No one ever took me seriously. All them schoolyard bullies, my own fucking family. All them bitches and bastards. And you, so fucking condescending, weren't you, to poor Ringo? All he wanted to do was to be a pal, to help? You thought I was dumb, I was rubbish. Now you'll see, man, the whole fucking world will know me. Abdul Karim will show them.'

Ringo's hands trembled. His eyes looked deranged. Fear for Muffin's life gripped Lawrence. He fought to keep himself calm, despite the desperation to shake the life out of the twerp, to find out where he'd taken Muffin. With a great effort he calmed himself.

He spoke, all pally-voiced. 'Hey, Ringo, sorry, Abdul. Chill, man. Let's have a talk. Tell me about what's going on.'

Ringo laughed. 'Yes, we will talk, you big fuck. I'll tell you exactly what you need to do to get your daughter back alive.'

Lawrence felt the smallest relief. 'Tell me. I'll do anything.'

'That's what I thought. Got a paper and pen?'

Late afternoon, back at the waiting room, Patel sat staring at an old Sherlock Holmes novel, but his mind was not really on it. His mother had taken a turn for the worse, they'd informed him five minutes after his sister had to rush off to retrieve her child from the babysitter. The kid had vomited her lunch, and the babysitter had to hand her back for health and safety reasons. Her husband was away in Sweden and was cutting short his trip to rush back. But he wouldn't be home till early next morning.

Patel had left the bag and its contents back at home. He didn't care if anyone wanted to come back to steal it. Not with a potential murder charge hanging over his head, Patel thought. The same instincts told him Clive would be alright to go back to Sylvia and resume his life with her, that they needn't fear from those ruffians again, and that Neha would stay put in the spare room and wouldn't skedaddle. The girl was a liar, but had integrity.

His phone buzzed. Patel leapt out of the armchair and grabbed it off the side table. 'Simon.'

'I'm sending you all that we've dug up on Sir Roger. I haven't been able to look at any of it. Just passing it on from our, erm, research department. Check your email.'

'Thanks, man. How's it going otherwise?'

'Deep shit, my friend. I'm in deep shit.' Simon sounded tired. 'Wave my career goodbye. I'll be fired in the morning.'

'Can you tell me about it?'

'I'm on an encrypted phone, but I won't give specifics. We just learned that five PE10s went missing from the MOD warehouse in Karachi.'

'What's a PE10?'

'Heard of C4?'

'Yeah?'

'This is a variation. British-made. There are several variations. C4 needs shockwaves to trigger. PE10 needs a different trigger. A particular vibration from a nano device planted in it.'

'And what would cause this nano device to vibrate?'

'A phone call.'

'Shit.'

'That's not all. PE10 can be remodelled to fit small structures quite easily, and the trigger range is a hundred metres.'

'Great if you aren't at the receiving end?'

'This is our much-lauded new action-against-terror strategy after the failure of years of drone attacks against the Taliban. Put these newfangled devices in innocuous everyday items and send them off to targets. They can be triggered by a phone call. Everyone's on the phone all the time, right? No one would suspect a thing.'

'Except, of course, the downside. When the darn explosives get stolen.'

'And they've made their way back to the UK.'

'Jesus Christ.'

'That's what we've been frantically tracking for the last few days. Good news is, the devices have trackers, and we've managed to retrieve four of the five devices, all headed to various parts of the UK, but the bastards managed to disable the tracker on the fifth device.'

'When was this?'

'We lost connection several hours ago, in the vicinity of Portsmouth, to which port all the devices arrived. But now, the PE10 will have been remodelled and infused into any innocuous item, anywhere in the UK, with no one the wiser. And when the shit hits the fan, I'll be carrying the can.'

'I wish I could help, mate.'

'I know you do. But the situation looks hopeless.'

'Don't lose hope yet. Keep looking.'

'And you too, man, don't lose hope.'

Patel put his pangs for his mother aside and opened the email attachments Simon had sent. He studied the reports – the dirt, as Simon would call it – on Sir Roger. Some controversial selections for the England teams over the years, then more recently, various financial irregularities, the feud with his stepson resulting in him suing over his mother's estate. Sir Roger's estranged wife had died suddenly of heart failure last year.

Police reports of his daughter Cynthia running away from boarding school, not once or twice, but five times. Juvenile record. Mostly drug use, the high-end type. Methamphetamine and cocaine. Fracas in London nightclubs. Almost weekly reports about the daughter's self-destructive activities from the time the mum died right up to six months ago. Then nothing. Apart from her being withdrawn from school two months before her sixteenth birthday.

Patel rifled through all the reports again. Some details from the court proceedings from the stepson's case, financial statements showing large sums being transferred from Sir Roger's into unnamed untraceable numbered accounts in various denominations, dozens of them, but nothing at all about the daughter. There was a mention of one police complaint, from a friend, that Cynthia was missing, but it had been withdrawn the very next day.

'Ah,' said Patel, as slowly the picture became clearer to him. 'Fuck,' he said.

He got up from the chair, felt himself shiver from the need to leap into action and the impossibility of leaving his mother when her life hung in the balance. He couldn't leave. He could only get others to move for him. They had no time to lose.

He rang Simon. 'Listen, pal. Tomorrow's cricket match at Lord's. I have a bad feeling about England's prospects.'

Chapter Twenty-Eight

Lawrence parked his car in the prepaid private underground car park, half a mile's walk from Lord's Cricket Ground. He got out of his car and walked along the row of parked cars till he came to a grey unmarked security van. He checked the number plate. BB3 456. This was the one. He used a key to unlock the rear doors and stepped into the back, crouching slightly. Inside, he shut the outer doors and turned on a flashlight. He faced a wall of different-sized lockers, some big, some small.

He located a locker, three down, four across from the left. One of the smaller ones. It had a panel with numbers, letters and symbols on it, just like a computer keyboard. He took out a piece of paper and studied the long series of characters on it. Some numbers, some letters, some characters.

Carefully, for he only had two chances to get it right, he keyed them in. Despite his care, his trembling finger, too big for the little keys on the pad, fudged one, pressing it twice. He cursed, pressed the clear button, and took a deep breath. He took out a ballpoint pen from his pocket, and using the tip of the cap, carefully entered the sequence again. An almighty pause at the end. Then a beep indicated that the code had been accepted. Sigh of relief.

He turned the knob and opened the locker. Inside, there was a mobile phone, looking like an ordinary smartphone on the market. Next to it, a premium ticket to the cricket match at Lord's.

Patel felt unable, for once, to be excited about the cricket match about to commence. He watched without feeling within himself the buzz among the fans queueing outside Lord's. Instead what he felt was a nerve-wracking tension at the enormity of the task that faced him, and the impossibility of success.

Apart from the usual security, there was nothing to indicate special measures were being taken to safeguard the event. No bomb squads sweeping every inch of the venue, no sniffer dogs deployed. No armed assault units waited in unmarked vans and buses around the stadium, ready to be deployed at a moment's notice, no plain-clothes officers mingling with the crowds, trying to spot a potential terrorist.

Simon had been unable to convince his superiors that there was a credible threat as Patel had no proof to offer. Simon had been unable to get hold of Sir Roger's archive of Skype conversations. His credibility was shot after the MOD break-in, and Patel's too, after his appearance at the Dubai shoot-out. Still at the hospital in Leicester, he'd forced himself to ring his old nemesis, Superintendent Skinner at Scotland Yard, who'd been surprised to be roused from sleep, but very willing to have a conversation with Patel.

When Patel had said his piece, and begged Skinner to rouse the anti-terror machine of the state, Skinner told him, with uncontained delight, 'Patel, I've often wondered, ever since I laid eyes on you, if you were for real.'

'Sir?'

'Cricket hero to zero, then a catcher of serial killers, two of them! And now, you've failed your first mental health evaluation, the report came in yesterday. Too much trauma, it seems. Perhaps you're a lover, not a fighter, eh? On top of all this, paparazzi photos of you in India and Dubai! They will be in the papers tomorrow, I mean today. And the best thing is, I was going to send you an email tomorrow, but this is better, telling you straight. You're suspended, pending investigation. Perhaps the trauma from India has messed you up permanently? What on earth were you doing in Dubai?'

'Sir, can we focus on the matter at hand, there is a terror threat at Lord's. The match needs to be cancelled to protect lives.'

Skinner just laughed, and hung up.

Patel punched his fist into the wall in frustration. The plaster cracked, and so did his knuckles. It hurt like hell, and it hadn't helped. The hospital security turned up, but he apologised and they let him be. Then his sister arrived, the doctor said his mother was stable again, and he'd thought, if not you, then who? If not now, then when? Something his primary school headteacher had loved to repeat in assemblies.

Now, he sat, a couple of plasters on his knuckles and a pair of ibuprofen in him, in his car in a disabled bay, staring intently at his laptop. Simon had been able to get him the CCTV feed from Lord's, and he was at the MI6 headquarters trying to plead his case to his superiors.

His head pounding despite the painkillers, he switched from camera feed to camera feed, poring over the grainy images of cricket fans pouring into the stadium to take their seats.

Lots of young white men and young brown men. Not a single obviously Muslim man. A lot of boisterous young university students in costumes. A group in T-shirts, each with a letter on the front. Together, they read, *TOOR*. For a moment he wondered why they wanted to spell the type of lentil used in Indian cooking, then realised they were meant to spell *ROOT*, as in,

Joe Root, the England captain. T and R had swapped places in the queue. He continued scanning the faces. A couple of Indian men in turbans. Not indicating Sikh, but a caricature of a Raja. A few young white women. Plenty of young Indian women talking at high speed, half on their phones, perfectly made-up with straight curtains of hair. Some dreaming, no doubt, of star-cricketer husbands.

Patel wouldn't be an option any more. Permanently retired – hurt from cricket, now a homicide cop with mental health issues on sick leave, and as of this morning, suspended from active duty, pending results of an internal investigation.

He wished he could walk around the stadium looking at all the faces in person. But he had a highly recognisable face. Especially if, as Skinner claimed, he'd graced this morning's tabloids.

The job could've been easier, he thought, if he had known what he was looking for. Rather than just a vaguely suspicious person, male or female, carrying a bomb that could be an everyday object.

Cricket fans for the most part had cosmopolitan looks. There were several young women in their late teens, and he couldn't see on the CCTV feed if they had green eyes. Or if their skin colour was the right side of wheatish, as his relatives would put it. Hair, he knew, could be dyed.

After several more minutes of fruitless search, Patel was fed up of sitting in the car. He got out, tense as a dog smelling a cat just out of sight. Five minutes to go before the match began. He stationed himself beside a catering truck, with a view of Bicentenary Gate, saw a female security officer ask a young Indian fan to step through the metal detector again. The machine beeped its OK the second time, and she was allowed through.

Patel felt a chill in the pit of his stomach. Did he miss it? He felt so sure that this was the place. MI6 wanted hard evidence. At least a tip-off from an insider that there was a credible terror threat at Lord's. They had nothing on Sir Roger.

Neha, aka Arifa Rahman, had sent him a message to say Sir Roger hadn't left his home all morning. How do you know? he texted back. I have access to live satellite imaging, she wrote back.

He heard a rousing cheer as the match began. People still came in; as always, there were dozens of latecomers.

Small mercy, he thought, that it was a weekday. Not a capacity crowd. The stadium half full. A few more fans arrived. All men. He heard cheers for what could have been a boundary. Something familiar about one of them. Just a young white man. Perhaps he had one of those faces you feel like you've seen before. He seemed nervous and twitchy. Slight smile on his face at no one in particular. The secret joy. Patel's blood froze. He'd seen that smile before. On two men. The first, on the Dales Ripper. The second, on the man calling himself Manu, who had hunted women in Bangalore.

The man looked around as a swarm of noisy cricket fans all arrived at once. Patel recalled where he'd seen him. At night, under a street lamp, from the other side of the allotment gates. One of the men harassing Clive. The one who had a famous name. Zappa, no. Ziggy, no. Ringo!

Before he could think, Patel launched himself towards Ringo. Ringo heard the sound of running feet, just had time to clock Patel's face, his smile starting to wither as recognition came to his eyes, when Patel winded him and held him immobile, spreadeagled on the floor.

'Get off, infidel,' shouted Ringo. Patel grabbed his hand just as Ringo flinched towards a hidden trigger on his torso. Patel cracked his fingers back, hearing a crunch. Ringo screamed his pain. Patel shook his hand till the trigger switch dropped harm-lessly by his side.

The next ten minutes went by in a blur as security officers swarmed them. Patel found himself whisked away to a secret location underground in a lead-lined vault. Here, they waited. Patel watched Ringo. Ringo was on his knees, words of prayer spilling out of him. Patel refused to leave him on his own. And they'd let him stay, after checking over his ID and con-sulting Simon.

Simon arrived, after having been blue-lighted across town along with a slew of counter-terrorism experts. He raised his eyebrows to Patel, too tense to speak, it being too soon to show relief.

The bomb disposal experts checked Ringo over, and carefully stripped him and handed Simon a thin vest. Simon gingerly held it. 'This is it?'

'Yes,' said a woman through her suit, sounding muffled. She unzipped the top of her suit, pulled it off her head. 'Harmless now, we've disabled the trigger.'

'Where's the rest?'

'This is it.'

Ringo laughed. 'Die, infidels,' he said, and wouldn't say any more. He reverted to his prayers, down once more on his knees.

'I'll take him in for questioning,' Simon said to Patel, his expression grave. 'Half the explosive material's still at large.'

Patel nodded, gutted that the job was still only half-finished.

Chapter Twenty-Nine

Patel found himself outside Lord's Cricket Ground once more. He went to the Grace Gate and, showing his ID to the security team, asked if Sir Roger had ordered an all-access badge for him. To his surprise, there it was. *What's he playing at?* thought Patel. He hadn't believed Sir Roger was exactly going to make it easy for Patel to investigate Lord's. Perhaps he wanted to appear above suspicion.

He headed for the pavilion and entered through the member's entrance, waving the badge and his ID, for good measure, at the security team. Where to? Where to start? Automatic pilot took him upstairs towards the middle-floor players' dressing rooms. Realising he had no business in either of them, he stepped out onto the middle-floor terrace, stared hopelessly at the vast, enthusiastic crowd, the majority of whom, as ever when they came to the UK, were Indian supporters. Needles in haystacks was about right. What was the capacity nowadays? Thirty thousand?

A collective 'Oooh' rang round the ground as a Jimmy Anderson delivery whistled past the edge of the bat and into the keeper's hands. Patel saw Jonathan Agnew leaning against the wall, watching, a pair of huge binoculars on a chair beside him.

'Aggers,' Patel said, wondering if he'd remember him after all these years.

Aggers took a moment, then said, 'Good heavens. Is it Vijay?'

'Shouldn't you be commentating?'

'Few minutes downtime. But how on earth are you? Well, bar saving the world from villainy, if the press reports are true.'

'Actually, now you mention it, could I borrow your bins a minute?'

'Oh, eh?' Aggers' journalistic nose caught a whiff. 'Something I should know?'

'Just looking for a friend. Won't be a mo.' Patel grabbed the binoculars and stepped forward to the white railing.

To his right, Kohli perched on the edge of a chair on the Indian dressing-room balcony. And for the second time in a week, Patel felt his own inner turmoil reflected in Kohli's features. Patel glanced at the huge electronic scoreboard and saw he'd been bowled for twelve by Stuart Broad. Slings and arrows. Patel gazed out. He'd never been at a cricket stadium before and been so disinterested in the match, or its outcome. He lifted the binoculars to his eyes, swept the stadium. Something about Ringo's attitude niggled at him. Sure, he'd been gutted at being caught, but had there also been a gleam in his eyes, almost triumphant, almost as though he'd sacrificed himself, as though he'd been expecting to get caught? As though the game was still to play for.

Patel searched the crowd. Once, twice, ten times, lingering on faces, until his eyes swam in his head.

'Sorry, old chap.' Aggers tapped him on the shoulder. 'Need 'em back, I fear. Duty calls.' But he gave Patel a long look before he left.

Patel walked back inside, into the hallway. He leaned against the wall, close by the open Indian dressing-room door. What to do?

Through the door, he heard Ryan Gonsalves, the number

eight batsman, complain loudly, 'These aren't my pads, man. Where're my pads? I need my pads!'

The kit manager, a man Patel vaguely remembered, came bustling out the door and hurried off downstairs. He was back a moment later with a huge kit-bag marked clearly, 'Gonsalves Kit 2'. Just in time too. There was a roar from the crowd. Patel looked up at a TV screen in the hallway to see a replay of Danwir rashly hoiking a bouncer straight down the fielder's throat on the square leg boundary.

Even desperate as he was, Patel winced in sympathy for Danwir as the screen showed him tearing off his helmet, muttering as he headed back towards the pavilion. Ryan bundled out of the dressing room, spying Patel.

'Good luck,' Patel told him.

'Thanks, bro,' said Ryan, looking cheerful. Patel watched him head downstairs, yellow pad-straps flapping, towards that most famous of all cricket rites of passage – the walk through the Lord's Long Room, past the throngs of MCC members and out onto the hallowed field. Patel felt that familiar pang of regret at his lost first career.

On the screen, the camera still lingered on Danwir's face, as he mouthed off to himself. Patel frowned. Over Danwir's right shoulder, he saw an out-of-focus image of a big man. Looked like he was a few rows up from ground level at the Nursery End. Great view he'd have: right behind the wicketkeeper. The blurry background couldn't hide the huge frame, the beard and topknot. Lawrence!

For some reason, Ryan's pads came into his mind. Something about ... what? He glanced in through the dressing-room door. Saw the next two batsmen kitted up and ready. Their straps weren't yellow. They were blue. All round the untidy room he saw pads with blue straps. The Indian team's pads were all blue.

Patel flew down the stairs and burst into the Long Room, knocking Danwir flat on his back. Patel stumbled sideways into a table. He heard the smash of glasses. He heard the crowd applause outside for the new batsman.

'Ryan!' he shouted and then hands grabbed him, threw him to the ground. Two huge security men pinned his hands by his side, tried to turn him face down. Walkie-talkies crackled and the crowd of MCC members called out in shock at the spectacle.

'I'm a police officer,' Patel shouted. 'ID in my jacket pocket. DI Patel.'

'Patel? Patel!' exclaimed the people around. Surely they knew him?

Maybe they did, but still the guards wouldn't release his arms. But another guard reached in and removed his wallet from his pocket and stared at his badge. He seemed unsure what to do next.

Patel yelled, 'You idiots. Get Ryan! He's got a bomb.'

The security beefs released him, in shock, still frozen to the spot. Several MMC members shouted, 'Bomb!' He heard the word taken up on the terrace outside. Patel pulled himself to his feet, snatched his ID back, then burst through the throng and out the doors, down the steps and onto the pitch.

He could hear people close by, calling out, shouting, 'Bomb ... Run! ... Go!'

A voice yelled, 'Stop or I'll shoot.'

'Police, police,' shouted Patel, turning towards the armed security, waving his ID but not stopping. 'Get Ryan! Gonsalves! He's wearing a bomb.' He could hardly make himself heard through the crowd uproar as word spread.

He saw that Gonsalves had already reached the middle and was staring blankly at him. But Patel sprinted across the field towards Lawrence. As he ran he yelled at the players, 'Get away from Ryan! Run!' But they just turned about in confusion. Patel heard screams now all around the stadium, but his eyes honed in on one man.

Lawrence did not leap out of his seat. He just stared at Patel running towards him.

'Hands where I can see them,' Patel yelled.

Lawrence slowly put his hands up. In his right, he held a mobile phone. Patel was still several yards away. He saw Lawrence's finger on the call button.

'Phone down,' Patel shouted.

He saw Lawrence hesitate.

'Don't do it, Lawrence. Look at these people!' His voice cracked with the strain of making himself heard. He skidded to a stop by the fence, ten feet from Lawrence.

They stared at each other.

'Just don't do it, Lawrence,' Patel called. He shook his head, suddenly exhausted beyond all reason. 'Just don't,' he said, almost a whisper.

Lawrence took his finger from the call button, let the phone drop.

High in the Nursery End stand, Patel was explaining for what seemed the hundredth time to the head of security. Lawrence was on his knees, hands behind his back in cuffs, a gun trained at his head. The stadium was almost empty. Whoever hadn't fled was being asked to leave in an orderly fashion. Somehow, there'd been no stampede. It seemed as if no one had been hurt. The cricketers had been shepherded onto team buses and straight away from the stadium to safehouses, as per protocol; all except Ryan, who was under arrest, being held in the locker room.

Out on the pitch, Ryan's pads lay where they'd been removed. The bomb squad had set up a perimeter and Patel watched as a robot edged closer on its little tank tracks.

The security head turned away to speak into his walkie.

Patel said to Lawrence, 'Speak to me.'

'Ringo's got my daughter. They said I had to make a call, the only number in the phone. That's it. One call for my daughter's life.'

'When did you need to make this call?'

'When I saw batsman number eight walk in to bat with yellow straps on his pads. If I did that, Ringo'd let Chloe go.'

'Ringo's in custody,' Patel said. 'He came to the match wearing half a kilogram of plastic explosive. All he'd say to us was "Die, infidels."'

Lawrence lost all the colour in his face. 'Oh god, where's Muffin?'

Patel said, 'I think I've an idea.'

Chapter Thirty

Patel switched the car engine off and coasted down the last hundred yards to Sir Roger's house. Not a single light seemed to be on. Patel found the darkness ominous. A house that had seemed so cheerful and welcoming only the previous afternoon now had wreathed about itself a foreboding dark.

Gingerly, he crept up to the front door. He couldn't see a CCTV but didn't want to take chances. He crept back to the car and phoned Neha. She did what she did best, cursing because her right arm was in a sling and she didn't have the patience to operate her laptop left-handed. Finally, after what seemed long minutes, she said, 'It's got an alarm.'

'Oh.' His mind raced, choosing and discarding options. If only the bloody cops would listen to him. He realised he now thought of cops, all cops, as different from him. How had things changed so much?

At Lord's, they'd arrested Lawrence. As they dragged him away he'd begged Patel to save his daughter. But he had no idea who Mr T was. Simon promised vaguely to look into it, and privately told Patel the matter would be passed on to the local cops, although the National Child Protection Agency would trigger the usual response.

'They'll be out in force as you know,' Simon told him. 'A

missing child trumps terrorism. Although I'll have to get back to interrogating Abdul aka Ringo now.'

Patel had been in the Leicester Royal's waiting room, where he'd turned a chair and a little table into a messy workstation, laptop and phone charger and bits of paper and printouts of police reports strewn around. He rang all his contacts in the police forces, and waited impatiently to hear of Chloe's rescue.

He'd urged them to look up Sir Roger, but this proved dicey. His police contact informed him they'd interviewed Sir Roger, who threatened to sue them if they so much as *thought* about casting aspersions on his character. Burnt already by the huge payouts on the bungling of the paedophile-ring investigations, the cops were keen to avoid slandering a celeb without adequate proof. And there was zilch, nada, to connect Sir Roger with Chloe or Ringo.

Something about their visit to Sir Roger at home kept bugging Patel. The nervous attitude, the impression of him walking on tiptoes, on eggshells, in his own home. It bugged him and bugged him, although it was a suspicion based on instinct more than any concrete thing. He thought about it, sighed, phoned Neha again. It took her an hour, then she got him the goods.

'He hasn't been out at all. I checked all the CCTV footage that's been uploaded in the local area around his house. Spotted his car briefly in the Sainsbury's, that's all.'

'That's no use.'

'Hang on, let me check. Yes, he used the card-only self-checkout. I got his shopping list.'

'Sorry, what?'

She said, 'I got the list of what he purchased from the local Sainsbury's. Wholemeal bread, Bourbon biscuits, orange juice, yogurt, apples, yoyos and Pom-Bears. They sell yoyos in Sainsbury's?'

Patel felt his head would explode with tension.

'Fuck!' he yelled. 'Sorry.' He gestured to the startled relatives at the other end of the room.

'What did I say?' said Neha.

'They're snacks. Kids' snacks.'

'Ah. And Pom-Bears is a toy?'

'No, they're teddy bear-shaped crisps. He's bought snacks for a little child. I used to live on those when I was three.'

'Fuck,' said Neha.

'Exactly!'

But try as he did, Patel could not get the cops to go and check Sir Roger's house again. Neha's digging, after all, was completely illegal and could not be presented in court as evidence. He had to do it himself.

Now, waiting in his car in the dark by Sir Roger's house, where his instincts told him Chloe was being held, his phone buzzed. Neha. Deactivated alarm @Sir R. You're welcome.

Patel tried all the windows he could reach. All locked. The kitchen door had a glass panel next to the handle. Didn't look very sophisticated. The type which locked if you yanked it up.

He took his shirt off, rolled it around his fist and smashed through the glass. He stuck his foot out to catch the shards that fell down. Bumped by his shoe as they fell, they didn't make too much of a noise. The shards that fell inside must've fallen on a thick doormat. No dogs were roused. The neighbours were too far off to hear anything.

Reaching through the broken glass, Patel unlocked the kitchen door. He crept inside. Slowly he moved from one room to the next, looking for Chloe.

He found a small bedroom in the middle of the house, with no windows facing out. A small glow lamp beside a single bed.

Patel paused at the door. He saw a small figure on the bed snuffle and move. As he was about to go in, he felt the cold muzzle of a gun press against his temple.

'Don't move,' whispered Sir Roger. 'You'll wake the poor little child. She's only just gone down.'

Holding the gun firmly against Patel's temple, Sir Roger pulled Patel away from the door and marched him down the hallway.

At the heavy door of his library, where Patel had been a guest a few times in his younger life, Sir Roger put the gun in his pocket and smiled his old smile at Patel.

'Hello again,' Sir Roger said, as though greeting an old friend. 'Come in and take a seat.'

Patel sat in an armchair by the fire, made up to blaze even in the late spring. Sir Roger strode to the sideboard.

'What are you drinking?'

'What you're having,' said Patel.

'Bourbon.'

Patel nodded.

They sat across from each other, holding their glasses. Patel was intensely aware of everything about him, especially the gun casually resting in Sir Roger's pocket.

Patel took a sip of the burning liquid. 'I trust you have no intention of running,' he said.

'Not at all,' Sir Roger said. 'And *I* suspect you have some questions. I saw you running across the pitch towards Ryan. I thought it would be quite something if Lawrence blew Ryan up just as you reached him. Quite the coup for my pay-masters. It's a shame you spotted Lawrence before he set off the bomb.'

'Lawrence thought he was making a phone call,' Patel said.

'Really? Is he that naïve? Did he think a father's sacrifice would be so simple? It's a life for a life. That's the rule.' There was venom in Sir Roger's voice, and Patel wondered to whom it was intended.

Patel said, 'You wouldn't have let any harm come to Chloe even if Lawrence had failed, or point-blank refused to go along with the plan.'

'Did you think so? I suppose you're right.'

The air seemed to go out of Sir Roger. 'Thank you. I guess you know more than I imagined.'

'Where's your daughter?'

Sir Roger looked at a loss for an answer, as if it was the last question he'd expected Patel to ask.

'What do you know about Cynthia?' he said.

'Not enough,' said Patel. 'Perhaps if you tell me the full story, we can help?'

'Ask me the right questions,' said Sir Roger. Patel couldn't tell if he was toying with him.

'You mentioned your paymasters.'

'Yes. I can't promise to give you anything useful. But I'm tired of this. This life. I'll tell you all I know.'

'I don't need the details of their identities. You can save that for my mate Simon and the anti-terror units, but I just need to know how you got involved.'

'Well, as these things stand, they lured me in with a harmless betting scam. A lot of money for little bets that did not change the outcome of the matches.'

'What was the bet, today?'

'Ryan was supposed to wear his special pads, with the yellow straps, to signal to the other batsman to get run out before the end of the next over.'

'Ryan didn't know?'

Sir Roger chuckled. 'Ryan didn't know his special pads were

packed with enough plastic explosive to take out himself, the wicketkeeper, three slips and a gully.'

'And that's not enough casualties, so there was Ringo.'

Sir Roger shook his head. 'Ringo is one of those, you know, zealous converts. It was his own plan, to double the impact. He'd wait for Lawrence to make the call and then blow himself up at the same time. And it would've worked too, but for you.'

'Ringo nearly pulled it off.'

Sir Roger nodded. 'The plan wouldn't have had a remote chance of success without his bright ideas.'

'To kidnap Chloe and use Lawrence instead of Majid.'

Sir Roger looked at him in wonder. 'Hey, you're a smart fella, you know that?' He sounded bitter.

'Not that smart. I haven't figured out Majid's involvement in all this.'

'Oh, Lord,' he said. He rubbed his face wearily. 'Majid, the poor slob. Nice guy for a movie hero, just made the wrong choices in life. Really. Got into all sorts of debts. Like me, I suppose. He thought he was organising another betting scam. Harmless stuff.'

'Did he find himself in too deep and run?'

'He found out he was going to die for a cause he never signed up to. Mr T arranged for him to make the phone call at the cricket match, same as Lawrence. Offered an extra lump of cash, which should have set the alarm bells ringing. Two hundred thousand pounds. We had our wires crossed, and when I visited Mr T at his house, in Stoneygate, Majid was still there. Then he left, and Mr T and I got into an argument.'

'About what?'

'About Majid triggering a bomb at a cricket match. Supposed to be at Nottingham. Yes, the one where you met me. But the explosives got delayed. And we lost our trigger man.'

'So how did Majid find out what was really happening?'

'Something made him suspicious, the two-hundred thousand, perhaps. When I arrived, Mr T gave him the code for the locker in the security van to collect the phone. He had to write it down, it's long and complicated. None of us could find a scrap of paper. I got a business card out of my wallet. Without thinking, I gave it to him. He wrote it down, took his money. Mr T gave him a bag to carry it in. He put my card into the bag too, and left. Then Mr T and I started arguing. I knew Majid would die making that call. Majid came back. He heard us arguing, understood everything and panicked. He made such a lot of noise getting out of there. Mr T and I chased him. We chased him all over the place in the pissing rain. We cornered him in some godforsaken place. Some kind of council wasteland. We couldn't find the bag. Too dark.'

His voice cold as ice, Patel said, 'How did you kill Majid?'

'I didn't. Mr T had a syringe all ready in an inner pocket. He had three or four in a small metal case, like a cigarette box. He only needed one. A cocktail of deadly chemicals that came out in the tox report as a drug overdose. He's got a Russian connection who supplies him the stuff.'

'What about DS Codman?'

'What about him? Just some bent copper in Mr T's employ.'

Patel breathed, in and out. The picture was much clearer, but for one more thing. He said, 'Are you telling me the truth because you don't intend for me to live to repeat any of it?'

Sir Roger laughed. 'No. I don't intend to kill you, Vijay. I did intend to kill myself, but I can't. Not with my daughter's life in the balance. I cannot carry on. I want that little girl to go back to her mummy. I've had enough of being Al-Qaeda's donkey. I'm telling you the truth so you can plead my case to whoever it is in charge of these things. MI6, the Home Minister? You're a national hero. They'll listen to you.'

Sir Roger's voice broke. 'I've been a terrible father, a terrible husband. I just want my daughter back, safe. Will you help me? I'll turn myself in and cooperate.'

Patel knew the pain of having a loved one on the brink of death. 'I will do my best, sir,' he said. 'Now, please hand me your gun.'

Social services arrived with the first police car. Patel felt an enormous relief to hand over the little girl to a PC and two social workers. They promised to take her straight to her mother as soon as she was checked over for injuries.

They left, and Patel helped two more PCs to secure the premises. Sir Roger continued to sit in his library, the fire now gone cold. Patel waited by the front door for officers from the Special Crimes Unit, so he could brief them before they met Sir Roger.

He heard a car in the driveway. A Leicester police car. DS Codman stepped out alone. At the sight of his face, Patel remembered something he'd forgotten in the drama of the last twenty-four hours. Neha aka Arifa had told him his mother had called Codman as soon as she'd fished Majid's bag out of the pond. So it must have been Codman, the burglar in the mask, who'd left his mother for dead.

With a yell of rage, Patel launched himself at Codman, who hadn't completely straightened himself after getting out of his car. The open door slammed against Codman's arm with great force. Codman shrieked in pain as Patel tackled him to the ground.

'You stabbed my mother,' Patel's spittle sprayed over Codman's face.

'Not me,' quavered Codman. Patel stepped on his arm. 'It wasn't me,' he cried.

'She is in intensive care. You put her there. She called you as soon as she found the bag. No one else could have known.' Patel grabbed his collar and pressed his knee into Codman's chest.

'No, no,' he whimpered. 'I just bungled the case like Mr T asked. I didn't send a cop as soon as she called me. That's all I did, I swear.'

'It wasn't him, Patel.' A weary voice spoke behind him.

Patel released Codman's collar, and he fell back. 'It wasn't this scumbag?' he asked, hoarsely.

'I can tell you exactly who it was,' said Sir Roger.

Chapter Thirty-One

Patel waited patiently, still hopeful of finding his quarry, two days after he learned that it was Mr T, or Tarsem, no second name, who'd attacked his mother in a bungled robbery attempt.

He had in his sight Annabel's Tea Rooms in the centre of town, squeezed between a high street optician's and a tennis shop. Two floors of offices nestled on top of the café, and the windows of the shops were where Patel's eyes were trained, along with the side passage to the café.

Neha hadn't been able to find anything on Tarsem. She located the GPS of his phone, which they got from Lawrence while he was still in custody, through Simon. It had been active at Tarsem's Stoneygate house, but by the time the police got there, it'd blinked off. Perhaps he had more than one bent copper in his employ. They reckoned he'd removed the battery. The police had failed to sniff him out, after a day of staking out his Stoneygate house, and a couple of other known addresses in Melton Mowbray and Kettering. He'd apparently vanished into thin air.

Patel's phone buzzed. Lawrence.

'Hey, glad they let you out.'

'Yeah, man, it was touch and go. But your pal Simon helped, I think. Still, I'm just out on bail. They're still charging me for attempted, even though they accept I didn't know what I was actually doing.'

'Thanks for the tip about the tea rooms. The police are concentrating on other possibilities, but I thought I'd cover this place.'

'Yeah, when I met him there I had this feeling he really knew the lady who ran the place. He acted like he owned it, you know?'

'Neha couldn't find any connection between Tarsem and the café, but you may be right.'

'I'm meeting my wife this afternoon, I mean I'm hoping to, but I thought I'd help you out, man. I'm just getting off the train.'

A small man emerged from the side passage, a hat low on his head, hands in the pockets of his trousers, whistling rather ostentatiously.

The hairs on Patel's neck prickled. 'The chick's emerged from the nest,' he said to Lawrence. 'He's on foot. Coming your way. I'm on his ass.' He followed, still on the phone to Lawrence, who said he'd wait outside the station.

On the curve from St George's Way towards the station, Patel decided to make his move. He needed to make sure he wasn't following the wrong guy.

'Hey, Tarsem,' he called.

The man barely paused at the sound of Patel's voice. Without even turning to look he began to run.

Patel began chasing Tarsem. But with no apparent effort, Tarsem was pulling away. Along the wide stretch down London Road, Patel rued his lack of fitness. Tarsem seemed to be in top shape. He was stretching the distance.

Then he saw, beyond the running figure of Tarsem scattering students and shuffling residents in his wake, the looming figure of Lawrence. He stood legs slightly apart, waiting for Tarsem to run into him.

Instead of slowing down, Tarsem sped up. Patel saw him run straight at Lawrence, who hesitated, unsure what to do, when at the last split second, Tarsem swerved around, carried on running. Lawrence, looking like a televised figure in slow motion, turned to stare after the running man disbelievingly.

Patel reached him, panting. 'Come on, man, get into gear.'

They both ran after Tarsem, who showed no signs of slowing. Lawrence kept pace with Patel, but he couldn't run any faster either.

When they reached the Victoria Park roundabout, they lost sight of Tarsem.

'Right,' Patel gasped. 'Let's split up. I'll go down straight, you work around the park. Fuck, I better call for backup.'

'Needle in a haystack,' grumbled Lawrence, looking at all the people in the park. Saturday morning. Busy time. 'That's it, he's gone, man.'

'Arrgh, I'm such an idiot,' said Patel as he kicked a lamp post, hopped scowling in pain. 'Double idiot,' he said. Why had he yelled his name, warned him off?

Patel's phone rang. Still hopping, he growled, 'This better be good.'

'Good? Not sure,' said Neha. 'Want the GPS location of one Tarsem? It just reappeared in the darndest place.'

Patel watched for a minute the struggling figure of Mr T, who was a great runner, but not much of a climber. He glanced at Lawrence, who grinned, then began shaking the allotment gates. Tarsem fell to the ground like an apple from a tree.

Patel bent over the groaning man and said, 'It just pulls open, you know?'

Just when Patel began wondering why his mother had changed her outfit three times in the middle of the afternoon, Padmini announced, rather brusquely, that she was going out for a coffee. Then stood there, glaring at him, as though expecting to be challenged.

'OK,' he said.

'Good,' she said, and still waited, but he wouldn't bite.

'With Mason,' she threw over her shoulder as she went back upstairs, with almost a flounce.

Patel supressed a smile. It was like living with a teenager. Speaking of which—

He got back to phrasing a reply to Arifa's text message from the previous night. He'd been trying to find the right words, which were proving elusive. After a few attempts, he just called her.

'Hey.' He could hear the bustle and screech of streetlife, plenty of car horns and auto honks. He felt a pang, somewhere between yearning and fright for the madness that was India. 'You're out somewhere?' he said.

'Yeah, I can't really hear you. Let me call you back in a minute.'

As he waited, he thought of how the Neha who'd appeared in his life had transformed into Arifa. At last he knew who she truly was, and he enjoyed the feeling of certainty. It had been draining, being unable to understand her secrecy, figure out her motivations, in the days they'd spent together. Now, at last, he could see her just as she was. A super-smart teenager.

She called.

'I thought you were grounded for a month?' he said to her.

'Of course I am. Even now, I'm in bed reading *Pride and Prejudice*.'

'Ha ha.'

'So did you find out?'

That's what she'd wanted to know in her text. What happened to Sir Roger's fifteen-year-old daughter? Patel had been unable to find words to write about the tragedy. So, he just said it straight.

'She died.'

'What?'

'Suicide. I guess she didn't put her trust in the British Foreign Office's efforts to bring back wayward children from the Middle East.'

'Did they not do anything?'

'Simon and I spoke to officials at the Foreign Office. They made noises about trying to get her back. But, you know, there's an official policy of hostility regarding any children who run away to join ISIS. We're not even sure if she'd gone to Syria or Lebanon. They certainly won't spend effort and money to investigate.'

Arifa said, 'Even for a white girl from the aristocratic classes?'

'I even considered approaching the tabloids, see if they'd run a campaign.' He'd dreaded approaching them, but determined to do all he could to save the girl, even letting the vultures rip him apart like carrion in exchange for publicising her plight. But he was saved that effort.

'How did she die?' Arifa sounded sad.

'I guess her captors told her Sir Roger had failed in his mission. She managed to text her dad's phone. That she decided to kill herself before they killed her. Simon told me about it.'

'MI6 have Sir Roger's phone?'

'Well, of course.'

'And he knows?'

'Yes. I cannot imagine what Sir Roger must be going through.'

'I can imagine.'

Patel understood that Arifa of all people knew what it was like to lose a loved one, despite their wrong choices, catastrophic decisions. She knew what it was like to go to any length to see justice done by them, even if it meant breaking laws or putting others in danger. And in Sir Roger's case, be an accessory to murder, kidnapping and terrorism.

Arifa said, 'I suppose this is Sir Roger's punishment. I keep thinking how nice he seemed when we met him.'

'He must have seen his daughter in you.'

Arifa laughed. 'Which is why he guessed my real age.'

'Your acting skills weren't up to scratch.'

'Your mother was fooled.'

'That's true. She usually prides herself on reading people.'

'Well, at least she didn't start matchmaking.'

Patel cleared his throat. 'Right, well, keep in touch. Let me know if you get into any universities here. I can scope them out for you.' Also scope out future employment for myself, he thought.

'No chance. I'm going to the US. Columbia.'

'I can just see you running amok in New York.'

'Yes, I bet you can.' She laughed. 'Right, I better go. I just got out to have some chaat. My mother will be raising hell.'

Patel could instantly taste the golgappas Vashist had made

him eat. His mouth watered at the same time as his stomach groaned. 'Remember ...?' he wanted to say, but he could sense her wanting to move on, with her day, her life, not be shooting the breeze with an old man like him.

'Keep in touch, then,' he told her. 'Goodbye.'

He knew she probably wouldn't. Which was fine. He'd only remind her of her lost father. Yes, he knew she saw a bit of her old man in him. Which would horrify his own mother, who'd had such a crush on Majid Rahman back in the day. He groaned out loud.

His mother came down the stairs again, said, 'What do you think?' She was in yet another outfit.

'Lovely,' he said, and decided to get out of there.

Patel stopped at Clive's house on the way to Allandale Road. He walked up to the front door and pushed in all the leaflets that had collected in the mail slot. Clive had turned up at their house in brand new Prada shoes, deliberately scuffed up a bit, beaming, and announced he and Sylvia were off to the land of Oz. Turned out no one wanted to claim the two-hundred thousand pounds in Majid's bag. So, finders keepers.

Technically, the money belonged to Padmini and Arifa. But Arifa did not want the tainted money. She had plenty of her own, and if she needed more, she could just hack into some billionaire's bank account. Padmini made the inspired decision to give Clive and Sylvia the money. Now they were off, first class, a carer in tow, to track down their son, Peter, the lost lamb.

Patel turned into the latest coffee shop to pop up on Allandale Road. Usually when a new business opened on this stretch, he wondered how long it would last. He had a feeling this one would. It had a good vibe, as his mother would say. He found a stool by the window, next to a little girl who was hunched over a piece of paper, crayon in hand, deep in concentration. He waited, without disturbing her.

Lawrence brought over a steaming little cup, the coffee in it the colour of his eyes.

'What do you think?' Lawrence said, beaming.

Patel said, 'Mmm, interesting. Quite strong, bit fruity?' What was he supposed to say?

Lawrence nodded. 'Yes. It's my own blend. Need to think of a name for it. Best coffee I've ever tasted. Maybe I'll call it just that. "Best coffee I've ever tasted".'

'Ah. Yes, why not?'

He smiled at the little girl. Chloe, or Muffin, as Lawrence called her, came over to show him the drawing. It was a circle with a line through it.

He studied it seriously and said, 'Future Turner prize. Well done.'

She seemed happy enough with the compliment, grabbed a sugar cube from his saucer and began sucking on it.

Patel turned to Lawrence. 'How's business?'

'Not bad, thanks, man. I plug the café in the media whenever they interview me about what happened.'

'You're a bit of a local celeb, now,' Patel said. Indeed, the people queuing for coffee at the till were glancing over, trying to look nonchalant while they did it.

Lawrence's smile faded as he said, 'Still working on getting Magdalena back.'

For the second time that day, Patel cast about for the right words. 'It must have been very hard to come to terms with, you know, how ...' He realised he couldn't say anything in front of Chloe, who'd sensed a change of tone in their voices and came to stand by him, still blissfully sucking on the sugar cube, and lining up the next one in her sights.

Patel wondered if Magdalena would ever be able to forgive Lawrence or herself for letting Ringo anywhere near their daughter. A certified terrorist. Plus finding out about Lawrence's true vocation, although now, of course, he was something of a good guy celeb. Lawrence tracking down Clive and saving his life, deciding to turn a new leaf, then being forced to commit a crime in order to save his daughter, and finally, being unable to actually commit the crime that would save his daughter. The media loved all of it, and so did the people of Leicester. Perhaps Magdalena would come around, after all. From what he could see, Lawrence was a terrific dad.

'That's enough sugar, Muffin,' Lawrence told Chloe, expertly pulling Patel's saucer out of reach just as Chloe made a grab for the remaining sugar cube. 'You're sweet enough,' he told her, and poked her gently in the ribs, making her squeal and laugh. The patrons all cracked a smile. A couple of the women made cooey noises.

Patel stood up to leave. Lawrence refused to let him pay. Patel put the money in the tip box instead.

'Thanks, man,' said Lawrence. 'Appreciate it.'

Patel knew the margins would be slim for a new café business.

Chloe ran back to the colouring corner to work on her next piece of 'art', and Lawrence came out to the pavement with Patel.

Slightly awkwardly, Lawrence asked, 'You back to Scotland Yard?'

'Oh, I don't know,' said Patel. 'I kinda like what you've done here, striking out anew, being your own boss.'

'Being your own boss is the best feeling,' Lawrence said.

Patel nodded, filed it away to mull over later.

'Do come in for your daily cuppa whilst you're still around, man.'

'Best coffee I've ever tasted,' Patel said, and Lawrence beamed as he waved him off, his bun nodding in the wind.

Patel smiled, walked away, thinking, *I've always preferred instant.*

Acknowledgements

My heartfelt thanks to my husband and first reader, Harry, for prioritising me and my work despite the pressures of his own career, and my son, Brân, for being unique and inspiring as only he can be.

I'd also like to thank all my friends in Leicester for accommodating, encouraging and inspiring me in so many ways.

A special thank you to **Kath Grainger**, friend *and* neighbour *and* reader par excellence, for some great feedback and the idea for the opening.

Bringing a book from manuscript to what you are reading is a team effort.

Dialogue Books would like to thank everyone at Little, Brown who helped to publish *Black Rain* in the UK.

Editorial
Sharmaine Lovegrove
Maisie Lawrence
Zoe Carroll

Sales
Caitriona Row
Ben Goddard
Rachael Hum
Hannah Methuen
Andrew Cattanach

Design
Charlotte Stroomer
Jo Taylor

Production
Narges Nojoumi

Publicity
Millie Seaward

Marketing
Emily Moran

Copy-editing
Jane Eastgate

Sensitivity reader
Gabrielle Johnson

Proofreading
Jill Cole